Who Goes Next?

By the same author

THE HARD HIT
SQUARE DANCE
DEATH OF A BIG MAN
LANDSCAPE WITH VIOLENCE
ACQUITTAL
THE BASTARD

WHO GOES NEXT?

JOHN WAINWRIGHT

ST. MARTIN'S PRESS   NEW YORK

Copyright © 1976 By John Wainwright
All rights reserved. For information, write:
St. Martin's Press, Inc., 175 Fifth Ave., New York, N.Y. 10010.
Manufactured in the United States of America
Library of Congress Catalog Card Number: 76-28065

Library of Congress Cataloging in Publication Data
Wainwright, John William, 1921-
   Who goes next?
   I. Title.
PZ4.W1418Wh3 [PR6073.A354] 823'.9'14 76-28065
ISBN 0-312-87010-8

The city. It had a new and fancy title; it was now known as a Metropolitan District—which meant its coppers were animated cogs in an even larger law-enforcement machine than before ... they were officers in a Metropolitan Police District.

Big deal!

They were northern coppers ... and don't you forget it. They changed their cap-badges ... and that's *all* they changed. And all the high-minded goons, squatting their lives away on cushioned chairs in Whitehall couldn't dent *that* argument; two cities they'd once been, and two cities they still *were*—one county constabulary it had once been, and one county constabulary it still *was*—and although (theoretically) a line drawn on a map had created a forensic 'Holy Trinity', the hell with that for a bag of marbles ... they were still *three*, and each counted the other two as something slightly inferior. Something they'd have to watch very carefully. Something which could, very easily, become an encumbrance, or even a hindrance.

Each city, therefore, remained *the* city. And the towns, villages and open countryside which separated the two cities remained *the* county constabulary.

'From the top,' said Gilliant. 'We set the example and, if we set a good enough example, the lesser ranks follow our lead. So, no parish-pump parochialism, if you please, gentlemen. We're big ... it's our first job to prove that "big" also means "better".'

Which was very nice pep-language ... particularly if,

like Gilliant, you'd been upped to Chief Constable of the newly formed M.P.D.

Gilliant waved a hand towards a side-table whose surface was almost hidden under a maze of bottles and glasses. He said, 'Pour your own drinks, gentlemen. Gin, whisky, sherry. Beer, if that's your tipple. Smoke, if you wish. Settle down, speak your minds and let's get as many kinks ironed out of this amalgamation re-shuffle as possible. The situation isn't of our choice ... all we have to do is make it work.'

The muttered grunts could have meant unanimous approval, unanimous disapproval, a mixture of both, or a series of prolonged burps brought on by badly cooked and hurriedly eaten meals. At this point in the first Senior Officers' Conference of the newly-formed M.P.D. nobody was giving *anything* away.

They were all high-rankers. They were all big men; big in authority, big in stature and big in self-importance. They had one common denominator. They'd all fought amalgamation, from the day of its first hint. They'd all hated the idea of gluing three perfectly good police forces into one bloody great montage of antagonistic coppers— one unwieldy and unmanageable conglomerate of differing police methods. They'd hated the idea, when the first circular, setting out future proposals, had landed on their respective desks. They *still* hated it. And the cloak of unconscious arrogance which is part of the make-up of every senior police officer precluded them from hiding their hatred.

Gilliant watched them, feet apart and firmly planted on the carpet of the huge office, and knew he'd a fight on his hands.

These men had to be tamed into a team ... and that wasn't going to be easy.

He understood them—he even sympathised with them

—but *he* was the top man ... and, before they left this office, that was the one bitter pill they'd all have to swallow.

It was (as Gilliant well knew) a 'territorial' thing; a series of jealousies, born of being boss-dogs in their own individual patches and now—thanks to the short-sighted lunacy of some jumped-up pseudo-expert at the Home Office—those patches had been destroyed. The official name was 'amalgamation' but, as far as these men were concerned, the real name was 'destruction'. Wholesale *destruction* based upon a bureaucratic day-dream that a new police force could be created overnight, and with the stroke of a pen.

Gilliant watched them move towards the drinks table. They reminded him of elephants, jostling each other at a water-hole. Rogue elephants, working elephants and at least one performing elephant ... that was the impression. But 'rogue', 'working' or 'performing', they had to be moulded into a single, perfectly disciplined troupe ... and *he* had to be the elephant-master.

As he watched, Gilliant smoked a cigarette. He handled the cigarette awkwardly, and like a man unused to seeking the solace of tobacco smoke. And those who already knew him, noted.

Gilliant indulged in cigarettes only when he was worried. *Really* worried.

As he was, at this moment.

The killer had waited eight years. Eight more minutes, or thereabouts, was no time at all. He rested the barrel of the rifle in the V of the tree's fork, and kept the thick bole of the ancient oak between himself and the gate leading to the field. The distance—the *exact* distance, measured weeks ago—was sixty-three yards, and the Zeiss, Hensoldt Diatal D.6X telescopic sight reduced that distance, in effect, to little more than ten yards. Less than half the length of a cricket pitch ... and the sight was already very accurately adjusted.

He eyed the rifle with an affection bordering upon the paternal. As if it was a living object, and capable of returning his relished love. It was, indeed, a magnificent end-product of the gun-maker's craft; a Husqvarna M.1622, .22, 6-shot, clip-loading, bolt-action match grade rifle.

Unregistered ... but, of course.

And, in eight minutes' time—or thereabouts—it would perform the function for which it had been smuggled from the U.S.A. and into the United Kingdom.

There was a gradual settling down. Each man had a chair, each man had a glass of his chosen booze. Most of them were smoking; cigarettes, a couple of pipes and, with one of them, a foul-smelling cheroot.

Gilliant had moved to one wall of the office, to where a framed Ordnance Survey map took up much of the wall-space. A thick black line marked the boundary of the new Metropolitan Police District, with a second thick black line following the run of the River Hewfraw, east to west, and dividing the new police area into roughly two equal parts. Red lines marked the limits of each police division and, within the red lines, green lines marked the limits of each section, within each division.

It was a huge, geographical jigsaw puzzle. Each piece fitted, perfectly, into the shape of its neighbours, therefore (theoretically) it *should* work. And, assuming the men gathered in Gilliant's office worked together—assuming they forgot their petty prides and self-esteems—it *would* work ... and (Gilliant promised himself, grimly) it was *going* to work, whoever's head had to roll to *make* it work!

He started quietly.

He said, 'Statistics. We'll start with those, gentlemen

'... in case some of you have skipped the cold figures we've been presented with. Approximately a million and a half acres. That's a lot of ground space ... by any yardstick. Authorised strength, ten thousand and three officers —don't ask me where they get the *three* from ... our lords and masters indulge themselves in their own brand of arithmetic. Let's call it ten thousand. If we ever reach that figure, I'll be a very surprised man. Our *actual* strength is well over three thousand short of our authorised strength ... a state of affairs I don't have to emphasise in this company. Less than seven thousand, for a twenty-four-hour coverage of a million and a half acres. And that includes two major cities. Lessford, in the south. Bordfield, in the north.'

He paused, then underlined the problem with the words, 'Lessford ... population approaching three-quarters of a million. Bordfield ... population approximately half a million, and growing fast. Add to that another million, or so, in the old county constabulary area, and *that's* what we're responsible for. Well over two million people ... possibly nearer three million.'

'God help us!'

The growled remark came from a large man, with a leonine thatch of snow-white hair. He sprawled in one of the chairs, scowled his obvious disgust at Gilliant and held a pint tankard of half-consumed beer in his right hand; hand wrapped around the body of the glass, fingers threaded through the handle ... the true beer-quaffer's grip.

'God,' said Gilliant, drily, 'is reputed to help those who help themselves. Let's start with the assumption that that's a true saying, Mr Harris.'

Harris sniffed.

Harris was from the original Bordfield City Police Force. Gilliant, on the other hand, had been the chief constable of Lessford City Police Force. But now ...

Prior to the official date of amalgamation, rumours had been rife. About the cold-blooded ruthlessness of this bastard Gilliant ... how he chewed nails, and spat rust when the occasion called for it. And Harris wondered. Harris knew all about chief constables. My Christ, yes! After the Robs Cully cock-up, Harris knew *all* about chief constables ... and how they cracked, like rotten twigs, when the pressure got *really* heavy.*

The killer watched his victim cross the adjoining field, and make for the gate. A man of habit. A farmer, harassed by the attention of wandering dogs who regularly chased and savaged his sheep; a good man (the killer didn't doubt he was a good man) driven to near-distraction by so-called 'pets' who had tasted hot blood after the joy of a quick chase.

The farmer had a twelve-bore shotgun under one arm. Loaded, no doubt. Ready to blast the life out of any canine sheep-worrier. He moved his head, left and right, as he scanned the surrounding fields for signs of dogs ... or the bloody aftermath of dogs.

The killer steadied himself against the trunk of the oak. He nursed the stock of the Husqvarna rifle against his cheek and lined the telescopic sight upon the gate which his victim must open.

Gilliant half-turned, tapped the glass cover of the map twice with the knuckle of his forefinger. Once above the Hewfraw line, and once below.

'Two regions,' he said. 'Not two *forces*—let's get any doubt about *that* out of the way—but two regions ... for easier handling. The North Region, with Bordfield its Regional Headquarters. The South Region, with Lessford its Regional Headquarters. Each region responsible for

* See *Landscape with Violence* (Macmillan, 1975).

day-to-day policing. Each with its own Assistant Chief Constable (Admin) and its own Assistant Chief Constable (Crime). Each with its own Head of C.I.D. ... *Regional* Head of C.I.D. But the buck stops here, gentlemen. Here, in this office ... which means I carry the can, but I *don't* carry passengers.'

Harris sipped at his beer, and guessed that *he* headed the list, now the tough talk had started.

He guessed right.

Gilliant said, 'Mr Harris, here—as you all know—has been promoted. Assistant Chief Constable (Crime) for Bordfield Region. Chief Superintendent Lennox—late Superintendent Lennox, of the old Lessford force—as his Regional Head of C.I.D.'

The obese man, with the bald head, the clothes of an old-time stand-up comic and the foul-smelling cheroot beamed his satisfaction.

Harris suppressed a sigh and, momentarily, closed his eyes in disgust.

A cold, humourless smile touched Gilliant's lips, as he added, 'You should work well, together.'

Somebody cut a laugh short, as Gilliant continued, 'Assistant Chief Constable (Admin), for Bordfield Region, Mr Child.' Again, the quick, humourless smile, as Gilliant added, 'I can personally vouch for Mr Child, Harris ... as one-time Head of my own C.I.D. He has the mind of an accountant, and the patience of a saint.'

'Does that mean ...' began Harris.

'It means "Administration" ... just that,' said Gilliant, flatly. 'His promotion is from C.I.D. to Uniformed Branch. He won't interfere ... I know him well enough to guarantee *that*.'

The quiet, solemn-faced man sitting in a chair in a corner of the office nodded, gently, as if in complete agreement.

Harris also nodded—once—then growled, 'Good.'

'I'm delighted.' Mild sarcasm touched Gilliant's tone. 'At least I've pleased *one* of my assistant chief constables.'

Harris compressed his lips and tightened his grip on his tankard. He looked anything but 'pleased' ... but remained silent.

Gilliant said, 'We now touch upon Lessford Region. South of the Hewfraw. A slightly larger region than Bordfield Region. With a somewhat higher population figure. Let me remind you, gentlemen. Mr Sugden, here—late chief superintendent of the county constabulary—is now Assistant Chief Constable (Crime) in Lessford Region. He was Head of C.I.D. in his old force. He has a reputation ... and I've every confidence in him. Mr Wheatley —my own old Assistant Chief Constable (Admin)— retains that post, as Assistant Chief Constable (Admin) in Lessford Region.'

The gaunt, sallow-faced man, who sat bolt upright in a chair near the window and nursed an untouched glass of sherry, failed to keep the bitterness from his eyes. Wheatley was an unpopular man, and had no delusions concerning his unpopularity. Of the whole company present in that office, he was the only one for whom the amalgamation hadn't meant promotion. Indeed, looked at from one angle, it had meant *de*motion. He'd been A.C.C. (Admin) to a city force, and was now merely A.C.C. (Admin) to a *region*.

The others were aware of this. They neither sympathised nor gloated. They just didn't look at him, and remained silent.

'I know Mr Wheatley,' said Gilliant. 'I know how much I can rely upon him.'

And that (thought Sullivan) is a double-edged compliment, if ever I heard one.

Wheatley recognised it as such and, for a moment, his nostrils quivered with suppressed anger.

'Head of C.I.D., Lessford Region.' Gilliant paused,

then looked directly at the man in question, as he continued, 'Detective Chief Superintendent Rucker—until recently Detective Chief Inspector ... until *very* recently, Detective Superintendent. *My* choice, gentlemen. And, for the record, there's been no back-door horse-trading. A certain amount of leap-frogging ... I agree. But tender corns are not my concern. Just as long as I get the man *I* want in the post *I* want him to fill.'

Rucker remained stone-faced. He raised his glass, sipped at the whisky and met Gilliant's gaze, eye-for-eye.

Rucker knew.

Sullivan also knew ... and wondered whether Gilliant *really* knew.

Wheatley was unpopular—no more than that—but Rucker was *hated*. Every man who'd ever worked under Rucker loathed his guts ... and this, despite the universal acknowledgement that Rucker was a fantastic (even frightening) thief-taker.

Trouble (thought Sullivan). As sure as God made green apples, we're going to have trouble once Rucker starts flexing his extra muscles.

The farmer stopped at the gate. He leaned the twelve-bore against the gate-post, lifted the hook from the stable and swung the gate open. He came through the gate and half-turned, to re-fasten the gate.

For almost three seconds his head was bent forward and motionless.

The cross-wires of the telescopic sight met at a point slightly behind—slightly above—his right ear. The V of the tree's branches held the Husqvarna rock-steady as the killer gradually increased the trigger-pressure.

The staccato explosion of the .22 rifle was dissipated, and lost in the open fields of the countryside; even the sheep, grazing less than fifty yards from where the killer stood, merely raised their heads in lip-nibbling curiosity.

The farmer folded forward, over the top bar of the gate, then slithered down to sprawl in the area of hoof-churned mud.

The killer used the sight as a telescope; watching the victim for any sign of continued life. He counted fifty, very slowly, before he lowered the rifle, left the hide of the tree and walked, almost nonchalantly, the sixty-three yards, to his victim.

The farmer was quite dead ... there being a complete and patently obvious absence of all 'life' in every victim of homicidal violence which no medic need verify.

The killer used the toe of a shoe to turn the victim onto his back. He worked the bolt of the rifle and fed a new cartridge into the breech. He raised the rifle to his shoulder and, from a range of less than two feet, sent a second bullet into the centre-forehead of the dead man.

The killer lowered the rifle, smiled at the corpse, and murmured, 'Don't worry, old man. You won't be alone for long.'

'Which leaves three.' Gilliant stepped forward, screwed his cigarette into a glass ash-tray, on the desk, then returned to his position alongside the wall-map. He pushed his hands into his trouser pockets, and said, 'Two deputy chief constables. A force as big as this has become *demands* two. There must be one man—*one* man—with absolute authority, twenty-four hours a day, seven days a week. Illness. Holidays. These things happen—these things come along ... and, without two men, each capable of taking over the reins, the force can be decapitated long enough to cause real trouble. Therefore, *two* deputy chief constables.'

He paused, then chose his words with obvious care.

He said, 'The post of deputy chief constable was offered to Mr Grafton ... the chief constable of the old county constabulary. After careful consideration, he declined the offer. As you all may have heard, he now holds a senior position in one of the more reputable private security firms ... and we all wish him luck.'

Nudge-nudge, wink-wink (thought Sullivan) but we all know the pompous bastard couldn't stomach the post of 'deputy' having once held the post of 'chief'.

'That was our misfortune,' continued Gilliant. 'Our luck changed, when Mr Bear accepted the offer, and threw up his post as assistant chief constable in one of the Northumbrian forces, to become deputy chief constable in *this* force. The other deputy chief constable I need hardly introduce. Mr Sullivan. Ex-Assistant Chief Constable (Crime) Sullivan, from my own old force. And gentlemen, let me leave you in no doubt. Mr Bear and Mr Sullivan are equal. There is no 'first deputy chief constable' or 'second deputy chief constable' in *this* force. They carry equal rank—they carry equal authority—and, whatever orders or instructions either of them give will have my unqualified backing ... always!'

The pause, this time, was slightly longer. It almost amounted to a defiance. A throwing down of a gauntlet to any of the men present who had visions of upsetting the applecart by playing Bear off against Sullivan, or vice versa.

Sullivan glanced across to where the apple-cheeked Bear sat, silently sipping a pink gin and smoking a pipe. A mischievous look flicked between the two and Sullivan's right eyelid dropped in a split-second wink of mutual understanding.

A good man (thought Sullivan). A man with a sense of humour, and a thousand times easier to work alongside than Grafton would have been.

Having introduced everybody present, Gilliant was laying down the general guidelines.

He was saying, 'Each region to have its own Administration Department. Its own Finance and Records

Departments. Stores. Planning and Housing Department. Its own C.I.D.—Crime Clearing House—Criminal Intelligence Office—Criminal Records Section—Fingerprint and Photography Departments. Each with its own Dog Section. Garage and Communications Branch. Road Traffic Operations and Accident Prevention Departments. Hackney Carriage and Vehicle Inspection Sections. Each, in effect, a separate force—but part of a single force ... a double-headed force, if you like. But with complete and absolute liaison, between the two regions.

'That's why you're here, gentlemen. In order that you're in no doubt about the way this new force will work. And I stress that ... *will* work! Pass what I've said down to your subordinates. To the various divisions—to the divisional officers—and from them, to the sections. To the man on the beat. To the detective constable doing routine enquiries. I want no man—or woman—in this force to be left in any doubt. The old order is a thing of the past. As from now, we start building new traditions ... which means we forget the old ones.' He raised his eyebrows enquiringly, scanned the assembly, and ended, 'Now, gentlemen ... questions. Anything you think I've missed? Anything you're still not sure about?'

There was a shuffling of feet, and each man glanced at his neighbour to see who, if anybody, was going to do slight battle with this new and confident chief constable.

Rucker spoke first.

His voice was a soft drawl carrying barely concealed contempt ... not, specifically, contempt for Gilliant but, rather, contempt for the whole of mankind. This being Rucker's normal conversational tone.

He said, 'The—er—flash bits. Regional Crime Squads. Task Forces. That sort of thing. The general public likes its quota of glamour ... presumably we pander to its tastes.'

'The public likes its criminals behind bars, chief

superintendent.' Gilliant met contempt with a flat, and flint-hard counter-argument. 'You do that, and they won't complain if they're saved the expense of what you're pleased to call "flash bits". Regional Crime Squads aren't our concern—*you* should know *that* ... they're strictly Home Office affairs. If we ever *need* a Task force—*or* a Commando Force—I'll let you know. And, if we *do*, it'll be because you people in this room aren't as good as I thought you were.'

'*Touché*,' murmured Rucker, and his lips moved into a twisted smile of sardonic approval.

'Or checkmate,' growled Sullivan. 'But we aren't playing games, Rucker ... and, if you think we are, move out of that new chair of yours and make way for somebody who has the right idea.'

'Oh, but we *are*—Deputy Chief Constable Sullivan ... *sir*,' drawled Rucker. 'The game of "Law".'

'The game of *discipline*,' snapped Gilliant, before Sullivan could reply. 'Demanding it, and accepting it. You've asked a question. You've been answered. No Task Forces. No Commando Forces. Not unless the job you've been given is too big for you to handle.'

Rucker lifted a packet of cigarettes from his knee. He selected a cigarette and lighted it from the flame of a lighter. A very ordinary, everyday series of movements. But, the way Rucker performed those movements—the deliberation and the finely timed pauses, between each segment of that normal, everyday series of movements ... it was sheer dumb insolence, honed to a fine art.

Sugden (thought Sullivan) has a real plateful bringing *that* bastard to heel.

'Nice game, darling?' asked the killer's wife.

'Moderate.' The killer eased the golf bag off his shoulder, closed the door of his estate semi, leaned the bag in a corner of the hall and stooped to peck his wife a dutiful 'hello' on the cheek she held ready. He said, 'That swing. I still tend to slice it a little ... and always into the same rough, on the seventh.'

'Practise,' smiled his wife. 'You'll get it right, in time.'

'I think it must be the grip.'

'I wouldn't know.'

'One day ...' The killer hoisted the golf bag onto his shoulder. 'One day I'll get the pro to watch. Maybe *he'll* know what's wrong.'

The killer's wife hurried towards the kitchen, as she said, 'A quick snack. Salami sandwiches ... okay?'

'Fine.'

'Then, we'll be able to do justice to Lucy's Cod Creole.'

'Lovely.' The killer turned towards the stairs. 'I'll have a quick bath, and change, before I come down ... after I've put the clubs away.'

'As you wish, darling. I'll have my bath, later.'

Such a typical exchange. Such an ordinary 'happy marriage'. A thousand and one—*ten* thousand and one—similar exchanges in near-identical homes, the length and breadth of the land ... the basic, contented, moderately happy family which, multiplied a few thousand times, formed the bedrock of normal, honest, English decency.

Except...

Fifty per cent of *this* 'happy family' suffered the scorch of white-hot murder in his brain. And *this* golf bag (always carefully locked away in what should have been the spare bedroom, but was very grandly called 'The Study') contained something far more lethal than golf clubs.

'Heaven forbid that I should be the one to suggest it,' said Gilliant, with a sigh, 'but what we need, at this particular moment, is a nice, meaty case. A real headline-breaker.'

'Always assuming we can handle it.' Sullivan's grunted

qualification to Gilliant's opinion left a large hole for doubt.

The others had gone. The triumvirate (the chief constable and the two deputy chief constables) upon which rested the ultimate success, or failure, of the newly formed Metropolitan Police District, had stayed on, in Gilliant's office, for a post-mortem chin-wag upon the recent high-level conference. The hard-bitten, 'you-will-you-shall-you-*must*' talk was no longer necessary. Emotional corsets could be unlaced and unpalatable truths could be touched upon.

Bear murmured, 'I don't know this man, Rucker, but...'

'You will,' promised Sullivan, grimly. 'You will.'

'As bad as *that*?' The worried frown looked out of place on Bear's round and cheerful face.

Gilliant said, 'Sugden should keep the lid on.'

'Can *anybody*?' asked Sullivan, doubtfully.

'Between us,' said Gilliant, flatly, 'we'll keep the lid on ... even Rucker can't intimidate *everybody*.'

'You—er ...' Bear hesitated, then spoke to Gilliant. 'You had a reason, presumably?'

'For the double-promotion?'

'From detective chief inspector to detective chief superintendent,' amplified Bear.

'To Head of C.I.D.,' growled Sullivan, bluntly. 'Talk about *creating* dissatisfaction.'

Gilliant said, 'Logically ... right. There was going to *be* dissatisfaction, who the devil got the job. Three detective superintendents. All expecting it. All at daggers drawn. None of them capable of imposing his personality upon the other two ... at least, that was *my* considered opinion. Make any one of them chief superintendent—Head of C.I.D.—and the other two might have smashed crime detection to hell ... out of sheer pique. But with Rucker.' Gilliant smiled. 'A double-promotion—a leapfrog—and those three detective superintendents have at least *some* common ground. Given time, they'll put their knives away. They'll work together.'

'Ah, yes ... but against Rucker,' murmured Sullivan.

'Rucker,' said Gilliant, musingly, 'will grow fat on it. He *likes* being hated. It's what makes him tick. He'll *make* 'em detect crime ... if only to demonstrate that one of them should be sitting in his chair.'

'And that, Winnie old cock, is what is known as "police diplomacy",' said Sullivan, with a chuckle.

'Winnie?' Gilliant frowned his non-understanding.

Bear's already red cheeks flushed a slightly deeper scarlet.

He said, 'The name, sir. Y'know ... the name. Bear—Pooh Bear—Winnie the Pooh ... so-o, "Winnie". It's a cross I've had to bear—oh my God, "bear"!—all my service.'

'You don't mind?'

'Nobody can rid himself of a nickname,' said Bear, heavily. 'Don't think I haven't tried ... but it can't be done. But ...' He moved his shoulders. 'As long as it's only used by equals, and above—and by everybody else when I'm not supposed to hear—I've grown to live with it.'

Sullivan said, 'It's a sign of popularity.'

'So they tell me ... except, it makes me sound a bit of a queer.'

'You should get your wife to write out an affidavit,' chuckled Sullivan. 'Carry it around with you.'

'And,' grinned Bear, 'don't think I haven't thought about *that*.'

Gilliant seemed not to have heard the exchange between his two deputy chief constables. He sat behind his new desk—a desk large enough to impress upon any stranger the magnitude of his new authority—and frowned the worry of his new responsibility at the virgin whiteness of his tooled-leather blotter.

He returned to his original theme.

He muttered, 'What we need at this moment is a big case. A difficult case. Something capable of welding all the bits and pieces into a single force ... something to give us our first taste of pride.'

And, had life been a motion picture, at that point there would have been a neatly timed 'dissolve', and the new scene would have shown two youths and a lurcher. A gate, surrounded by churned mud. Then a slow 'zoom in' to the body of a thickset man whose blood still oozed from the back of his skull and into the black stickiness of the mire.

'Leave him, eh?' said the first youth, and there was a tremor in his voice.

'For Christ's sake!' The second youth looked shocked at the suggestion.

'Why not? It's not our business.'

'We can't just *leave* him.'

'He's dead. What the hell ...'

'How the hell d'you *know* he's dead?'

'He looks it. Hell's bells, he's *dead*.' The lurcher smelled fresh blood, and began to wriggle its way beneath the bottom bar of the gate. The first youth snarled, 'Ketch! Back ... *heel*.'

The lurcher wriggled itself into reverse, pulled itself free of the gate and squatted alongside its master's foot. It looked longingly, and tongue-lolling, at the fresh meat and spilled blood beyond the gate.

The second youth wasn't too far from panic.

He said, 'Look! We've gorra tell *somebody*. We can't just leave him there.'

'Who?' asked the first youth.

'The police. The coppers.'

'Oh, bloody hell. If we do *that* we're ...'
'We've *got* to.'
'All right.' The first youth weakened. 'But—y'know ... just that we were out for a walk. Not that we were after rabbits.'
'Look, they're not gonna ...'
'The bloody cops! They'll do *owt*.'
'Not when there's a dead 'un. Not when we've found a ...'
'We don't *know* he's dead.'
'Well, *I* bloody well know.' The second youth turned to walk back the way they'd come. 'And *I'm* gonna tell the coppers. For Christ's sake ... what else?'
'Hang on.' The first youth leashed the lurcher, then hurried after his companion. He called, 'Hang on a bit. We might as well both end up holding the mucky end of the stick.'

Sugden could contain himself no longer.

He checked that the road ahead was clear of traffic and pedestrians, held the Rover steady, then turned his head and eyed the fat man with open disapproval.

He said, 'Is this some sort of off-beat joke, or summat?'
'Eh?'
'The—er ...' Sugden lifted a hand from the steering wheel and waved it in the general direction of his newly acquired Head of C.I.D. 'The gear? The get-up? What the hell is it? The local university rag week ... summat like that?'
'Oh!'

Lennox looked mildly surprised. Not shocked. Not hurt. Not insulted ... merely mildly surprised.

'When they said,' continued Sugden, coldly. 'Y'know ... when they told me you'd be working, more or less, alongside me. They warned me. "He's a bit of an eccentric," they said. "A bit of an odd-ball."'

Lennox voiced his mild surprise, as he murmured, 'Why should they think that?'

'Why, indeed.' Sugden breathed heavily through his nostrils, returned his attention to the road ahead, and said, 'You're not an "eccentric", mate.'

'Of course not.'

'You're stark staring barmy. You—a detective chief superintendent—and ... well, God knows where you could *buy* an outfit like that, these days.'

'Oh, you couldn't,' admitted Lennox, cheerfully.

'That I'm prepared to believe.'

'I buy my clothes to last,' explained Lennox. 'This suit, for example. Thirty years' wear and tear ... and as good as new.'

'I wouldn't say "as good as new",' contradicted Sugden, grimly. 'Thirty years old. And it looks it. And it stinks ... what the hell *does* it stink of, by the way?'

'Cats.'

'Rats? How the devil can it ...'

'*Cats.*' Lennox grinned, a little shamefacedly. 'The missus—she breeds 'em ... see? And—y'know—I nurse the kittens sometimes. And—we-ell, y'know ... they tend to piss all over your lap, sometimes.'

'Holy Christ!'

'I—er—I didn't think it was so obvious,' apologised Lennox.

'Aye ... it's obvious. It makes me feel like puking.'

'We'd better stop the car first ... eh?' suggested Lennox.

'Are you being funny?'

'No. But if you're going to be ...'

'A figure of speech,' said Sugden, in a flat voice.

'Good. I'd hate to think ...'

'We'd better get together, Lennox,' interrupted Sugden. 'Let's say, tomorrow—tomorrow afternoon ... we'll—er—decide how a Head of C.I.D. should dress. *And* smell.'

* * *

'Which farm?' asked the desk sergeant.

'Appleyard's,' said the second youth. 'It's down a lane off the Lessford Road. About two miles beyond ...'

'I know where it is,' cut in the desk sergeant. He turned from the counter and called through a hatch which connected the public counter area with an inner office. He said, 'Appleyard's farm. Report of a Sudden Death. A shooting job, by the sound of it,' he turned to the youths and asked, 'Which field?'

'Long Meadow,' said the second youth. 'That's about ...'

'I know.' The desk sergeant turned to the hatch, again, and called, 'At Long Meadow ... that's almost a mile south of the farm itself. How are we for cars?'

A voice from beyond the hatch said, 'Alfa-Seven-Three. That's on Lessford Road. And Alfa-Four-Zero ... they're out that way. A statement from a witness to a road accident.'

'Forget the statement,' snapped the desk sergeant. 'Get 'em both there. And I want details ... as soon as possible.'

The desk sergeant fingered back the cuff of his tunic, glanced at his watch, and ended, 'Log it out at seventeen-thirty-five hours.'

The two youths were edging their way towards the door. The lurcher strained at its lead as its nose identified an interesting smell near the public counter.

The desk sergeant said, 'Not so fast, lads.' His smile carried a professional fusion of friendliness and warning. 'Names and addresses, before you go. And proof of identity, if possible. We'll be round for statements, later.'

'I told you,' groaned the first youth, softly. 'I bloody well *told* you.'

And, ninety-nine times out of a hundred, that's how it starts.

Murder ... it starts with what is officially called a

'report'. Information given, often unwillingly, by some 'why-the-hell-can't-I-mind-my-own-business' member of the public. A stammered, disconnected yarn, told over the public counter of a police station—sometimes muttered into the mouthpiece of a telephone—noted, logged and then investigated.

It starts as a 'Sudden Death'.

A corpse, where there shouldn't *be* a corpse. A dead 'un ... some member of the public who's been inconsiderate enough to die, other than in bed. A 'coroner's job'.

And, more often than not, that's all it is. A 'Sudden Death'.

People die, and death doesn't concern itself too much with convenience. It has, at its disposal, twenty-four hours a day—seven days a week—and, if it feels like indulging in sick humour, it snaps its fingers and that's it ... Bingo! A heart attack. A stroke. An eight-wheel lorry nudging the victim in the small of the back. Anything. Anywhere.

Death is the biggest Joker in the whole of the pack.

And, when death snaps its bony fingers unexpectedly, what was once a human being becomes a 'thing'. It becomes 'property' ... specifically, the 'property' of whichever coroner is responsible for the district in which the ex-human hits the deck.

The next-of-kin take second place. Friends, trade union colleagues, fellow club-members—all and everybody else —step to the rear of the stage and H.M. Coroner claims the limelight. He suddenly 'has a body'—death has presented him with an albeit unwanted gift ... and *he* decides.

And because they are (among many other things) 'Coroner's Officers' coppers are lumbered with the sometimes messy task of viewing the corpse, collecting the data and completing a 'Sudden Death Report' ... from which report the Coroner decides what action he's going to take, to rid himself of this 'thing'—this 'gift'—which has suddenly been dumped in his lap.

Hence the re-routing of Patrol Cars Alfa-Seven-Three and Alfa-Four-Zero ... because, although Sudden Deaths are ten-a-penny, every murder *starts* as a Sudden Death. And (as all coppers quickly learn) ... you never *know*!

'Deputy chief constable!' Mary Sullivan chuckled as she made the remark. 'I wish they could see you *now*.'

'The help I get from this bloody family,' grumbled Sullivan. 'A bit of encouragement might go a long way.'

'You're doing fine, dad.' Steve Sullivan grinned up at his father. 'The Sistine Chapel should look like a Giles cartoon by the time you've finished ... just don't fall off the steps.'

A little unsteadily, due to a slight wobble on the stepladder, Sullivan descended to the bare floorboards. He placed the can of paint on the floor, alongside the stepladder and carefully bridged the top of the can with the paintbrush. He wiped his paint-messed fingers down the ancient jacket and trousers.

He breathed deeply, before he spoke to this highly comical duo who happened to be his beloved wife and son.

He said, 'This room ... it's supposed to be *my* den. If, and when, we ever move into the damn place.'

'Of course, dear,' said Mary.

'In that case, why the hell can't *I* have a say in a colour scheme.'

'What's wrong with the colour scheme?' asked Mary, innocently.

'Beige ceilings. Now, who the hell ever heard of beige-coloured ceilings? Ceilings are supposed to be *white*.'

'Not always,' contradicted Steve.

'I'm not asking *you*,' growled Sullivan. 'If you were allowed to run riot, we'd have zebra-striped bogs.'

'Now that,' mused Steve, 'wouldn't be a bad ...'

'For Christ's sake!'

'Richard Sullivan.' Mary put as much mock outrage into her voice as she was able to muster. 'Kindly watch your language ... they may not like too much swearing here, at Upper Drayson.'

'In that case, they can ...'

'And what's wrong with a beige-coloured ceiling?'

'*Or* stone-coloured walls?' added Steve.

Mary ended, 'In the long run, it saves work.'

'How the hell can it save work?' Sullivan stared non-belief.

'That pipe of yours,' explained Mary. 'This is your den ... agreed?'

'We've already decided. But, for the life of me, I can't see ...'

'You smoke that pipe of yours. You'll smoke it in here. All day—*every* day—and, in no time at all, the tobacco smoke will turn a *white* ceiling into a *beige* ceiling.'

'And every wall stone-coloured,' added Steve, mischievously.

'So, why not *start* with that colour?' asked Mary. 'Unless, of course, you feel like re-decorating the room every six months.'

'Oh!'

'Long-term planning ... see?' Steve rammed the defeat home.

'What about grub?' Sullivan surrendered, by changing the subject. 'Picnic in the kitchen, as usual?'

'Chicken sandwiches and lots of hot, sweet tea.'

'For the workers,' added Steve.

'And that,' growled Sullivan, 'let's *you* out.'

'For heaven's sake! I've ...'

'You've designed the bloody place. All right,' continued Sullivan, hurriedly, 'I'm not saying it's *badly* designed. But, by Christ, after what it's cost to ram you through the sausage-machine they call a university, in the hope that you'll one day be an architect, don't start trying to kid *me* it's been designed on the cheap. And, having designed it, all you've done ever since is stroll around with a self-satisfied expression on your face while everybody else has sweated their guts out making lines on a piece of paper into something capable of keeping out the weather.'

'The gratitude of the man!' gasped Steve. 'I spent hours —*hours!*—measuring up, planning all the ...'

'It's a wonder you didn't rupture yourself lifting the pencil up and down.'

'Chicken sandwiches?' murmured Mary Sullivan.

'Aaah!' said Sullivan senior.

'Aaah!' said Sullivan junior.

And, within the next five minutes they were seated on canvas and tubular-steel chairs, around a card-table, in the kitchen of their new, but not yet moved-into, house. Noshing away for dear life.

The Sullivan family. The *family*—not the copper ... not the newly appointed deputy chief constable. And a mere handful of the seven thousand coppers under his control would have believed that *the* 'Sullivan' was capable of such simple pleasure; that he was, at heart, a very ordinary bloke, who loved his wife and loved his son, and enjoyed the mutual Bing Crosby–Bob Hope back-chat with the latter.

It looked like rain—one of those mid-July downpours—and the detective constable had a decision to make.

His name was Enfield—D.C. Enfield—and, along with the four Motor Patrol constables, from Alfa-Seven-Three and Alfa-Four-Zero, he'd viewed the body of the dead farmer from all and every angle ... but never nearer than from the muddy area around the gate.

'It looks bad,' he said, quietly.

Constable Buckle, from Alfa-Seven-Three, said, 'It could be. Y'know ... it just *could* be.'

'That second one, through the forehead,' agreed Enfield. 'Or, maybe the second one was the *other* one. But *two*. That makes it look bad.'

'Aye.' Buckle nodded his agreement.

Constable Vine—also from Alfa-Seven-Three—said, 'Still—y'know ... it's possible. Some silly sod arsing around with a small-bore. Or a ricochet, maybe.'

'*Two* ricochets?' P.C. Buckle was old enough to be Vine's father; the difference in age was acknowledged and respected. They worked well together as a squad car crew; youth and energy combining with experience to form a good team. The elder man shook his head, slowly, at his younger colleague, and said, 'It won't do, Tim. One of 'em *has* to be deliberate. Short of a miracle.'

'That—that means ...' P.C. Vine swallowed, and didn't end the sentence.

P.C. Black, from Alfa-Four-Zero, said, 'We'd better get the circus rolling ... eh?' He looked at Enfield for the go-ahead.

'Tell 'em,' said Enfield, sadly. ' "Suspected Foul Play." No more than that, for the moment.'

'Will do.' Black turned to walk towards the parked squad cars, about twenty yards away in the grass of Long Meadow.

'Meanwhile.' Enfield eyed the gathering clouds anxiously. He said, 'A good downpour, and the consistency of that mud's likely to be affected. And there ... there ... and there.' He leaned forward, and pointed. 'Footprints. See 'em. Spiked. Now *he* isn't wearing spikes.' Enfield nodded towards the corpse. 'The two Herberts who found him ... I doubt if *they'll* have spiked shoes. So-o, that means those footprints could be important, and —y'know ... it looks like rain.'

'Boxes.' Police Constable Denver, the second officer

from Alfa-Four-Zero, looked pleased with himself, as recollection of something he'd read in one of the standard 'What-To-Do-At-The-Scene-Of-A-Crime' booklets filtered into his memory. 'What we need is boxes. One for each footprint. Then, if it rains, they won't ...'

'Great,' said Enfield, sarcastically. 'Pick a few up, and put 'em in position.'

'Eh?'

'Why,' said P.C. Buckle, heavily, 'do we always have to be lumbered with *one* thickheaded barmpot.'

'Look—all I said ...'

'No boxes,' interrupted Enfield, soothingly. 'So, what else?'

There was a moment's silence, then Buckle snapped his fingers, and said, 'Signs. Those "Accident Ahead" things. Those temporary "Police No Parking" signs. There's about half a dozen in each squad car. Put 'em up —one over each footprint—then drape those accident jackets over 'em ... those gaudy things that make us look like glorified Wombles. Tents—y'know ... a tent over each one of 'em. Right?'

Enfield grinned his approval, and said, 'Thanks for coming, mate.'

'Any time.' Buckle turned on Denver, and snapped, 'All right—jump to it, lad—you know what we want ... chop-chop.'

Denver scowled his embarrassment for a moment, then sprinted away, towards the parked squad cars.

So, why should anybody want to kill an honest, hard-working farmer?

By eight o'clock that evening, that was the big question. Bill White had farmed land all his life—and his father before him—and, because of his nature (and despite a bit of a temper when he was upset), he was a well-liked man in the community. All right—he'd no time for skivers and idle buggers ... but what the hell sort of motive was *that* for murder?

'He used this pub?' said the detective inspector.

'Aye.' The landlord nodded. 'Every night of his life, for the last forty years. So I've been told. I've been here more than twenty years ... and he's never missed a night since *I* came.'

'A bit of a boozer?'

'A pint and a half. Never more, never less. Steady. Steady as a rock ... whatever else, Bill White wasn't a boozer. He just liked his evening drink.'

The D.I. had decided to concentrate his enquiries in the village.

Long Meadow was, by this time, stiff with coppers. Uniformed and C.I.D. A detective superintendent was working his ears off, organising the chaos at the scene of the crime. Photographs. Plan Drawing. Organised Search Detail. Lifting of Footprints. The whole dolly-bag ... and, with all that man-power available, one detective inspector would have been superfluous.

So-o, the D.I. had decided to concentrate *his* initial enquiries in the village ... specifically, in the taproom of *The Fighting Cocks*.

'Somebody killed him,' he said, gently, as he raised a partly-consumed glass of ale to his mouth.

'Aye ... we've heard.'

'Who?' The D.I. replaced the glass on the surface of the bar-counter.

'God knows.' The landlord looked shocked at having been asked the question. He said, 'Look, sir, if anybody here could name the sod who ...'

'All right. Who *might* have?'

The landlord shook his head in bewilderment.

'Let me put it another way,' teased the D.I. 'Somebody shot him—right? ... Eventually, we're going to arrest somebody for it. Who would you be *least* surprised to see us arrest?'

'There's—there's *nobody*. He was a ...'

'Who here, for example?' pressed the D.I. 'Who, among this lot, would you be *least* surprised to see arrested and charged?'

'None of 'em.' The landlord looked outraged. 'They all knew Bill. They all liked him. He was one of the ...'

'They didn't *all* like him,' said the D.I. softly. Grimly. 'Nobody's *that* popular.' He turned his head to glance at the other occupants of the half-filled taproom, and said, 'Who, here? Who, here, won't be too sorry to see him go?'

'Look—I keep telling you—he was a well-respected man. He was a ...'

'He's dead,' said the D.I. mercilessly. 'That makes him "well-respected" ... *now*. "Speak no ill of the dead", and all that crap. But go back a bit—go back a week—and try to forget he's dead. Somebody here didn't like him. I'm not saying they *killed* him—don't get me wrong ... but don't try to kid me that everybody in this bloody room is going to put a personal wreath on the coffin.'

'No.' The landlord hesitated, then said, 'No ... I reckon not.'

'Who?' insisted the D.I.

'Look—I don't like ...'

'*I* don't like murder,' said the D.I., coldly. 'Presumably, you *do*.'

'Nay—be damned!—you've no right to ...'

'I've a right to ask questions. I've a right to demand answers.' The D.I. sipped his beer. 'Now—c'mon, stop being coy—somebody here, in this room, isn't likely to sleep any less easily because Bill White's next bed is already reserved in the public morgue.'

'You've a hell of a way of putting things,' breathed the landlord.

'I have,' said the D.I., 'one hell of a *job* ... but I'm going to do it.'

'All right.' The landlord moistened his lips, glanced at a short, dark man sitting alone in one corner of the room. He said, 'Him. I'm not saying he killed Bill—for Christ's sake, I'm not saying *that*—but ...'

The D.I. waited.

The landlord remained silent.

'But *what*?' asked the D.I.

'Bill shot his dog,' mumbled the landlord, miserably. 'Y'know ... upped with a twelve-bore, and shot it. Said it was sheep-worrying. Harry swore it wouldn't. But—y'know—I dunno ... who knows *what* a dog gets up to when it's on its own. *I* wouldn't like to say.'

'But Bill White shot it?'

'Aye.'

'And Harry ... what's his other name?'

'Gascoinge. Harry Gascoinge.'

'A gypsy name?' The D.I. raised interested eyebrows.

'Aye.' The landlord nodded. 'Just outside the village. There's a van—two vans, in fact ... that's where he lives. Him and his missus. And a son. For about five years, now. They don't cause trouble.'

'But Bill White shot his dog?'

'Aye ... a bitch, actually. A nice animal. Sally.' The landlord looked more and more wretched. 'They—er—they were never apart. Y'know ... wherever Harry went, Sally was there.'

'But not when Bill White shot her ... presumably,' mused the D.I.

'No.' A vertical crease folded itself between the landlord's eyes. 'No—I reckon not ... come to think.'

The D.I. tasted his beer then, off-handedly, asked, 'Does he have a .22?'

'Harry?'

'Uhuh.'

'I—er...'

The landlord closed his mouth, and stared down at the bar-counter.

'*Has* he?' insisted the D.I.

'I—er—I dunno,' muttered the landlord.

'The hell you don't know!' For the first time the D.I. put authoritative bite into his voice.

The landlord looked up, and said, 'Look, mister, I don't wanna drop any of my customers in the ...'

'You're going to answer my question, mate,' said the D.I., grimly. 'Here—or at the nick ... does Gascoinge own a .22?'

The landlord nodded.

'Licensed?'

'I—er—I reckon not. There's a lotta guns round these parts...'

'That aren't licensed. I know.' The D.I.'s voice held disgust as he ended the landlord's sentence for him. 'That's half the bloody trouble with you people. You think a gun's part of ordinary, everyday country equipment.'

'Harry Gascoinge wouldn't murder anybody ... not just for the sake of a dog.' The landlord looked sad-eyed but, at the same time, truculent. He looked into the face of the D.I. and said, 'You're a townie, mister, aren't you?'

'Lessford,' agreed the D.I.

'Aye.'

'Does it make some sort of difference.' The D.I. was on the immediate defensive.

'Aye ... a lot of difference.' There was continued respect for the law in the landlord's tone, but the respect was modified by mild contempt for this representative of that law. He said, 'This is a village pub ... see? Not one of your town boozers. I know my customers. *Know* 'em. Not just as people who buy my beer, but as neighbours. As *friends*. Come Christmas, we merrymake together.

Come a wedding—come a funeral—come a birth—that sort of thing... and we're all one. Y'know... a real community. All right, we have a squabble now and again. Like between Bill and Harry. But it blows over. It doesn't last long. And—look, mister detective—we don't go around *killing* each other ... see? We leave that sorta game to the townies ... we respect *life* a damn sight too much.'

'We'll see,' said the D.I. softly. He finished his beer and, before he turned to leave the taproom, he added, 'I'll let you know how valid your argument is ... when I've had a go at Gascoinge.'

The bits and pieces of a murder enquiry ... the mundane little heartbreaks, the unreported ripples of emotion, the sudden bitternesses and much-too-late regrets.

They never hit the headlines, because they aren't 'news' in the accepted sense of that word. They don't have blood attached.

The newly-widowed Muriel White, sitting in an armchair in the farmhouse kitchen; weeping silently, and with a policewoman's arm around her bowed shoulders; tears rolling, unheeded, down her middle-aged cheeks.

And her voice a droned whisper of self-condemnation.

'Poor White. His socks. Last thing he said, afore he went out. He'd worked a hole in his heel, and I'd darned it all lumpy. In a hurry—y'know ... that much to do. And I'd darned it all lumpy. And t' last thing he said. Would I undarn it, when I'd time. Darn it up again. 'Cos it were all lumpy, and it hurt him when he walked. Them were t' last words he spoke to me. That I'd darned his sock all lumpy.'

A nephew, in Northallerton; a disgusting youth. Yapping and worrying at the heels of his parents as they washed and dressed, prior to hurrying off to give what comfort they could to the mother's bereaved sister.

'You won't forget to mention it, will you? To my Aunty Muriel. About my Uncle Bill's watch. A half-hunter—a smashing watch—and he said it were mine if owt happened to him ... last time I saw him. About four years back. Remember? Went out of his way to tell me. "If owt happens to me, it's *yours*." That's what he said. His very words. So, you won't forget to mention it to my Aunty Muriel, will you?'

A brother—a fellow-farmer—near Guisburn; four years younger than the dead man; a nurser of grudges and a man who squeezed perverted enjoyment from unintended affronts.

'Told yer ... didn't I? Just wait long enough ... that's all. Wait long enough, and it all comes home to roost. Half that flaming farm shoulda been mine. Fifty-fifty. But no ... the old man said it all had to go to our Bill. Bloody will an' all! By God, I wish we'd seen a good solicitor ... that's what *I* wish. Anyroad, it's too late—he don't have *any* of it now ... does he? "Gather ye rosebuds while ye may" ... eh? We-ell, he's gathered all the rosebuds *he's* gonna gather. Now it's *my* turn.'

A conversation, between a farm-worker and his wife; a good man, with a good mate ... but a man who knew his worth, but knew he had never been paid his worth.

'We can't afford a wreath,' he said, bluntly.

'Charlie! We *have* to send a wreath. He's your gaffer.'

'Aye ... well.'

'And he's not been a bad gaffer. You can't say he's been a *bad* gaffer.'

'Not as bad as some.'

'Well ... then.'

The farm-worker hesitated, chewed his lower lip, then said, 'All right. If it'll keep you happy.'

'It's only right, luv.'

'But only a little 'un, mind.'

'No ... I'll pick a nice little 'un.'

'And the card. Nowt soppy. Just "from" ... then our names.'

'Aye. That's all.'

'I'll be there,' he warned. 'I'll be at t' box ... so mind what I've said.'

She murmured, 'I know, Charlie. I know how you feel. But—y'know—we *should* ... to show we're Christian folks, like t' rest.'

A neighbouring farmer; a blunt, unemotional man. A man used to taking full advantage of everything ... including death. He and his herdsman sat on twin churns, alongside the entrance to a well-equipped dairy.

The farmer mused, 'A hundred and twenty head, I reckon ... don't you?'

'All that,' agreed the herdsman. 'I'd say nearer a hundred and fifty.'

'Happen.'

'And good grazing.'

'Good grazing, and a river to sup at,' agreed the farmer.

'If she'll sell,' murmured the herdsman.

'She'll sell,' said the farmer confidently.

'Auction?'

'Be buggered for a tale! Private treaty ... we want no rich-me-quick city bleeders upping t' price past all reason.'

'I reckon she'll go for auction,' said the herdsman.

'No ... not if I get my price in first.'

'And—don't forget—there's his brother. He might want a say.'

'Him!' The farmer's lips curled. 'He hasn't two pennies to scratch his arse wi'. Up Guisburn way. By God ... there's some bonny bloody farms up on *them* tops.'

'Still ... you never know.'

'You need brass to buy land, these days, lad,' said the farmer, dourly. 'Brass—or a bloody good overdraft ... and you need even more brass to work it. That brother of his wouldn't know where to start looking. No-o ...' The farmer sucked his upper lip meditatively, for a moment, then said, 'Let's see him planted. Then I'll make a fair offer to Muriel—cash on the table ... she'll not refuse. Not if I let her stay on at t' house.'

'Happen.' The herdsman didn't sound fully convinced. He repeated, 'Aye ... happen.'

Consternation, aggravation and speculation.

Some of the bits and pieces of a murder enquiry which never hit the headlines.

Mind *you* ...

At the actual *scene* of the crime the words and music would have made *West Side Story* look like a T.V. ad. for Walls ice cream.

Preston was in charge. Preston was a detective superintendent. And Preston believed in all-action, all-noise, all-chaos police methods. There were (give or take a few helmets) about a hundred coppers in and around Long Meadow by eight o'clock that first evening, and every last one of them sweating, or swearing, or both.

Preston had that effect upon people.

Photography Section had recorded everything, from every angle, from every distance. The only thing that hadn't been photographed was the skyscape. But, at the tentative suggestion that it might be an idea to hare off back to the dark room, and there busy themselves producing a few score pictures, Preston had barked an immediate negative.

'I might want some more photographs yet.'

'Of what?' asked the P.S. sergeant who, himself, tended towards the testy side. 'Blades of bloody grass? That's about the only thing we *haven't* shot.'

'Watch it, sergeant.'

'Knackers.'

'This is a murder enquiry, and ...'

'Gerraway? And here I've been thinking it was a flower show.'

By the gate, a detective constable was squatting on his haunches alongside the area of mud.

He called, 'This cartridge case, sir ...'

'Leave it!' howled Preston. 'Don't touch it. Just put it into a cellophane envelope, for lab examination.'

The D.C. looked nonplussed.

'You've got him,' said the Photography Section sergeant, sarcastically. 'He's here for the rest of his service ... working out how the hell he's going to leave it where it is, not touch it and, at the same time, put it in a bloody envelope.'

'I'll have you, sergeant. So help me, I'll ...'

'All measured up, sir.' One of the Plan Drawing 'specialists' joined the verbal ding-dong. 'Okay if we go back to the office, now? We could get the plans finished and a few photostats knocked off before ...'

'No. Hang on a bit. I might want ...'

A squad car P.C. hurried up and said, 'Sir. Word from the mortuary. The one through the forehead. He was dead at the time, according to the P.M. And, if he was on his back, there should be a bullet in the mud, somewhere ... compliments of Dr Carr, and could he have it as soon as possible?'

'Two,' murmured the P.S. sergeant pointedly.

'Eh?' Preston blinked.

'Bullets. Two holes—two bullets ... unless, of course, he had it on a piece of string, and used the same bullet twice.'

'Have you taken all the photographs we might need?' choked Preston.

'And more.'

'Good. On your way, sergeant. Get 'em developed ... and a complete set on Mr Rucker's desk, *tonight*.'

'With pleasure.'

The P.S. sergeant waved a hand to a trio of plain clothes men who were standing around nursing cameras and tripods, and the four of them hurried off towards two parked shooting brakes.

The squad car P.C. muttered, 'Sir. Dr Carr asked me to...'

'Shurrup!' Preston turned his growing irritation in the direction of the Plan Drawing wallah, and snarled, 'All right—if you're *sure* you've missed nothing ...'

'I'm sure, sir.'

'Same applies. Get back to Beechwood Brook. Draw your pictures ... and photostats on Mr Rucker's desk, before morning.'

'That's asking a lot, sir. We have to ...'

'Asking? Who the hell's *asking*? I'm *ordering*, lad. Jump to it. Get your pencils cracking, and make it an all-night session if necessary.'

'Yes, sir,' sighed the P.D. wallah. 'We'll deliver the goods, if it's at all possible.'

He, too, motioned to two of his colleagues and made his way towards a car parked on the grass of Long Meadow.

'Dr Carr, sir. He seemed very anxious ...'

'We're *all* anxious, constable. Carr's anxious. I'm anxious. Everybody's bloody anxious. It's a damn good job some of us can keep our heads.'

'Yes, sir.'

'Hey ... you, there.'

The D.C. squatting alongside the area of mud looked up at his lord and master.

'Got that cartridge yet?' shouted Preston.

'I'm—er—I'm just getting it, sir.'

'Good. Get cracking. And all the casts ... have they been taken?'

'Sir?'

'The plaster casts, for God's sake. The footprints. All that "Henry Moore" stuff. Have they got it all?'

40

'Yes, sir. I—er—I think so.'

'For Christ's sake! Don't you *know*?'

The D.C. chanced his arm, and said, 'Yes, sir. I know ... they've taken all the casts.'

'Right,' bawled Preston. 'Get the cartridge, then start poking around in the mud, till you find the bullet. It's there, somewhere.'

'In ...' The D.C. swallowed, then pointed a finger at the horrific mix of mud, blood and brain tissue. 'In *there*?'

'Where the head was. Start grubbing around till you find it.'

'W-what with?'

'With your hands ... what else?'

The D.C. breathed, 'Oh, my God!' and fought to disassociate his mind from the rest of his body, as he set about one of the most disgusting tasks of his whole police career.

Preston didn't notice. Preston was already yelling instructions and counter-instructions to every officer within hearing distance. This was Preston's way of bobbying; the 'three-ring-circus' way—a way favoured by many high-ranking coppers ... and not, necessarily, the *worst* way.

One grass-green recruit couldn't understand it. He asked an old hand, and the old hand wasn't being deliberately cynical when he gave the answer.

'Y'see, son, it works this way. He shouts loud enough. He tells everybody to do summat then, five minutes later, he tells 'em to do summat else. That way, he can't go wrong. Somewhere, among all that bawling and blather, he has to be right ... at least *once*.'

The killer sipped brandy, smoked a moderately expensive cigar and exchanged after-meal small-talk with his host. The man in whose house he was a guest was a deputy manager at a busy provincial bank; a man 'going places' in the banking world; a man who had learned the art of conversation as part of an evening's entertainment.

His name was Stanley Boyd.

His wife, Lucille Boyd, was in the kitchen with the wife of the killer.

Boyd was saying, 'One must, of course, appreciate that "absolute security" is rather like "absolute truth". An unattainable perfection.'

'A bank, surely?' murmured the killer.

'Security, old boy.' Boyd settled himself deeper into the comfort of the well-cushioned armchair. 'It comes from the mind of a man. A puzzle, if you like. A conundrum. And a conundrum thought up by the mind of one man, can be answered by the mind of another. Therefore, "absolute security" is a myth ...'

(... *By this time they'll know. They'll have found White's body. Somebody. They'll have realised it was murder. They'll wonder why White. They'll never guess. There's no link, so they'll never guess ...*)

'... unless, of course, you have a community which deals solely in cheques and credit cards. That's the nearest you're ever likely to get to "absolute security". No money ... as such. Merely the transfer of wealth. Numerals, moved from one set of figures to another.'

'It's a fascinating thought.' The killer dragged his mind back to the conversation.

'I think so ... naturally.'

'But a bit cold-blooded, don't you think?'

'The cool, crisp feel of a fiver.' Boyd smiled part-agreement. 'It's a primitive thing we'll never rid ourselves of, I'm afraid ...

(... *Primitive. Like killing. Supposedly difficult. Supposedly an act few people can bring themselves to commit. To slaughter a complete stranger. A man you don't known—except by name—and to squeeze a trigger and* drop him as easily, and as dispassionately, as a slaughterman might drop an ox. The beauty of it. The sheer ...)

'... the barter thing.'

'The—er—barter thing?' The killer frowned puzzlement.

'Barter ... y'know.' Boyd moved the hand holding his cigar in a tiny wave. 'Half my pig for a hundredweight of your potatoes. That sort of thing. The pig—the potatoes —they're both something you can handle. Something you can feel. Wealth you can actually touch. The same with the fiver. You can handle it. It has substance. More substance than ink, drying on the page of a ledger.'

The man called Crispin was terrified.

His terror had lasted eight long years and, with each day of those years—with each hour, almost—it had mounted a little. It was now his whole life. He inhaled it with each breath. It was a tiny tremor which accompanied every heartbeat. It wrapped itself around every mouthful of food he chewed, and threatened to choke him when he swallowed. It rattled the cup against his teeth—a miniature tattoo of desperation—each time he drank at the tea.

Judas Christ!

Eight years ago *he'd* dealt in terror. The 'beat-up', the 'going-over', the 'dusting-off' ... he'd been an acknowledged expert in the art of inflicting pain. He'd had men—and women—screaming for mercy ... and getting none.

Free-lance aggro merchant. Top line. Best in the business.

But Durham nick!

That bloody place could tame wild tigers. It had a name; the toughest granite-house in the country ... The Moor was a Butlin's Holiday Camp, by comparison. The real bastards ended up in Durham and, when they came out, they weren't bastards any more. They'd been boned and reduced to jelly.

Like *him*.

Shit-scared that all their past bastardy was going to catch up with them; that, round the next corner, somebody was waiting, with an iron bar in his fist.

Crispin's eyes never stopped moving. Every face—every corner—in the grimy café was searched and re-searched for the first sign. A sign that, one day, *had* to come. The split-second prelude to broken bones and mangled flesh ... the only retribution recognised by the sub-humans who peopled Crispin's twisted world.

It was going to happen. As sure as hell ... they knew he was out, and when they traced him it was going to happen.

He gulped down the rest of the tea, then scurried from the café and into the deepening gloom of the evening.

Crispin—Wally Crispin ... a one-time King Rat who'd been reduced to a terrified mouse.

Topographically, Long Meadow was part of High Dale Farm, and High Dale Farm was within the area originally policed by the officers of the Beechwood Division of the one-time county constabulary. Such simplicity had, needless to say, been shot to hell and beyond by the machinations of Whitehall-based masterminds and, via the magic word 'amalgamation', High Dale Farm was now part of a 'Metropolitan Police District' and, because it was south of the River Henfraw, it was within the Lessford Region of the M.P.D. Which, in turn, meant that Sugden was its A.C.C. (Crime) and Rucker was its Head of C.I.D.

Neither Sugden nor Rucker were ex-county constabulary coppers ... which enamoured them not at all with the bulk of the boys and girls engaged on the initial murder enquiries, because they *were* ex-county constabulary coppers.

Nor was that all.

Beechwood Brook was still a full-sized police division (albeit, now of a Metropolitan Police District) complete with its own divisional officer. And, only a few months before the amalgamation re-shuffle, that divisional officer had stepped into the shoes of a legend ... a strictly 'county constabulary' legend.

Ripley had once lorded it over Beechwood Brook, and after Ripley had come Blayde and, having worked his nuts off trying to prove that he was a fit and proper person to shine the shoes of the great Ripley, Blayde was now lumbered with a duo of high-ranking C.I.D. slobs who were heavy-footing it within the sanctuary of his (Blayde's) D.H.Q.

Life was getting slightly trying for Chief Superintendent Blayde.

'I'd like to know what goes on,' he said, bluntly.

'We've decided to use the Recreation Hall as the Information Room,' said Rucker.

'*We?*'

Rucker pinned this stroppy uniformed chief superintendent with a cold, sardonic stare of near-disbelief.

Blayde returned the stare, and said, 'Can I assume you're not using the word "we" as a form of royal pronoun?'

'As far as I'm concerned, you can assume just what the devil you feel like ...'

'And, as far as *I'm* concerned,' snarled Blayde, 'the Recreation Hall of this particular divisional headquarters remains just *that*—a Recreation Hall—until I receive some sort of official notification to the contrary ... with reasons attached.'

'Hold it!'

Sugden jumped in before the verbal flare-up got completely out of hand. He closed the door of the Recreation

Hall to keep long-eared constables out of harm's way, then turned his attention to Rucker.

He said, 'Chief Superintendent Blayde knows about White's death ... does he?'

'If he doesn't he must be ...'

'I know,' interrupted Blayde, furiously. 'And the reason I know is because a patrol sergeant *mentioned* it to me.'

'Rucker?' Sugden's voice was low-pitched and dangerous.

'What does he want?' sneered Rucker. 'An illuminated address, on vellum?'

'He not only "wants", he's going to *get* the respect due to his rank.'

'Time-wasting protocol ... is that what you mean?'

'You left a word from the end of that question, Rucker,' snapped Sugden.

'Oh, yes ... *sir*.'

'Don't forget it. *Never* forget it.' Sugden turned to Blayde, and continued, 'My apologies, chief superintendent. As divisional officer, you should have been notified. You have my word that, as from this moment, you'll be kept up to date with all developments in the case.'

'Thank you, sir,' said Blayde, flatly.

'For the record, then. At seventeen-thirty-five hours today, we received a report of the death of William White, of High Dale Farm. He was found shot through the head, in Long Meadow. It's being treated as murder ...'

'Because it *is* murder ... chief superintendent,' murmured Rucker.

'We'd like the use of this Recreation Hall as an Information Room.'

'With pleasure.' Blayde bobbed his head.

'We'd also like as many men as you can spare, as back-up officers to the C.I.D. men staffing the Information Room.'

Blayde switched his eyes from Sugden to Rucker, then back to Sugden.

'May I offer a suggestion?' he said, softly.

'Please.'

'Let this division take over the staffing of the Information Room ... totally.'

'The hell!' breathed Rucker.

'Let *me* take over personal responsibility ... under your orders, of course.'

It was a challenge—a quietly spoken defiance of Rucker's newly acquired authority—and Blayde's tone made small effort to hide the fact.

Sugden knew coppers. He knew that the peculiar demands of their jobs, plus the personalities of men who could do that job well, was a breeding-ground for antagonisms amounting to near-pathological hatreds. The basic nuts and bolts of coppering—that the Police Service fought a never-ending war against bastards ... and it *took* a bastard to *beat* a bastard. The most closely-guarded secret of law-enforcement; the eternal gamekeeper-poacher argument.

And this (as Sugden knew) was one of those moments that surfaced occasionally. Chief superintendent versus chief superintendent. C.I.D. versus Uniformed Branch. Rucker versus Blayde.

Sugden knew what he *wanted* to do ... but he also knew what he *had* to do.

Rucker was a damn fine detective—whatever criticism could be levelled at the man, that single, all-important fact could never be denied ... *but he had to be tamed.*

Sugden's tone was as stone-faced as his expression, as he said, 'Thank you, Chief Superintendent Blayde. That's a generous offer. I'll accept it, gladly. The Post Office should be installing extra telephones, tomorrow morning. Four ... if you think you need more, let me know. That means Detective Chief Superintendent Rucker, here, can concentrate all his energies on keeping the actual enquiry moving. Feeding all information back to here ... where you'll supervise the collating of it into the Murder File.'

'And the Murder Log?' asked Blayde.

'That, too.' Sugden nodded. 'It's already been started, of course. Detective Sergeant Tallboy—one of your own C.I.D. officers—has it under way. He can move in here, and continue the log under your supervision.'

'Ripley's son-in-law,' murmured Blayde.

'Does that make a difference?' The question held hidden barbs; Sugden wasn't taking sides—pro-Rucker, or pro-Blayde—and that, too, had to be made clear.

'No difference, sir,' said Blayde, gently.

'Good. In that case, I'll leave the organising of the Information Room to you. There's a meeting—an unofficial get-together—scheduled for midnight. Here ... if that's convenient.'

'Quite convenient, sir. I'll have the place ready.'

'Good. You'll be present, of course. To see how far we've progressed. To plan the first full day's enquiry.' Sugden turned, treated Rucker to a quick, humourless smile, and ended, 'That's it, then, Mr Rucker. As you suggested ... this is the obvious place for the Information Room. And, thanks to Mr Blayde, you're free to push the enquiry as hard as possible.'

'I'll push it ... *sir*.' Rucker's tone was as cold, and smooth, as polished ice. 'Have no fear along those lines ... I'll certainly *push* it.'

Harry Gascoinge had a knack. He kept his head motionless, but missed nothing with his eyes. The eyes matched the mahogany tan of the face and the jet of the long, brushed-back hair and, in the claustrophobic confines of the caravan—reflecting, as they did, the soft light from the two brass oil lamps—they seemed to have a life separate from that of their owner. They reminded the detective inspector of twin animals, caged and everlastingly seeking escape.

In the shadows, at the back of the van, Gascoinge's wife sat on a cushioned bench and watched her husband being interrogated. She was a huge, muscular woman—almost twice the weight of her whipcord man—but with the deferential silence of a good 'traveller's' wife.

It was a game—this question and answer routine—a game of tag, played with words. It had ancient rules; rules hammered out centuries before, when the wanderers and the law-enforcers had first clashed. It also had deep and subconscious hatreds. The hatreds of the oppressed and the oppressor; hatreds which were birthrights and instinctive.

The D.I. struggled to subdue these illogical and unfounded hatreds. There was that about the man Gascoinge which the D.I. admired—a simple dignity and a refusal to *quite* conform—but the age-old hatreds made the voice of the detective unnecessarily sharp-edged ... made him *sound* offensive, when he *wasn't* offensive.

'I understand you have a gun,' said the D.I.

'Who told you that, sir?'

The 'sir' was not servility. It wasn't even deliberate good manners. It, too, was part of the game; it carried a subtle mockery ... the mockery of the untamed for the would-be tamer.

The D.I. smiled, and said, '"Information received." That's all I can tell you, Gascoinge.'

'People say things,' murmured Gascoinge.

'Have you a gun?' The D.I. made it a direct question.

'Where would I get a gun, sir?'

'That's no answer, Gascoinge.'

'What sort of a gun, sir?'

'A .22 rifle.'

'I'd need a certificate for such a gun.'

The D.I. nodded.

'Who'd give *me* a certificate, sir?'

'People have guns, without certificates,' said the D.I.

'And, when you ask, they tell you?'

'No ... not always.'

'They'd be fools, wouldn't they, sir?'

The D.I. said, 'On a murder enquiry, the fools are those who tell lies. And those who refuse to answer questions.'

'You think I murdered White, sir?'

'No.' The D.I. smiled, again. 'If I thought *that*, we wouldn't just be sitting here, talking.'

'No, sir ... that, we wouldn't.'

The interior of the van was spotless; it smelled of cleanliness and sweet herbs. It was a warm night, with the promise of thunder in the air, and the warmth and the smell of the herbs and the closed-in comfort of the caravan made the D.I. feel drowsy. He'd had a long day, and it was almost eleven o'clock ... and, with luck, bed was well within thinking distance.

He sighed, 'Can we do a deal, Gascoinge?'

'I wouldn't know, sir.'

'White shot your dog,' said the D.I. 'Had that happened today—just before White was killed—I might have considered you as a possible suspect.'

'For a dog?'

'For Sally,' said the D.I.

'She was a fine bitch.'

'I know dogs,' said the D.I., gently. 'I know what they can give ... and what an owner might do. On the spur of the moment.'

'She was a fine bitch,' repeated Gascoinge.

'But not after a time lapse. Dislike, probably. Probably something even deeper than dislike. But not murder ... not when the blood's cooled.'

Gascoinge said, 'Are you asking me, sir? Are you asking me whether I killed White?'

'No. I know you didn't.'

'Know?' For the first time, Gascoinge moved his head, and looked directly at the D.I.

'Pretty sure. *Very* sure.' The D.I. nodded. 'I'm asking you to let me *prove* you didn't.'

'How?'

'The gun. The .22. Let me have it, Gascoinge. Forget the certificate offence ... I won't push it. Just let me have the gun. Ballistics will prove it wasn't the murder weapon.'

The woman spoke for the first time.

She said, 'Why should we trust you, sir?'

Gascoinge's eyes reflected his wife's question.

'Dammit, because I ...' The D.I. closed his mouth on the sudden spat of anger. He moved his shoulders in a resigned shrug, then said, 'It wouldn't mean anything.'

'What's that, sir?' Gascoinge sounded mildly interested.

'To you people,' said the D.I., heavily. 'It wouldn't mean a thing.'

'What?' insisted Gascoinge.

'Because I've *said* so. My word ... my promise, if you like.'

'You mean we aren't people of honour? Is that what you mean, sir?'

'No.'

'What then, sir?'

'You don't think *we* are,' said the D.I. 'You don't trust us. Maybe you have your reasons ... I dunno. But, it's a pity. We're people of honour, too. Most of us.'

'You?' asked Gascoinge, solemnly.

'I like to think so.'

Gascoinge lowered his gaze and stared at the floor of the caravan for a moment. Then he looked back at the face of the D.I. and said, 'If I have a sporting rifle, sir—*if* I have one—could you prove it didn't kill White?'

'Not me, personally. But Ballistics could prove it. Easily.'

'But, if I have a rifle—*if* I have a rifle—I should have a certificate?'

'You should have a certificate,' agreed the D.I.

'I'd be in trouble with the police, if I hadn't?'

The D.I. chose his words carefully.

He said, 'This is a murder investigation, Gascoinge. To get at facts, we're prepared to overlook minor law-breaking. I'll be honest. I couldn't guarantee the return of your gun ... not unless you were first granted a licence. And—again, to be honest—I doubt if you *would* be granted one. But, the fact that you haven't a licence ... that could be overlooked.'

'By you?'

'By me.' The D.I. nodded.

'By those men who give you orders, sir?'

The D.I. met Gascoinge's gaze and, in a quiet, but very deliberate voice, said, 'They'll be given a rifle. They'll be asked to check that it isn't the murder weapon. If it *isn't* ... that's all! No name will be mentioned. Nobody'll be told where the rifle came from. Nobody!'

Gascoinge moved his head in acceptance of the promise. He stood up, moved to the far end of the caravan and, from its poor hiding place at the rear of a high shelf, he took an ancient, but well cared for, single-shot .22 rifle.

The weapons were being collected.

Blayde, having been recognised as the divisional officer of Beechwood Brook, wasted no time on half-measures. The modern D.H.Q. building had rooms to spare, and the Recreation Hall was only one of them.

The Women Police Constables' Retiring Room (one of a handful of architectural baubles thought up by the planners of this over-expensive, status-seeking building) was cleared of its armchairs and turned into a 'reception centre' for weapons rounded up by uniformed and C.I.D. officers, throughout the evening and early night.

The Firearms Register was consulted. Squad cars, Panda vans and privately owned, 'mileage allowance' vehicles called at houses, farms and outlying smallholdings; registered firearms were asked for—regardless of their calibre—and receipts were given; the firearms were labelled and carefully stacked in the Women Police Constables' Retiring Room ... on the million-to-one chance that the murder weapon was not merely registered, but was also readily available to the first enquiring copper.

People closed their eyes, and slept ... or *tried* to sleep.

The killer slept. His conscience was easy; he'd thought it all out for years—lived with the scheme, until the scheme had become part of his life—and whatever qualms he might once have had concerning the slaughter of people whom he didn't even know no longer troubled him. Some, indeed, were already dead ... White, and the others, were merely joining them.

Crispin tried hard to sleep, but succeeded only in spasmodic snatches of shallow unconsciousness. He was huddled under an overcoat, in a corner of a bedroom, in an empty and condemned house on the outskirts of Darlington. The vandals and the vermin had combined to further wreck what was already derelict; the windows had gone, much of the roof was missing and the incoming weather had made crumbly goo of large stretches of old plaster; the place stank of rats and mice, and the rotting floorboards were thick with droppings beneath the resting places of starlings. The place was a death-trap, in that the joists were unsafe and even the walls could not have withstood sudden, or excessive, wind-pressure, but Crispin was unaware of this secret danger ... his sleeplessness being, not the result of fear for his safety, but because he was hungry, cold and haunted by the knowledge that eight years inside one of the toughest jails in the United Kingdom had squeezed him dry of all the spit and vinegar necessary for his own brand of 'manhood'.

Sheila Bentley slept soundly and comfortably. She slept on a spring-interior mattress and between brushed nylon sheets ... not knowing that this was the last night's sleep of her life.

Mind you ...

Everybody didn't sleep.

Everybody didn't even *try* to sleep.

Certain flatfeet, for example ...

A brief, pre-conference chin-wag was in progress, within the privacy of Blayde's office. Sullivan was there. So was Sugden, Preston and, of course, Blayde himself. Rucker was *not* present ... an oversight on somebody's part, perhaps. Or, on the other hand, perhaps not.

Nobody mentioned Rucker's absence.

There was an air of amiability—almost companionship—between the four high-ranking officers. Pipes had been stoked, and cigarettes had been lighted. Blayde (the only uniformed officer of the quartet) had his tunic unbuttoned. Sullivan was perched precariously, with one cheek of his backside warming a corner of the ultra-modern desk, which was the centre-piece of the ultra-modern office. Sugden and Preston sprawled, feet wide apart, in two of the equally ultra-modern (albeit surprisingly comfortable) easy chairs which were also part of the office furniture.

And Sullivan was saying, '... and the chief wanted it. A big case. Something to weld the force together.'

'I wouldn't call it "big",' observed Sugden ... a remark which he conveniently forgot, within the next few days. 'Straightforward murder. Up, and down ... shouldn't take too much bringing home to roost.'

'Murder's big enough, for starters,' grunted Preston.
'Tell me.' Sugden addressed the question to Blayde. '"Appleyard's" Farm ... right?'
Blayde nodded.
'Farmed by White. Why not *"White's"* Farm?'
Blayde glanced at Preston for the answer.
Preston said, 'High Dale Farm ... see? Originally—donkey's years back—it was farmed by Dick Appleyard. He was there when I first came to the division. Then he emigrated. Australia, I think. Maybe New Zealand. One, or the other. White took the place over, but y'know what these hayseed communities are like ... it's still "Appleyard's" Farm. Always will be.'
'Before I came,' added Blayde. 'White was already there, when I arrived.'
'We "townies".' Sullivan grinned. 'You ex-county blokes'll have to keep us in line, as far as country lore goes. Otherwise we'll look real berks.'
'If you don't mind my saying, you already *do*.' Sugden's counter-grin robbed the observation of any offence. 'What the hell's that on your hair?'
'Eh?' Sullivan lifted a hand and rubbed the palm across his grey and close-cropped thatch.
'It—er—it looks like paint,' observed Blayde. 'Light brown paint.'
'It bloody well *is* paint,' grumbled Sullivan, self-consciously. 'The joys of do-it-yourself home decorating. A beige-coloured ceiling, no less.'
'Very modern,' murmured Preston.
'I have a "with it" family, superintendent.'
'But you're definitely *without* it?' chuckled Sugden.
'Cubic ... but hen-pecked,' agreed Sullivan, with mock resignation. 'But—seriously—is it *too* obvious. I'd hate to be a distraction at the briefing.'
'We go through the motions,' said Blayde, philosophically. 'It's all pre-packed patter, and they've all heard

it before. Nobody'll be listening. Nobody'll be watching. It'll be the usual exercise in sleeping with your eyes open. I doubt if they'd notice, if we all trooped in there wearing bright blue wigs.'

'And,' added Sugden, teasingly, 'nobody's likely to have the gall to laugh at a newly-appointed deputy chief constable.'

Sullivan sniffed, then said, 'Which reminds me. I've asked Harris and Lennox along. Y'know—to sit in ... just in case the enquiry spreads into their region.'

'Good idea,' commented Blayde.

Sugden's chuckle repeated itself, then expanded into a laugh, as he said, 'Poor old Harris.'

'Y'mean Lenny?'

'Lenny,' agreed Sugden. 'I've worked alongside him for a few years.' He raised his eyes to the ceiling, and ended, 'Ye Gods!'

Preston said, 'A good thief-taker ... I'm told.'

'Er—"unusual". Good—*very* good ... but a one-off job.'

'Harris,' said Sullivan, 'needs a sense of humour ... that's all.'

'Harris,' corrected Sugden, 'needs the patience of Jesus Christ ... *that's* the first requisite, when you're working with old Lennox.'

'Unorthodox.'

'Stark staring bloody mad ... but doesn't know it,' said Sugden.

Blayde looked serious, as he said, 'Lennox is a great copper. Don't let the externals fool you. A lot of it's an act. In a tight corner, I'd ask for no better man to guard my back.'

Blayde's solemn defence of Lennox dampened much of the jocularity.

Sullivan glanced at his watch, and said, 'We'd better get in there. It's almost midnight.'

'Just one thing,' said Preston. 'The plaster casts of the footprints. Spiked shoes ... so I'm told.'

'Golfing shoes,' said Sugden. 'Carr'll go into the details. But, golfing shoes. Eleven spikes—four on the heel, seven on the sole ... the spikes are peculiar to golfing shoes. Men's ... size ten.'

'That should help.'

Blayde said, 'Beechwood Golf Club. Less than a mile, across the fields to the fourteenth hole. A little more than a mile, to the clubhouse. Five-hundred members ... thereabouts. It cuts it down ... but not much.'

'Was White a member?'

'Good Lord, no.'

Sullivan hoisted himself from the desk corner, and said, 'Come on, chaps. They'll all be in there by this time ... anxious to hear the usual guff.'

The 'usual guff'. From Sullivan, himself ...

'... And those are the details, gentlemen. I expect an all-out effort. No cutting corners. As little duplication of enquiries as possible. Statements, wherever possible. Every detail—however apparently insignificant—fed into this Information Room, without delay. Nobody flying off on a personal tangent. This is a team job. If we work well—if we work together—we should end up with the first successful murder enquiry of the new force.'

From Dr Joseph Carr, M.Sc., Ph.D., director of the Area Forensic Science Laboratory ...

'... Estimated time of death, between four and four-fifteen. Murder. Premeditated. Forget any "ricochet" theories, gentlemen. The one through the forehead was a *coup de grâce* ... he was already dead, but the killer wanted to be absolutely sure. A .22 bullet, from a rifle. Bolt action. We have one of the bullets ... the one from the forehead. We have a cartridge ... presumably, the one ejected after the first shot. We have the shoe-casts ...

golfing shoes. Give us a bullet, or a cartridge, from the same rifle. Give us the rifle. Give us the shoes ... or casts made from footprints left by the same shoes. We'll perform our little conjuring act, never fear. We'll link them together for you. We can forge *that* much of the chain.'

From Sugden ...

'... Chief Superintendent Rucker has overall charge of all enquiries. He'll be guiding the physical side of the investigation. The footwork. The graft that, eventually, brings home the bacon. He'll keep you on your toes. If he doesn't, I *will*. The Information Room ... that's Chief Superintendent Blayde's pigeon. Here—where we are at the moment—is where *everything* is reported ... and, without delay. I'll repeat what Assistant Chief Constable Sullivan has already emphasised. This is a team job. Any would-be glory-boys ... and God help 'em!'

The 'usual guff'.

Followed by the usual questions.

Sullivan (old hand that he was) knew all about the 'any questions, gentlemen?' gimmick with which each speaker —including himself—ended his spiel. Some of the questions were genuine; asked by men who didn't *quite* understand the set-pattern rigmarole of a murder case. But other questions—more than half of them, in fact—were asked by would-be blue-eyed boys anxious to attract the attention of the high-rankers; asked by eager-faced tearers-up-of-trees, each busting a gut to be noticed ... to be *known*.

Carr answered these non-questions with the innocent patience of the expert who is forever worried by the possibility that he isn't being fully understood.

Sullivan gave them grunted, one-word replies ... like the quick brushing off of annoying gnats.

Sugden (to Sullivan's secret delight) was blunt, to the point of rudeness. To one particular eager-beaver query, he snapped, 'If you don't know the answer to *that*, you don't deserve to carry the rank of detective sergeant. If you *do* know, why the hell ask?'

'I—er ...' The scarlet-faced time-waster fought to salvage some self-respect from his shattered attempt to steal the limelight. '*I* know the answer, sir. It's just that—y'know ... if some of the others aren't quite sure about...'

'In that case,' interrupted Sugden, coldly, 'they can ask *you*. And, if they do, let me know. I'm anxious to know how many passengers we're carrying.'

It was the one moment of moderately high tension in the whole conference. It did two things. It chopped a pompous D.S. off by the knee-caps ... and it set the tone of Sugden's authority, as A.C.C. (Crime).

For the rest, it was boring, and it had all been heard before.

So-o—some poor old stick of a farmer had been murdered ... it was a crying shame, but so what? Guns were everywhere, these days. Murders were ten-a-penny and, of all the run-of-the-mill killings this was just about *the* most 'run' of *the* most everyday 'mill'. Twenty-four hours from now—forty-eight, at the most—and His Nibs (whoever His Nibs was) would be 'helping police in their enquiries' ... and they'd all be back to tracing nicked cars, or hounding the snouts about the latest spate of shopbreakings.

Ah, well ... that was bobbying.

One day more—one day less ... and roll on that bloody pension!

Except, of course ...

'What's her name, again?' asked Lennox.

He held the telephone in his right hand and, with his left, he pulled a pad of lined foolscap to within writing distance. He contorted his obese body until he could hold the earpiece to his right ear with his left hand, grabbed a pencil from the desk top with his right and, on the foolscap, scribbled the words 'Sheila Bentley. Ashfield Comprehensive'.

Then, he rumbled into the mouthpiece, 'Okay. Pass the word. I'll be down ... and tell whoever's handling things at the scene to keep the kids clear.'

'You have some sort of gripe, I understand,' said Rucker, softly.

'If, by the expression "gripe", you mean a complaint...'

'By the expression "gripe" I mean a complaint,' agreed Rucker. 'I could, if you wish, put it in Chaucer's English —or Norman French—but, for the moment, we'll be crude and colloquial. *Gripe.* You have some sort of gripe ... right?'

'Your men are interfering with the members' play.'

'Well ... well ... well,' murmured Rucker.

The two men and the woman were in a large and airy room. There was a picture window, from which could be seen the Number One Tee of the course. The room itself was a clutter of lists, golf bags, old clubs, an unopened box of golf balls, an odd mix of good class furniture, a trio of desks, a couple of wall cabinets and a chest of filing drawers. There was also a faint odour of beeswax, linseed oil and embrocation ... the odour associated with manly pursuits and healthy, outdoor activity.

The woman—a tweed-skirted, hand-knitted-pullovered creature of zero feminity, with the jaw of a world heavyweight champion—said, 'Major Ingle, should I ...'

'Leave us,' interrupted Rucker, smoothly. 'What I have to say to your boss isn't for your shell-like ears. And I don't usually yell "Fore!" before I go into action.'

'I have no intention of taking orders from ...'

'Be available, my dear.' The stiff-backed secretary of

Beechwood Golf Club stroked his moustache with the back of a forefinger, and said, 'Y'know—within reach ... available to show Chief Superintendent Rucker out, when I've—er—finished with him.'

'Yes, major. Of course.'

She marched to the door, and left the office.

'Now ...' began Ingle.

'Not yet ... *Major.*' Rucker's slow smile was that of a tiger within reach of a particularly succulent lamb. He drawled, 'You may be a lad with the she-men but, when *I'm* conducting a murder enquiry, you take your turn in the queue. I'll "finish with *you*" first, then—if you still have the energy available—I just *might* let you have your say.'

'My complaint concerns ...'

'Your complaint doesn't even interest me ... *Major.*' The smoothly inserted interruption was a deliberate, and calculated insult. 'This place—this glorified, over-expensive putting green you're in charge of—has a certain membership. How many?'

'I'm damned if I see why I should ...'

'You'll be damned if you *don't*,' warned Rucker, gently. 'A man was shot to death, less than a mile from here. The killer wore golf shoes. Presumably, even *you* can add two and two together.'

'I find your attitude highly objectionable.'

'Quite—I'm paid to be objectionable ... and I haven't even started yet. I'll ask you again. What's the membership of this place?'

'If you think you can ...'

Rucker snapped, 'Ingle, I'll ask you the same question a *third* time. But the third time of asking won't be here ... it'll be at Beechwood Brook Police Station. *After* I've charged you with Obstructing the Police in a murder investigation. And, if you think I'm bluffing, *make* me ask you a third time.'

'Five hundred,' said Ingle, hurriedly. 'About.'
'No.' Rucker shook his head. 'Not "about". The exact membership. And, if you don't know, look it up ... now!'

Ingle breathed heavily, then said, 'Five hundred and thirty-two.'

'Good.' Rucker nodded solemn satisfaction, then said, 'In which case—and for your information—my men will require five hundred and thirty-two statements. Plus five hundred and thirty-two corroborative statements. Plus statements—and corroborative statements—from you, and from the female who apparently thinks you won the war, single-handed. Plus statements—and corroborative statements—from every man, woman and child who has the dubious honour of treading the turf of this club. I don't give a damn how inconvenient the taking of those statements happen to be. I care even less how, or whether, they interfere with the childish waving about of golf clubs, or the hitting of inoffensive balls. Those statements are going to be taken ... *Major*. With, or without, your puny consent. My men have orders. Every last one of those statements are to be taken, today.'

'That's utterly ...'

'Any pompous stupidity, and *I'm* to be notified.'

'Just who the devil ...'

'That's why I'm here, little man. Putting *your* priorities in order.'

'And if I don't care to ...'

'You'll suffer. You'll be deflated. *Anybody* who fancies himself as a cop-tamer will be deflated ... that I promise. Pass the word along to your five hundred and thirty-two playmates. To co-operate. In the long run, it'll be quicker ... and far less painful.'

Ingle glared, then choked, 'Rucker. I warn you. I have friends ...'

'Congratulations. I haven't.'

'Friends in authority. Friends who can ...'

'I don't give a damn,' snarled Rucker, 'if you're on boozing terms with the Almighty himself. Your "friends" don't frighten me, little man. On a murder enquiry, they *daren't* frighten me ... they daren't even *try*.'

'Really? In that case you're in for a ...'

'Shall I tell you *why* they daren't frighten me?' Rucker's voice dropped to a sneering purr. 'Because—and they know it—any back-door scare tactics, and I'll nail *them* as readily, and as happily, as I'll nail you.'

Ingle hesitated. He moistened his lips and touched his moustache, nervously.

Then, he muttered, 'I've—er—I've heard stories about you, Rucker.'

'Is that a fact?'

'Stories about what sort of a ...'

'Stand in my way,' said Rucker, coldly, 'and you'll be able to *tell* stories about me. Meanwhile, I'm doubling the number of men on duty at this place. They'll talk to who the hell they like. They'll go where the hell they like. They'll take statements from who the hell they like. And they'll interfere with as many games of golf as they like. Understand? And you, little man, will stand there, smile and like it. Otherwise ... God help you.'

Rucker turned and walked from the office.

The square-jawed female was waiting in the corridor, beyond the door.

'I think your soldier-boy friend needs you,' murmured Rucker.

'What?' She blinked.

'He needs a quick dose of self-esteem. He's just had his epaulets chewed off.'

Police Sergeant Poynings said, 'A sad thing, sir. A very wicked thing.'

Which, in view of the fact that the subject-matter of the remark was murder, and that the victim of that murder was a moderately attractive, perfectly healthy and (until her violent death) an unusually happy woman, seemed an uncommonly trite and unnecessary utterance. Death is rarely other than sad, and murder is never other than wicked.

But Lennox knew exactly what the sergeant meant.

'Sad, old son,' he agreed, heavily. 'Sadder than usual.'

And it was, too.

Sheila Bentley had been secretary to the headmaster of Ashfield Comprehensive School, in the city of Bordfield. She'd been one of those ever-young spinster ladies who have a natural affinity with children of all ages. She'd been a mother-substitute to the younger pupils, and a confidante to the puppy-love-saddened teenagers. She'd been a close friend to every master and every mistress, and the very rock upon which the headmaster had built a highly successful triple-stream establishment of learning.

She was far more than 'one more murder victim'—far more than 'one more dead woman' ... she was, as far as any human being ever can be, irreplaceable.

'How?'

As Lennox asked the question he checked that the coppers already at the scene were doing their job effectively; that this particular part of the school's forecourt—the rectangular marked-out parking lot for the use of the staff's cars—was being kept clear of hundreds of already-weeping pupils; that, as other squad cars and other officers arrived, they were deployed to seal off the school and its surrounds from the gathering sightseers.

'A shot through the head.' P.S. Poynings answered Lennox's question. He pointed to a tree-lined cul-de-sac, across the road from the school frontage. 'From up there ... from what we've gathered, so far. From a parked car.'

'Make? Number?' asked Lennox.

'Dunno, sir.' Poynings looked sad at having to break

the news. 'A dark-coloured car ... no better description than that. Y'know what it's like.'

'Don't blame yourself, sarge,' soothed Lennox. 'And don't blame *them*. They're not coppers. Who looks at car numbers, when there's a corpse to look at?'

'Aye—I know ... but a bit of luck wouldn't do much harm, now and again.'

The walkie-talkie clipped to the lapel of the sergeant's tunic crackled out a metallic call-sign and Poynings lifted the set to his mouth and answered. The luck he'd just mentioned seemed to have arrived.

He re-clipped the set into position, and said, 'You heard, sir.'

'Abandoned, Spar Road ... with a spent .22 cartridge on the floor, by the driver's seat.'

'Could be it,' said Poynings.

Lennox glanced down at the rag-doll figure sprawling by the doors of the Woodwork Classroom.

He said, 'Hang around here till the doc arrives, sarge. Keep things under control. I'll push off to Spar Road. I'll keep you informed.'

'Yes, sir.' The sergeant frowned at the dead woman, and murmured, 'It is, y'know. It's a real sad thing, sir.'

The detective constable said, 'Your name, sir, please?'

'Procter,' replied the member. 'Harold Procter.'

'Tell me, Mr Procter—between four o'clock, and quarter past four, yesterday—where, exactly, were you?'

'At work. At my office ... till—er—about five-thirty. I can't be certain to the minute, but five-thirty is *about* the time I left for home.'

'Not here, at the links?'

'No. Not yesterday.'

'You'll have witnesses, of course, sir?'

'Witnesses?'

'People who'll verify that you were at work, between four and four-fifteen?'

'A whole office-full, officer. I'd say about a dozen ... at least a dozen.'

The detective constable said, 'Thank you, sir. Now, if I could have a short statement, please. And the name of a couple of the people who can corroborate your whereabouts, at the time of the murder.'

'If it'll help. I can't see how it can, but ...'

'Negative statements, sir.' The detective constable smiled. 'You'd be surprised how many statements we have to take, in order to prove what *didn't* happen.'

'Ah ... y'mean *elimination*.'

'That's about the size of it, sir.'

'Eliminate everybody ... eh? And what you have left is the murderer.'

'Not quite everybody.' The detective constable's tone was soft, and solemn. 'Everybody, but one. The bloke we're after ... nobody can eliminate *him*.'

'Which division is this?' asked Lennox.

'Daiton Division, sir,' said the squad car constable. 'We're about half a mile inside the divisional boundary.'

'Good lad.' Lennox's pudding-shaped face beamed appreciation at the 'local knowledge'. 'Get on the squawk-box. Pass word to the Operations Room. My compliments to the Daiton divisional officer—notify him of what's happened—ask him if he'll let me have as many men as he can spare, for immediate house-to-house. Then notify Fingerprints, Photography and Ballistics ... get 'em out here, fast. Then Mr Harris ... put *him* in the picture. Got all that, son?'

'Yes, sir. I'll ...'

'Fine. Then you, and your mate, stand guard over this car. Nobody touches it till the dabs are taken. Nobody touches the cartridge till the bang-bang brigade have given it the once-over. And *nobody* picks up any "souvenirs" ... got it?'

'Off pat, sir,' said the squad car constable. 'Any cock-ups, and they won't happen here.'

'That's my boy,' said Lennox, approvingly. 'I'll be back at the school ... consulting my navel.'

'Were you playing golf here, yesterday, sir?'

'Actually—yes ... I was. Yesterday morning I had a quick round with ...'

'Yesterday afternoon, sir. Between four and four-fifteen?'

'No. At that time, I was in Manchester. No ... actually, I was on my way back from Manchester. From a sales conference.'

'When did you leave Manchester, sir?'

'About—lemme see—no later than quarter to four. Between half-three and quarter to four.'

'Driving your own car?'

'Yes.'

'Alone?'

'Yes ... on the trans-Pennine motorway, in fact.'

'I'd like a short statement from you, if you don't mind, sir.'

'Certainly.'

'And the name of somebody you were with at the sales conference, please.'

'How many? I can give you a dozen names, if that's all you ...'

'Just one, sir. A couple, at the most.'

'Lemme see, now—a baronet ... would he do?'

'Fine.'

'And a fellow-director. He should lend weight, don't you think?'

'Fine, sir. Their names, please.'

* * *

The headmaster (a Mr Martin) couldn't help, and was almost self-condemnatory *because* he couldn't help. Yes, he'd been the last person to see Miss Bentley alive; well, perhaps not *the* last person—but *one* of the last persons ... the last person, he supposed, who'd actually spoken to her. She'd left his office; they'd been discussing timetables—things like that—and who, among the senior pupils, might be suitable for the role of Becket in a proposed school production of *Murder in the Cathedral* ... she was (*had* been!) a tower of strength as far as the school dramatic society was concerned. They'd miss her. *Everybody* would miss her. Then, she'd left the office, and he'd seen her through the window. Crossing towards the Staff Room ... that room, over there. The prefabricated building. 'The Nissen Hut' ... that's what everybody called it. It wasn't, of course. In fact, it was a good idea ... the Staff Room, separate from the main building. Checking that coffee and biscuits were ready for the break —as always ... that was another thing she could *always* be relied upon to do. And across the front of the Woodwork Classroom—this place ... another prefabricated building. To keep the noise from all the classrooms, you see. And she'd walked in front of the doors ... and then ... and then ... She'd just stumbled—that's what it had looked like ... as if something had hit her at the side of the head, and she'd stumbled sideways, and then ... But, of course, it *had*, hadn't it? Something *had* hit the side of her head! And he hadn't—y'know—it was hard (almost impossible) to remember, but he was sure he hadn't *heard* anything. A gunshot. He was almost sure he hadn't heard anything ... almost *sure*. He'd been inside the office, you see, and what noises he could hear had seemed like normal traffic noise. He could almost imagine the sound ... *now*. In retrospect. He could almost convince himself that he *had* heard the shot ... but he thought not. Imagination ... they didn't want imagined evidence, did they? Oh, yes, he'd seen the car. He was *sure* he'd seen the car. Noticed it—no more than that... but, to that extent, *seen* it. A dark coloured car. Probably dark blue. Probably dark green. He wasn't sure ... just that it was dark coloured, and that it had driven out of the cul-de-sac, and driven off towards Lessford. In the general direction of Lessford. No—he was sorry, he was so *sorry!*—but he hadn't noticed either the make, or the number. Or who was driving it. Or how many people were inside. Or—or *anything.* He hadn't realised, you see. Miss Bentley stumbling, and the car driving away ... there'd been no reason to connect the two. Not at that time. Which was stupid of him, he supposed ... *criminally* stupid. He should have known. He should have guessed ... but how *could* he have guessed? Who would want to do this terrible ... He meant—*why?* Why, in God's name ...

'Don't blame yourself, Mr Martin.' Poynings glanced at his watch, then said, 'I dunno how these things are organised, but I think you should close the school for the day.'

'Oh!' Martin ran worried fingers through his iron-grey hair.

'Close the school for the day,' repeated Poynings. 'The Education Committee will understand ... I'm sure they will. And the pupils will be better at home, till we've sorted things out. We'll be able to interview 'em later—tomorrow, maybe ... and the staff. But—er—y'know ... if you could see it in your way. To—er—close down for the rest of the day.'

'Yes. Yes.' Martin shook his head, and blinked some degree of objectivity into his mind. 'You're right, of course, sergeant. I'll send the pupils home. And the staff. I'll—er—I'll stay on—and a couple of housemasters ... just in case we can assist in any way.'

'Couldn't ask for more, sir. Thank you.' Poynings looked beyond Martin's shoulder, and added, 'Now—if you don't mind—here's the ambulance, and the doctor.

Take my tip, sir. Busy yourself with clearing the school ... eh? The next few minutes could be a bit upsetting.'

'Mr Kitley?'
'Yes. Why?'
'Mr Harold Kitley?'
'That's my name. What's all this about?'
'I'm a police officer, sir. We're checking the movements of members of this golf club, between four and four-fifteen, yesterday.'
'Why?'
'It's to do with the murder of Mr White. You've probably heard, or read ...'
'Are you suggesting I'm in some way involved?'
'No, sir. It's just that ...'
'Then why pester me with all these ...'
'Routine enquiries, sir. That's all.'
'Yes ... I've heard all about "routine enquiries".'
'They're necessary.'
'Tell me, officer, am I obliged to answer your questions?'
'It'll help us, sir. It'll ...'
'Am I obliged to *answer* them?'
'No, sir. You're not. But ...'
'In that case, I'll wish you good-day. I'm a very busy man.'
'Look, sir. This is an important ...'
'So is my time. Good-day, officer.'

The bullet had spent itself in the soft planks of the door to the Woodwork Classroom. The spent cartridge was there, on the carpet of the abandoned Ford Capri. The ballistic boys did the rest; it was as elementary as adding two and two, and coming up with four ... as elementary, and as certain. The same calibre, the same make of bullet ... the same *gun*.

'So,' said Sullivan, bluntly, 'where's the link?'

Lennox scratched his pot-belly, meditatively.

'Fleas?' enquired Rucker, sarcastically.

Lennox continued to scratch. If he heard the remark of his gaunt opposite number, he ignored it.

'There has to *be* a link,' insisted Sullivan.

'They didn't know each other,' rumbled Lennox. 'That much we've established.'

'Have we?' asked Rucker, doubtfully.

Sullivan frowned, and said, 'Come again?'

'The handful of people we've asked *say* they didn't know each other,' amplified Rucker. 'But, so far, all we've done is ask "Did White know Bentley?" or "Did Bentley know White?" Nobody's yet done any serious leaning. Everybody's been very polite.'

'Early days, old son,' said Lennox.

The fat detective switched scratching points. He moved from his stomach to a point about six inches below his left armpit.

Rucker said, 'When the hell did you wash last?'

'Eh?'

'I have the impression you're lousy.'

Lennox grinned, and said, 'Some sorta rash ... overwork, I think.'

'That'll be the day!'

The three men shared a table in a café, less than a hundred yards from Beechwood Brook D.H.Q. It wasn't a particularly posh café. Its main fare was boiled ham sandwiches and moderately good tea. But even top-line coppers require to eat, occasionally, and the café was beyond the orbit of the organised chaos of the divisional headquarters. It was late afternoon and, apart from Sullivan, Lennox and Rucker, the café was empty. They could, therefore, talk off-the-record 'shop' without being overheard.

'The golf club?' asked Sullivan, as he drained the last of his tea.

Rucker said, 'It's being given the once-over. A first, gentle probing ... then, if any of 'em get too high-hat, we can start turning the thumb-screw.'

'The Capri?' Sullivan asked his next question of Lennox.

Lennox stopped scratching, and said, 'Car hire. Taken out yesterday evening by a "John Smith". Usual documentation produced—driving licence, certificate of insurance ... false name, false address. The Powder Puff boys are going over it for prints. So far, nothing ... I'm not hopeful. The boffins are poking around on the pedals, searching for mud-clues. Hair-clues. *Any* bloody thing!'

'Time-wasting,' murmured Rucker.

'What the hell else?' asked Sullivan.

'We're getting nowhere.'

'We *never* "get anywhere", Rucker. Not till the final dash. Not till we feel a collar ... then we've *got* there.'

Rucker curled his lips, and said, 'The great British public. Blind, deaf and out of its tiny mind. A man gets shot—a woman gets shot ... there's a rifle, somewhere. The damn thing makes noise when it's fired. There's a motor car—not a small motor car ... a Ford Capri. And it's parked in a street, God only knows how long. There's a man—a killer—strolling around with his hands in his pockets ... but nobody notices him. Nobody notices the fornicating motor car. Nobody has eyesight keen enough to recognise a flaming rifle. Nobody hears the damn thing go off, when it's fired. And—already—they're screaming the roof down, demanding an immediate arrest ... the great British public! What the hell do they think we are? Where the hell do they think their own responsibility stops? Or don't they think they *have* any responsibility?'

'They're worried,' growled Sullivan. 'Scared.'

'And we're *not* worried?'

Lennox stripped a cheroot of its jacket of cellophane, as he mused, 'She ain't a golf buff ... she ain't a member of Beechwood Golf Club. The first thing we checked. She ain't matey with any member. She doesn't buy eggs—milk, that sort of thing—from White's farm. We've checked *that*, too. The bloke who hired the car. He paid cash. The description—it could fit *anybody* ... any of us three, at a pinch.'

'Not *you*, for God's sake,' sneered Rucker. 'That would be *too* easy.'

'I don't have two heads, old son.'

'No ... but you've a triple-sized gut. And those clothes are unique, outside the confines of a seaside picture postcard.'

'People keep saying rude things about my dress sense. I'm damned if I can see ...'

'There's a connection,' cut in Sullivan, brusquely. 'Cut down on the Nervo and Knox act, you two. Work together ... or do I have to tell you? A killing in the North Region, a killing in the South Region. The same killer ... or, so it seems. We start with that assumption. We're one force, with two of everything. Mr Harris and Mr Sugden. You two ... two of *everything*. Now, for Christ's sake, don't tell *me* we can't nail a gun-happy lunatic who's set himself up in competition. We nail him up fast, and we nail him up tight ... and the first thing we have to come up with is the link. And don't tell me there *isn't* a link. White and Bentley. There's a common denominator, and all we have to do is find it ... from then on, we can free-wheel to the bastard we're after. A suggestion. Switch roles for twenty-four hours. Rucker, you take the Bentley killing. Lennox, you take the White case. Work together ... *together*, you understand. Use the one Information Room. Treat it as a double-murder. Switch as much as you like—as often as you like—treat it as a single enquiry. Anything! Work in double-harness. In company, if you think it'll increase the chances of an early arrest. But give me action. Find that damn connection ... whatever it is.'

That evening, the killer used his own car. It was a Mini. A red Mini. One of a thousand similar cars which whizzed and nipped along the roads and streets of the newly formed M.P.D.

Lamps, set into the waist-high concrete wall which surrounded the roof park merely accentuated the darkness of its huge floor-space and, beyond and below the wall, the sodium yellow of Lessford street-lighting formed a transparent haze of gold beyond which the lights of the city, and the traffic of the city, moved and twinkled like the glitterings of a massive kaleidoscope.

It was summer—mid-July—and a cricket-bag (supposing any living soul had seen the killer) would not have looked too conspicuous. Nevertheless, and for obvious reasons, he had hoped nobody *would* see him.

The roof park was deserted. Two unoccupied cars, and a van, were the only vehicles there.

In one corner, within a yard of the surrounding wall, the lift's entrance and exit was boxed in with a concrete, cubic structure and, within the narrow passage, between this structure and the wall, there was complete darkness. Complete solitude. Complete secrecy.

The killer smiled his satisfaction.

The position of the multi-level car park. The position of the protruding lift-shaft. Even the elbow-rest level of the surrounding wall. Everything ... *perfect*!

Weeks before he'd worked out the exact distance between his firing point and the stage door. He'd calculated the possible wind-speed between the canyons of the streets, below, and the allowance which might be needed ... but which *wouldn't* be needed on such a still night as this. The odds, in favour of some innocent pedestrian moving into his line of fire ... long odds but, if necessary, odds which he was prepared to eliminate via a first shot with which to drop the pedestrian. He'd practised firing from darkness into artificial light—practised squinting through the magnification of the telescopic sight, from the shadows and at a poorly lighted target—and he could do it ... he knew damn well he could do it. Given two seconds—no more—and the head of his intended victim would stop a .22 slug ... and the intended victim would be as dead as the other two.

He was God. He held the decision of life and death in his hands ... in the gentle squeeze of one forefinger. And, up there, above the scurrying nightlife of the city, he *felt* like God. Omnipotent. Avenging. Merciless.

He opened the cricket-bag, lifted the Husqvarna from its nest of soft dusters, checked that the magazine was fully loaded, fed a cartridge into the breech, turned the dial on the telescopic sight to the *exact* distance, then leaned the rifle against the wall and watched for the opening of the stage door.

'An odd name, Grieve,' observed the detective constable. 'Y'know—spelled that way ... a bit out of the ordinary.'

'Think so?'

'No offence, of course. Don't get me wrong. I'm not being ...'

'No offence taken, lad. I've had more smart remarks than *that* about it. I couldn't care less. Amos Grieve ... that's my name, and I'm stuck with it.'

The man with the uncommon name was in his mid-fifties, slim, fit, sun-tanned and with deep lines cutting into the folds of his face and producing a permanent morose expression.

He said, 'I'm no Tony Jacklin, constable. I'm just the pro, at a run-of-the-mill golf club ... and Ingle never lets me forget it.'

'Ingle?'

'The club secretary—Major Ingle ... a stiff-necked sod, who'd have us cut the greens by numbers, if he could get away with it.'

'You don't like him?'

'He knows it. The dislike's mutual.'

The D.C. glanced around at the clutter of the pro's shop, and remarked, 'You work late.'

'All hours,' agreed Grieve. 'Whilever there's anybody at the Nineteenth, I'm expected to be on hand.'

'The club house?'

'Don't call it that, lad. The "Nineteenth" ... they think it sounds better. Booze-hall-cum-knocking-shop-cum-liar's-conference-hall ... if you want the *real* description. But—y'know—when they're nicely oiled, one of 'em sometimes trots around here, and buys something. Even a complete new set of clubs ... I've known *that* to happen. It's a living. And I like the game ... which compensates for a lot.'

'Healthy?'

'The best game on God's earth.'

'Okay.' The D.C. got down to business. 'You coach 'em. You run this shop. What else?'

'You name it,' sighed Grieve.

'Specifically?' insisted the D.C.

Grieve said, 'It's a bit of a shambles. A place like this needs some sort of staff ... even a place like *this*. The greens have to be kept in trim. The fairways. Even the rough needs trimming occasionally. The bunkers have to be raked. Then, there's the Nineteenth. Apart from the steward, and his wife, there's the waiters and the cleaners. We put on a meal—of sorts ... that means a cook and kitchen staff. It all adds up. Say two dozen—average ... it fluctuates, like a bloody yo-yo. Some of 'em double as caddies. Weekends—and whenever there's a club competition—some of the locals come in for caddy work. If you can make head or tail of it, lad, let me know. I'll be grateful ... it's sometimes beyond *me*.'

'But you have overall responsibility?'

'Under Ingle ... but all Ingle does is sit behind a desk, dream up cockeyed schemes, and do sod-all.'

'So-o,' mused the D.C., 'half the time you don't know where a lot of 'em are. You've to take a lot on trust.'

'I chase 'em, whenever I can. Whenever I've time. My first priority's coaching. My second's this shop. After that ... I try my best. I go over the course once a day. Sometimes twice. That's about the only way I can keep track that what should be done is *being* done. We don't get too many grumbles. Those who do ... they'll grumble that the Pearly Gates are made of cultivated pearls. You know the sort.'

'In every walk of life,' sighed the D.C. 'Which is why I'm going to have to ask for a statement. A fairly long one, I'm afraid. A detailed list—as detailed as possible—of the people who work under you. Where they were—where they *should* have been—between four and four-fifteen, yesterday. Including yourself. Whether, to your knowledge, they knew White. And, if they knew him, whether they liked, or disliked him ... any hints they might have dropped.'

'It's likely to be a session,' said Grieve.

' 'Fraid so.'

'Sit down,' Grieve waved a hand towards a chair. 'Make yourself comfortable. I'll get some coffee organised. We might as well have *some* degree of comfort.'

The shot was perfect. The killer couldn't have asked for more. The sight brought the victim to what almost seemed touching distance. The low wall gave the rifle rock-steadiness.

Even the victim co-operated.

He opened the stage door, then paused on the pavement and looked up at the sky, as if to check that rain clouds were not gathering. Paused ... and stayed perfectly still.

The cross-wires found their mark just above, and to one side of, the right eye. The trigger eased back against the gentle increase of pressure. The Husqvarna jerked, ever so slightly, as it sent the .22 bullet speeding towards its target and, through the magnification of the sight, the killer saw the tiny hole punched into the skull, before the victim's knees buckled and he fell forward on the pavement.

The killer jerked the bolt of the rifle, and the empty cartridge tinkled onto the floor of the roof park before the rifle was returned to the cricket-bag.

He dropped the cricket-bag onto the carpet of the Mini, between the front and rear seats. He drove from the multi-level car park and, within minutes, was lost in the traffic of the city.

A red Mini. One of a thousand similar cars which whizzed and nipped along the roads and streets of the newly formed M.P.D.

Rucker and Lennox (at Sullivan's suggestion) had switched roles. Rucker was pushing the Bentley killing ... and Rucker didn't give a fourpenny damn whom he annoyed, or whom he upset.

He was in the sitting room of a detached house in one of the more salubrious residential areas of Bordfield, and the man he was chopping down to size was (very obviously) unused to the role of 'choppee'; *he* was used to talking to lesser mortals, like this ... and the experience of being at the receiving end of such talk tended to higher his blood pressure.

The man's name was Freeman—Patrick Freeman—and he was dressed in scarlet nylon pyjamas, silk dressing-gown and soft leather slippers. The dampness of his hair bore witness that he had not long bathed, and his attire was proof that he was contemplating the comfort of his bed. Rucker (being Rucker) hardly noticed such trivia; he was there till doom cracked ... or until he had answers he was prepared to accept.

The detective sergeant was merely there for the ride, and the experience. He'd *heard* of Rucker. Now, he was getting a front-row seat ... and the performance was tending to make his hair stand on end.

'You've no damned right to ...' bawled Freeman.

'Don't make me laugh,' said Rucker in a soft voice.

'What the hell's that supposed to ...'

'You hire cars, Freeman. What legal knowledge you possess stops short at required tyre pressures, and speeds in built-up areas. Murder is way out of your league. Don't make the complete monkey of yourself by trying to quote law to *me*.'

'I'm not quoting law to ...'

'And don't back-pedal. You were just about to yammer on about "rights". What "rights"?'

'The—the—the ...'

'Start with the assumption they don't exist, sonny. Not when a murder enquiry gets into its swing. Start with *that* assumption ... you'll be a damn sight nearer the truth.'

Freeman fumbled a cigarette from a silver box, on a side-table, as he said, 'I've already told a detective sergeant all I know about ...'

'Good. Now you're going to tell a detective chief superintendent. Congratulations. You're going up in the world.'

'All I know. Everything.' Freeman snapped a table lighter into flame and lighted the cigarette. The smoke from the glowing tip magnified his combination of fury and apprehension.

'Not everything,' contradicted Rucker.

'Everything,' insisted Freeman. 'Every question he asked, I answered. I didn't ...'

'Do you usually hire cars out to murderers?' asked Rucker, innocently.

'How the hell was *I* supposed to know ...'

'I'm not interested in "suppositions". I'm interested in the truth.'

'All right. I didn't ...'

'Smith?'

'Eh?'

'The name he gave ... John Smith?'

'Yes. That's the name on the driving licence.'

'And you believed him?'

'Why not?'

'Why *not*?' Rucker's mouth twisted into a sneer. 'I thought the Welfare State had eradicated suckers who still fall for the "John Smith" gag.'

'People *are* called ...'

'Which authority issued the driving licence?'

'It was a phoney driving licence. I keep ...'

'It had an issuing authority. It didn't look *that* phoney ... did it?'

'Would I have ...'

'Answer 'em. Don't ask 'em. Did it look phoney?'

'No. Did it hell.'

'So ... which issuing authority?'

'I didn't notice.'

'What was the number?'

'The number?'

'On the driving licence, dummy. They have numbers ... didn't you know?'

'Of course I ...'

'So, what was its phoney number?'

'I didn't check.'

'What the devil *did* you check? That an unknown man had a piece of pasteboard that *looked* like a driving licence? Is that all?'

'Yeah,' admitted Freeman, reluctantly. 'That's about

all. And that he had a certificate of insurance.'

'Number?'

'I don't know.'

'Issued by?'

'Eh?'

'You nebulous clown, an insurance certificate is issued ... by an insurance company. The name of the company covers half the blasted certificate. Which company issued the certificate?'

'I—I forget.' Freeman smoked his cigarette in quick, nervous journeys to, and from, his lips.

There was a moment of contemptuous silence.

Then, Rucker asked, 'Do you keep books? ... other than the *Tiger Tim Annual*, I mean?'

'Yes. We keep books.'

'What do you put in 'em? Pressed flowers?'

'Look, copper, don't be ...'

'Call me "copper" again,' warned Rucker, softly, 'and you'll leave a following cloud of dust.'

'All right. But I don't like ...'

'Murder?'

'Eh?'

'That's the subject-matter, Freeman. Murder—double-murder ... and one of your cars was right there, in the middle of it. For all we know, *you* might be the man we're after.'

'What the hell ...'

'Mightn't you?' asked Rucker, gently. 'From where I'm standing. A cock-and-bull yarn about hiring an expensive car, to a stranger. Without moving a muscle to check his identity. Without checking his driving licence. Without checking his certificate of insurance. Without making any sort of even half-sane entry in what you laughingly call your "books". You could be, Freeman. Never forget that —you just *could* be ... and without bringing gnomes and fairies into the argument. Don't get stroppy, sonny. Otherwise I might think you *are*.'

Freeman breathed, 'Christ!' backed away from this murderously effective detective, felt for the arm of an easy chair, and sat down. He whispered, 'Oh, my Christ. You don't *really* think ...'

Rucker said, 'The ball's in your court, Freeman. Play it well, and—who knows?—you might sleep in your own bed, tonight.'

'Anything,' gasped Freeman. 'Just ask the questions ... anything.' He waved a hand towards the empty twin to the armchair he was using. 'Sit—sit down, please. Y'know ... as long as you like. Any questions. As long as you like. I'm—er—I'm here to help.'

'That you are,' agreed Rucker, coldly. He turned to the D.S. and added, 'Your pocket book, sergeant. Use the chair. I'll stand. As from now, it's recorded. Every word. Every tin-pot excuse. How a would-be-murderer can get his hands on a car, as easily as *that*.'

The detective sergeant said, 'Yes, sir.'

He settled himself in the vacant armchair, flipped his notebook to the first clean page and waited, with his ballpoint poised.

Lennox, too, was conducting what might, loosely, have been called an 'interview'. Lennox had plumped for Muriel White, the widow of the recently murdered farmer and (typical of Lennox) he'd brought along a middle-aged policewoman sergeant; a woman who'd worked her way through years of the brand of sorrow which only a working copper comes across ... the aftermath of major lawlessness, which never hits the headlines but which, very often, is far more awful than the crime itself. The W.P.S. had brewed tea, laced with brandy, and was fussing around the bereaved woman with *just* the right amount of cold-blooded efficiency; the balance had to be perfect ...

enough respect to convince the heartbroken woman of their sorrow, but enough briskness to keep the tears at bay.

The W.P.S. knew her job.

Mind you, Lennox helped. In the first place, he didn't *look* like a copper ... any sort of a copper, much less a detective chief superintendent. The baggy, eye-searing-patterned suit. The jazzy, Fair Isle pullover. The bow tie ... which looked as if it might light up, or spin round like an aeroplane propeller (or both) at any moment. The almost hairless, Christmas-pudding head, atop the gasometer-shaped figure. The complete lack of anything remotely resembling dignity.

An out-of-work music hall comedian ... certainly.

A high-ranking police officer ... *never*!

One of the farm cats had found a nest on Lennox's lap and, as his podgy fingers stroked and tickled its neck, it purred pure feline contentment.

They were in the farm kitchen. Stone-flagged, but warmed by the heat radiating from the closed-lidded Aga which claimed almost half of one wall-length. The sink, the fridge, the deep-freeze, the Welsh dresser, the plain-topped table ... they were all above-average sized but, within the spacious kitchen, they didn't look out of place.

Lennox unwrapped a cheroot. He performed the operation one-handed, in order not to disturb the cat.

'D'you mind?' he asked. 'They—er—they tend to pong a bit ... if you aren't used to 'em.'

'It's all right, sir.' Mrs White nodded, and a sad, nostalgic smile added itself to the misery of her expression. 'White used to smoke twist. I'm used.'

Lennox lighted the cheroot—still without disturbing the cat—and rumbled, 'It's necessary, luv. We don't enjoy doing it ... but it's very necessary.'

'More tea?' suggested the W.P.S.

'No. No thank you.' She turned to Lennox, and continued, 'Whatever I can do. Just tell me.'
'Your hubby. He was a well-liked man.'
She nodded.
'But—sorry, luv ... *somebody* didn't like him.'
'Somebody,' she agreed.
'Any idea who?'
She shook her head.
'Was he a—y'know ... was he a secretive man?'
'He kept himself to himself, if that's what you mean.'
'Uhuh.'
'He had his opinions ... but he didn't air them much.'
'Tell me about him, old pet,' said Lennox, gently.
'About him? Or about his opinions?'
'Either. Both. Just talk about him ... anything that comes into your head.'
She chewed at her lower lip, started, 'He was ...' then almost broke down. She sniffed, dabbed her eyes with a handkerchief, composed herself and, in a steadier voice, continued, 'He was a good man, sir. That's not just because I'm his wife. He was a good man. Not too—y'know ... "romantic" is what a lot of people might say. He wasn't "romantic". He wasn't a fly-by-night. He didn't fancy himself. Y'know ... fancy himself. At—at anything. Just farming. He was a good farmer ... and a good husband. Considerate. Not flashy. Y'know—not flashy—but ... considerate. He took his time. He thought things out. Then, when he'd made up his mind—when he was sure—he couldn't be moved.'
She gazed into the distance of memory for a few moments, then continued, 'He bought this place, seven—maybe eight—years back. It wasn't much. Not then. It had been let run down. But White could see the potential—y'know ... what *could* be done with it. It was hard work at first. For us all. White, his father ... me, too. I've worked in the fields from sun-up to sun-down ...

many a score times, those first few years. White almost broke his back, getting the place into shape. And his father—he tried to keep pace ... I think it killed him. He died four years back. But, by that time, it was as they wanted it. Mainly pasture. A few head of cattle, but mostly sheep. White always said sheep would pay, in the long run. Keep the dogs off. Pen them in winter ... they don't need much else. They lamb. Give them good grass. They don't ask for much else. Mutton and wool ... that's what re-paid the overdraft. English lamb. English mutton. English wool. White swore by them ... and he was right. On this sort of land, he was right.'

There was a silence—a silence of unspoken memories —and Lennox eased the silence to one side, by murmuring, 'But graft?'

'Oh, my God!' She sighed, heavily. 'No holidays. Not since we came here. Market, once a week ... that's all. He used to say we didn't need a holiday. With a place like this—with views like we have—we didn't *need* a holiday. He was a worker, sir. None better. The hours he put in! But—y'know—the few times he *had* to be away it was misery. He couldn't get back fast enough.'

She dabbed at her moistening eyes.

The W.P.S. said, 'Come on, Mrs White. Have some more tea. It'll help.'

'No ... no thanks, dear.' The sigh was deep and frame-shuddering, then she had control of herself once more.

'You were saying?' urged Lennox, gently.

'Just that—y'know ... he hated every minute he wasn't here. At the farm. He was in hospital once. Nothing, really ... a broken ankle. It was awkward to set ... something like that. He had to stay for two days. They said a week, or thereabouts ... but he discharged himself, after two days. He couldn't stand being away. And once, on jury service. At Lessford. Just the one day ... and he went on alarmingly. And, another time, they talked him into attending an N.F.U. conference, at York. He was supposed to stay overnight ... it was going to be another two-day affair. He left, the first evening. He wouldn't stay. Y'know ... he really *loved* this place.'

'The isolation?' suggested Lennox.

'Yes.' She nodded. 'That, and the countryside. And he could only stand people for so long. Just for so long. Then he wanted the peace of this place.'

'Nice,' murmured Lennox. He inhaled smoke from the cheroot, scratched the neck fur of the purring cat, and repeated, 'Nice. No neighbours ... he didn't like neighbours?'

'That's about it,' agreed Mrs White.

'Let's see ... how far is it to the village?'

'Four miles. All of four miles ... along the footpath across the fields. Nearer six, by road.'

'And those are your nearest neighbours?'

'Not counting the Gascoinges.'

'The Gascoinges?'

'Harry Gascoinge and his missus. And their son. They're gypsies. They have a couple of vans at one corner of the land. Near a coppice. Out of the way—and they're clean—*real* gypsies ... they aren't a nuisance. Gascoinge helped, sometimes. At lambing. Fixing fences. That sort of thing. He helped, sometimes.'

'Friends, were they?' asked Lennox.

'We-ell ...' She twisted and untwisted her fingers in embarrassed knots.

'They *weren't* friends?' Lennox gently reversed the question.

'It—it was Sally, y'see,' said Mrs White, miserably.

'Sally?'

'Gascoinge's bitch. White swore he'd come across it, chasing sheep. I dunno—you can never be sure, with dogs ... but I'd be surprised. White swore he saw it. And he shot it. With a twelve-bore. If it *was* ...'

She shook her head, slowly.

'It was your hubby's bread and butter,' murmured Lennox. 'We know all about it, in this job, luv. Sheep-worrying. Every year. You can't blame a farmer for protecting his living. Even these things.' He glanced down at the cat, and scratched it behind its ear. 'You'd be surprised how much damage they can do. Bloody fools who can't keep their pets under control.'

She sighed, and said, 'Yes—I know ... but she was a grand dog.'

'Gascoinge wouldn't like it, of course.'

'They—they weren't speaking.'

'Childish,' said Lennox, sadly.

She nodded, with equal sadness.

'But no more than that? No more than not speaking to each other?'

'White didn't bear grudges.'

'And Gascoinge?'

'He swore it wasn't Sally. I think it went deep.'

'Deep enough to kill?' asked Lennox, quietly.

'I don't think so,' she whispered, then she seemed to realise what she'd said and, in a stronger voice, said, 'No! I'm sure. Harry Gascoinge's not a bad man ... and that was a wicked thing for me to say. No ... I'm sure Gascoinge wouldn't have killed White, for the sake of a dog. Not even for Sally.'

Lennox lifted the cat from his lap and placed it gently onto the floor of the farm kitchen.

He said, 'Now—no arguments, luv ... tea. You need it, and I could do a cup. And—I'm sorry—I've a few more questions I'd like to ask. Let's take time off, for a cuppa.'

Freeman would have given five years of his life for a drink ... even tea. But he daren't even make the suggestion. Rucker was 'leaning' and when Rucker pulled out all the stops the unfortunate bastard at the receiving end wondered what was coming next; from which direction, and with how many barbs. Therefore, Freeman didn't suggest time off for a drink—he even made the smoking of his cigarette an apologetically necessary appendage to sanity ... which, with Rucker in full spate, it almost *was*.

'You saw him,' said Rucker.
'Well—I only ...'
'This man "Smith". You dealt with him ... personally?'
'Yes, but ...'
'Therefore, you saw him. Good God, man, you *saw* him. You weren't wearing a blindfold.'
'No. I—er—I—I saw him. More or less.'
'More or less? What the hell does that mean?'
'I—I wasn't taking particular notice. I was ...'
'You were trusting him with a particularly expensive car.'
'Yes, but ...'
'To drive it away.'
'Yes—I know—but ...'
'As far as *you* knew, to drive it round the nearest corner and flog the bloody thing.'
'People—people don't do ...'
'You have a very innocent mind, Freeman.'
'They *don't*,' wailed Freeman.
'He committed murder. *Double*-murder. D'you think he's too nice a man to steal one of your beautiful motor cars? D'you *still* think that?'
'No—of course not—it's not that. It's ...'
'You getting all this down, sergeant?' Rucker asked the question to the detective sergeant.
The detective sergeant scribbled away, furiously and, without looking up, said, 'Yes, sir. Every word.'
'Good. At this rate, we should be able to sell the serial rights to *Comic Cuts*.' Rucker flipped his attention back

to the writhing Freeman, and said, 'Description?'

'Eh?'

'You saw him. His description?'

'I keep telling you. I don't ...'

'Don't be a bigger fool than God made you. What sort of a man *was* he?'

'He was just—y'know ... just a ...'

'Could you have handled him?'

'Eh?'

'If he'd turned awkward. Could you have slung him out ... without the help of the Brigade of Guards?'

'I—er—I ...'

'*Could* you? Could *you* have handled him?'

'Ye-es. I—er—I think so.'

'Were you sitting down?'

'What?'

'When this highly technical transaction was taking place. Were *you* sitting down?'

'No. No ... I was standing up. Behind the ...'

'Was *he* sitting down?'

'No. He was standing up. At the other side of the ...'

'Is the floor level?'

'Look—I can't see what ...'

'You're not expected to "see" anything, Freeman. Your job is to answer questions. Is the floor level?'

'Yes ... of course it's level?'

'Fine. Now, did you look up at him, or down at him?'

'I just—I just *looked* ... that's all.'

'You just "looked"?' sneered Rucker.

'Yes—that's all ... I just ...'

'You "look" at Blackpool Tower, bonehead. But you're a few feet shorter.'

'Oh!'

'Up? Or down?' insisted Rucker. 'Use that apology you pass off as a brain, and *think*. Remember! You're there ... His Nibs is hiring a car ... he's talking to you, and you're talking back ... now, *come on.* Level? Up? Or down?'

Freeman drew on the cigarette, his face creased into a scowl of concentration, then he said, 'Up ... I'm sure. Up. A few inches up. He was a few inches taller than me.'

'A few inches?'

'Yes. A few ...'

'*Two* inches is a lot, Freeman.'

'Oh!'

'So, don't get carried away with yourself. How tall are *you*?'

'Five-eight—five-eight-and-a-half ... about that.'

'Six inches would make him a blasted giant. Three inches would make him six foot ... as near as dammit. That's my height ... just short of six foot. How does that compare?'

'About—about the same ... I'd say.'

'Take your time. Don't over-enthuse.'

'All right. Not quite ... not *quite* as tall as you.'

'Five-eleven? Any advance on five-eleven?'

'No. That's about right. Five-eleven ... that's as near as I can get.'

Rucker turned to the sergeant and said, 'Five-eleven—thereabouts—and skinny. Slim build.'

Freeman began, 'How d'you know ...'

'You could have handled him. You could have thrown him out ... and you're no Mr Universe. So, if he isn't a runt, he's skinny. He isn't over-endowed with either flesh or muscle. Or is that too involved?'

'I'm—I'm sorry.' Something akin to reluctant admiration touched Freeman's expression. He screwed what was left of his cigarette into a stand ash-tray, and muttered, 'I should have remembered. I—I know I should have remembered ... and I feel a bit of a fool.'

'You *are* a fool—and not merely "a bit" of one ...

but don't get above yourself. So are most people.'

'Oh!'

'Right-handed, or left-handed?' Rucker refused the interrogation any real interruption.

'I—er... right-handed. Yes. Right-handed... I'm sure.'

'He signed that pathetic register you keep... with his *right* hand? If you're not sure, for God's sake, say so.'

'I'm sure. His right hand.'

'Ballpoint. We have the register... we know he signed with a ballpoint. His? Or yours?'

'His, or my, what?'

'Pen. Ballpoint. Did he use his own, or did he ...'

'Oh—er—mine. The one on the counter.'

'Was it handy?'

'It was *there* ... to be used, if necessary.'

'I know it was *there*,' sneered Rucker. 'Not for one moment did I think you had to nip out and buy the blasted thing. But what the devil do you mean by "there"? Alongside his hand. A few feet away. In the next room. In the ...'

'On the counter,' cut in Freeman.

'How far away from this "register" article?'

'About two foot... maybe a yard.'

'Not exactly handy?'

'Handy enough. I mean ...'

Rucker murmured, 'Freeman—take it from me... not exactly *handy*. Certain professions—bank employees, schoolmasters, even coppers—require the constant use of a pen. People in those professions carry their own pens around with them. Savvy? They're not likely to walk even a yard, to use a strange pen, when all they have to do is take their own out of their pocket. As a general rule, buck navvies *don't* carry pens around in their pockets. It's a pointer—no more than a pointer... but, with witnesses like you, pointers are all we can hope for.'

Freeman nodded his silent defeat. As from that

moment, he offered no resistance. Rucker had licked him, by sheer professionalism ... plus scorn-filled insults. The detective sergeant scribbled the duologue into an official record of the interview and he, too, marvelled at the police expertise of Detective Chief Superintendent Rucker.

Rucker said, 'Right, the pen—the ballpoint—was about a yard away from the so-called "register". Did this "John Smith" yobbo make a move—*any* sort of movement—towards his own pocket, before he decided to use your pen?'

'I—I don't ...'

'As if he *might* have a pen of his own handy? As if using *your* pen amounted to a change of mind?'

'No. No ... I don't think so.'

'I suppose that's all we can hope for ... that you "don't think so".'

'People don't notice these things,' said Freeman, heavily.

'As sure as hell *you* don't. Right ... let's take the "register". We have it. It's been examined. No fingerprints ... why?'

'How do ...' Freeman closed his mouth, then said, 'Yes, I do. He didn't take his glove off.'

'Glove? D'you mean *gloves*?'

'No. He—er—he took the right glove off, to hold the pen. But not the left glove. He—he rested his left hand on the page ... and the right hand on top of his left.'

'So-o. His right hand—his *ungloved* hand—didn't touch the paper?'

'That's—that's right.'

'But *did* touch the ballpoint?'

'Yes, but ...'

'I know,' said Rucker, flatly. 'And, ever since, everybody within a radius of ten miles has used the fornicating pen. Prints! We could start a new fingerprint system with 'em all. And every one of 'em smudged to hell, and useless.'

'Look—if I'd known ...'

'If you'd *known* you wouldn't have hired him the car. We can take that for granted. How did he hold the pen?'

'Eh?'

'The pen? People hold pens and pencils in some very cackhanded ways. What about him? Between the thumb and first finger?'

'I really can't ...'

'First and second finger? Second and third finger?'

'For God's sake! He just ...'

'I've even known some lunatics hold a pen between the third and little finger ... how they handle the thing, like that, is beyond me. But how did *he* hold the pen?'

'I—I don't ...'

'You *know*, Freeman. You were there. You watched him. You *saw* ... therefore, you *know*. How?'

'Honestly. I don't ...'

'He's shown you the duff driving licence ... which you haven't even bothered to read. He's shown you the certificate of insurance ... which, in your infinite wisdom, you've seen fit to ignore. You've shoved this "register" thing under his nose. He's reached across—borrowed your handy ballpoint—and now, he's writing his name. *He's writing his name!* Get it? One gloved hand on the page. One ungloved hand holding the pen—making damn sure it doesn't leave fingerprints on the paper ... *come on.* How's he holding the bloody pen?'

'Like—like everybody holds a pen. Like most people.' Tiny beads of sweat dotted Freeman's forehead and upper lip. He glanced at the D.S., and said, 'Like he's holding *his* pen. Normally. And—and—and ...' Freeman seemed to choke; seemed unable to mouth whatever words he wanted to say.

'Get it out,' purred Rucker. 'There's something else ... get it out.'

'His—his hand was dirty,' whispered Freeman.

'Dirty?' Rucker pounced on the word, with the speed of a cat pinning an escaping mouse.

'Yes. Y'know ... dirty.'

'No—I don't know ... tell me.'

'Just—y'know ... *dirty*,' moaned Freeman.

'Filthy? Is that what you mean?'

'No. Not exactly *filthy*. Just ... dirty. Ingrained dirt.'

'Ingrained?'

'As if it was there ... in the pores. As if he couldn't wash it off. The hand—y'know ... it wasn't *unwashed*. Not that sort of dirt. Ingrained. Under the skin, almost. In all the cracks of the fingers.'

'Miner's dirt?' suggested Rucker. 'Collier's dirt?'

'No-o ... not exactly that.'

'All right, mechanic's dirt. You employ mechanics, don't you?'

'Yes.'

'Their hands ... the oil and grease. In time it gets bedded into the skin. It takes some shifting. *That* sort of dirt?'

'More or less ... but not quite. Partly that, I think. But something else.'

'Oil—grease—worked into the skin ... plus something else?'

Freeman nodded.

'And the nails?'

'Not—not *manicured*. Washed—y'know ... washed. Even brushed, I wouldn't be surprised. But still—y'know ... discoloured.'

'Will you settle for a "workman's hands"?'

'We-ell—I dunno ... I can't be ...'

'As opposed to a so-called "white-collar worker". Somebody who *uses* his hands ... at his work. At his *dirty* work. Not the hands of a surgeon. Of a concert pianist. For Christ's sake, Freeman, you know what I'm getting at. Stop being deliberately dumb. The hands of a manual worker ... is that what you're saying?'

'Er—yes—I suppose ... except ...'

'Except? Except what?'

'The gloves. They were driving gloves—y'know ... expensive.'

'Every Tom, Dick and Harry drives a motor car, these days. And they all fancy themselves as Brands Hatch grand prix wallahs. That means the bits and pieces that go with the image. Driving gloves aren't ...'

'These were racing gloves.' Freeman stuck his heels in and met Rucker's contemptuous stare with a blink. 'Open at the back. Fastened at the back of the wrist, with a good press-fastener. Take my word for it ... they were expensive gloves. Racing gloves. And they aren't on sale everywhere.'

'All right ... expensive driving gloves.' Rucker nodded reluctant acceptance. 'He could have nicked 'em ... but let's say he didn't. They knock the image. That's what you're getting at ... right? A manual worker—a yob who, on the face of it, has to *hire* a car—and he wears jazzy driving gloves. What colour?'

'Black. Soft leather, with air-holes punched down the sides of the palms. I tell you, they were ...'

'You,' said Rucker, gently, 'are going to tell me *everything*, Sonny Boy. You've already remembered a lot ... a lot you hadn't previously remembered. But we've only just started. Settle back in that chair, Freeman. We've a long way to go. I'm going to take you over every inch of that man. Every second he was in your sight. And you're going to remember—you are going to *remember*! ... if it takes all night.'

Rucker and Lennox were busy. Each was 'interviewing';

each, in his own individual way, was probing the two wounds of what each still thought was a double-murder. Each was making slow and painful progress.

But by this time, it was a *triple*-murder.

The two Heads of C.I.D. were occupied, therefore Sugden—Assistant Chief Constable (Crime) to the Lessford Region of the newly formed Metropolitan Police District—had (figuratively speaking) to roll up his sleeves, and take to the streets.

And, in a city of three-quarters of a million souls, a skull-shattered body, draped across one of the central pavements and leaking blood all over the litter-strewn flagstones is a big draw.

'Get 'em back,' snapped Sugden. 'Clear the whole bloody street.'

'Yes, sir.' The motor patrol sergeant turned, and passed the order down the line. 'Right—clear the street ... everybody! You—you—you ... get to that far end, and stop everything. Cars, pedestrians ... everything. You—you—you ... the same at the other end. Clear the whole bloody street. Send 'em home to their beds. And don't stand any nonsense.'

The half-dozen uniformed coppers slowly sheep-dogged the rubber-necking crowd beyond the parked police vehicles and to the extreme ends of the street.

'You were first at the scene?' asked Sugden.

The M.P.S. said, 'Yes, sir. We all got the call. I was here first ... along with another squad car. The C.I.D. arrived within a couple of minutes. Then the ambulance and Doc Carr. The rest have arrived, since. The C.I.D. lads are searching the crowd for witnesses. Doc Carr's in the theatre ... trying to find the bullet, I think.'

'Who is he?' Sugden stared, stone-faced at the murdered man.

'Arnold Westerfield. That's his stage name ... real name Arthur West. He's a good actor. I've seen him a few times. Amateur—it's an amateur company ... but as good as a lot of professionals.'

Sugden sniffed.

'They're doing Rattigan's *The Browning Version*,' volunteered the motor patrol sergeant. 'Westerfield's taking the part of Andrew Crocker-Harris. He plays the part well.'

'He's taken his last curtain call,' said Sugden, drily.

'Er—yes. Yes, sir. It's a pity.' The M.P.S. looked slightly shocked at the apparent flippancy of the A.C.C. (Crime). In an almost accusing tone, he added, 'I knew him slightly. He was a nice chap.'

If Sugden noticed the implied criticism he ignored it. He was running his finger along the scar on the woodwork of the stage door; the mark gouged by the bullet, after it had done its killing work and ricocheted off into the corridor beyond the door.

'From up top, somewhere,' he mused.

'Sir?'

'A downhill shot. Through the head, then a glancing blow at the partly open door ... ending up inside, somewhere.'

'Dr Carr's searching for the ...'

'Aye. You've said.' Sugden squinted up, beyond the overhead street lights. 'Roofs,' he murmured. 'Are they being searched?'

'Not yet, sir. We've only ...'

'As soon as possible, sergeant. At a guess, that's where the killer positioned himself. Any roof within view of this door ... I want it thoroughly searched. Get people out of bed, if necessary. Anything. Just get to those roofs ...'

'Another .22.' Doctor Carr appeared at Sugden's elbow. On the doctor's open palm rested a slightly misshapen pellet of lead. Carr added, 'It was in the skirting board.'

Three uniformed constables and a C.I.D. man, who

had been helping Carr in his search for the bullet, re-entered the street.

The motor patrol sergeant pounced upon them, and said, 'You four ... the surrounding roofs.' Another squad car braked to a halt a few yards away, and the M.P.S. continued, 'Take the men from that car. Every roof within sight of this door. Every upper room, with a window facing in this direction. As fast as possible ... and, if you need help to get to the roofs, contact the fire brigade.'

The quartet trooped off, and collected the two men from the squad car on their way.

'Dead, of course.' Sugden jerked his head at the sprawling body.

'As a nit,' agreed Carr, unprofessionally.

Sugden growled, 'That's one more Richard Burton won't have to worry about.'

'The same killer?'

'What do *you* think?' said Sugden, sourly.

Carr nodded.

A shooting-brake holding fingerprint and photography experts rolled to a halt along the cordoned-off street.

'Here come the cameras,' sighed Sugden.

'Assuming,' said Carr, sombrely. 'Let's work on the assumption. Where's the pattern?'

'God only knows.'

'An open field. A school playground. A busy street. An elderly farmer. A middle-aged secretary. A comparatively young man. Two men, and a woman ... who, as far as we know, have never even *met* each other. Where's the *pattern*, Sugden?'

'There isn't one.' Sugden qualified the remark, by adding, 'Or, if there is, we haven't tumbled yet.'

'There's one answer,' said Carr, gently.

'Don't even suggest it, doc.'

'A pathological killer.'

'Don't even *suggest* it, doc,' repeated Sugden, harshly.

'If we have *that* we have real trouble.'

The man called Crispin squeezed himself between bales of hay in the stackyard, and prepared himself for another night of mild dozing which was a substitute for sleep. He hated the countryside; he hated its bleak night breezes which, even in July, brought shivers and goose-pimples; he hated the stillness, punctuated by unidentifiable noises —scufflings and distant banshee screams, as some secret creature killed some other secret creature—and the ripple of barks as a score of dogs, in a score of distant and separated farms, took up the call of its neighbour ... a wave of yappings, and snarlings, and howlings which, in his imagination, swept from one end of the land to the other.

Crispin hated the countryside ... but he was terrified of the towns.

The towns and the cities had once been *his* jungle, wherein he'd prowled and maimed. Where he'd ruled by fear, and where he'd committed abominations in the sure knowledge that his victims wouldn't *dare* take their complaints to the law.

Until he'd gone too far.

Until he'd committed murder ... eight years ago.

And eight years inside H.M. Prison, Durham, had transformed a tiger into a kitten.

And men knew this, and men were waiting for the first sight of his face. Men with long memories, and scores to settle. Town men. City men. Men who were what *he* had once been.

Terrible and terrifying men.

He squeezed deeper into the gap between the bales, and the misery and self-pity swept over him like one of the waves of barking from the distant dogs.

The detective inspector who'd interviewed the landlord of *The Fighting Cocks*—who'd interviewed Gascoinge—

now had the job of questioning Sheila Bentley's sister. The cases had, already, become so entwined; he'd started with the White killing and was now deep into the Bentley killing. There wasn't a man on the force who doubted that the same finger had triggered off both shots. Detect one, and you detect both—you detect all three ... although, at this moment, the D.I. was one down on the up-to-the-minute count. He still thought it was a *double-killing*.

The house was a red-brick semi, with a front lawn and a privet hedge. One of a thousand—one of a million—the standard British, brick-built dog-kennel, which the standard British man-and-woman-in-the-street calls 'a house in a respectable residential area'.

The D.I., and his accompanying policewoman constable, had been into scores of such houses, and scores of such front living rooms.

The only unusual thing about the set-up was the woman herself ... Violet Bentley.

'Tea, or coffee?' she offered. 'We don't keep anything stronger in the house ... not even for medicinal purposes.'

'No. Neither, thank you,' said the D.I.

The W.P.C. said, 'No thanks.'

'Please yourself. I always understood you people *lived* on tea, coffee and cigarettes. By the way, you'll oblige me by not smoking in this house ... I detest the smell.'

'Of course not, ma'am.'

'Miss.'

'I beg your pardon ... miss.'

Violet Bentley lowered herself into an armchair, straightened her skirt, and said, 'You're here to ask questions, I presume?'

'If—er—if you feel up to it, miss.'

The Bentley woman smiled. It wasn't a nice smile. It wasn't even a *womanly smile*. It went with the corncrake

100

voice. With the severe, 'bun' hair-do. With the thin-lipped mouth. With the complete absence of make-up. With the cold appraisal of grey-green eyes.

She said, 'For your information, inspector. I'm no hypocrite. I didn't like my sister over-much when she was alive. I'm not the type of person to play-act heartbreak now she's dead.'

The D.I. said, 'Oh!'

'Sister-love is a grossly over-exaggerated fiction. I know very few sisters who actually *like* each other. I know none who positively *love* each other.'

The D.I. said, 'Oh!' again.

The W.P.C. murmured, 'I have a sister—two, in fact ... and you have my word, Miss Bentley, *I* love them both.'

'You may think you do ... but you don't *live* with them.'

'No—that's true—but ...'

'That's the acid test. No two women can share the same house, except on terms of armed neutrality ... and that includes sisters.'

The D.I. glanced the W.P.C. into silence, cleared his throat, then said, 'Right—er—Miss Bentley. Can we disregard your own feelings for the moment, and get down to brass tacks. Somebody shot your sister. Murdered her. One way of moving in on the murderer is to find out as much as we can about his victim.'

'*His?*'

'She was shot. Women don't usually go in for guns.'

'What an uncommonly innocent remark to make, inspector.'

'I'm sorry. I don't follow your ...'

'Madame Fahmy. Elvira Dolores Barney. Long before the Women's Lib crowd claimed equal rights—the nineteen-twenties, nineteen-thirties ... and *they* shot their victims to death.'

'We think a man,' said the D.I. doggedly.

'As you wish.' She moved her shoulders in a couldn't-care-less shrug.

The D.I. said, 'Your sister, miss. What sort of a person was she?'

'Man-fond.'

'You mean she had men friends?'

'I mean that *all* men were her friends. She was a simpering ninny, as far as men were concerned. She'd work herself to a standstill, to earn a smile from something in trousers.'

'That sort of information doesn't help much,' grunted the D.I.

'What sort of information had you in mind?'

The D.I. rubbed the side of his face, meditatively, then said, 'A man ... all right—forgive me, if I disagree, miss—but we have to start an enquiry with *some* sort of firm supposition. We think a man ... and, pending evidence to the contrary, the investigation is concentrated upon pinpointing some man. A man who, presumably, knew your sister.'

She smiled, sardonically, and said, 'You've cut down the whole male population of the world, inspector. You've reduced it to a mere hundred, or so ... at a guess.'

'She knew so many men?'

'I've already said ... she was man-fond.'

'In what way?'

'She liked men.'

'What I mean is ...'

'I doubt if she was a trollop, if that's what you're getting at.'

'Ye-es. That—er—that was what I ...'

'I couldn't be sure, of course.'

'Oh!'

'She was certainly a tease. She egged men on ... but,

knowing her, I doubt if she had the courage for promiscuous fornication.'

The D.I. stared a little.

She added, 'For all I know, she died a virgin. It wouldn't surprise me.'

The D.I. said, 'We'll let you know, miss. After the P.M., I'll make it my personal business to call in, and let you know.'

Violet Bentley paled a little. The rat-trap mouth compressed itself into an even thinner line. The nostrils quivered, slightly.

The D.I. had had enough. He, too, could deliver verbal shocks ... and, in his opinion, knock-for-knock time had arrived.

He snapped, 'You'll pardon me, miss, but the differences between yourself and your sister aren't important—not unless *you* shot her ... which I doubt.'

'I find that an objectionable remark, inspector,' she snapped.

'It was probably meant to be, miss. Even though I didn't like making it. There are channels, via which you can make an official complaint ... that's up to you. My job's to winkle out information. Your sister's been murdered. We're sure—as sure as we can be—that she was killed by whoever killed the farmer, William White ...'

'Yesterday?' She sounded genuinely surprised.

'Yesterday,' said the D.I. 'Now—without going into a long-winded rigmarole about her morals—did your sister know White?'

'How do *I* know?'

'You're her sister ... the chances are you *should* know.'

'I'm sorry. I *don't* know. I can make a guess ... that she didn't.'

'Okay. Why make that guess?'

'He was an elderly man, as I understand it.'

'Late middle-age.'

'Too old for Sheila. She was something of a cradle-snatcher.'

The W.P.C. muttered, 'Thank God I haven't a sister like *you*.'

'Constable!' snapped the D.I. He turned to the elder woman, and said, 'Did your sister play golf?'

'Golf?' Violet Bentley looked surprised at the question.

'Did she play golf?' repeated the D.I.

'Not to my knowledge.'

'She didn't own clubs, for instance?'

'Not to my knowledge.'

'Did any of her men friends play golf?'

'The chances are that some of them did. She had enough.'

'Did she ever visit Beechwood Golf Club?'

'I've already told you—as far as *I* know, she didn't play golf.'

'Socially,' said the D.I. 'As a guest. There's a club house. It's not unusual to invite guests for dinner—for a drink ... that sort of thing.'

'Oh, that's *quite* possible. Free meals. Free drinks.'

'Do you know any of these men you're on about?'

'Sheila was the attraction. Not me.'

'For heaven's sake, she was your sister! You lived together. She'd mention names. She *must* have mentioned names.'

'No.' Violet Bentley shook her head.

'That's almost impossible to believe. I mean—damn it all—you both lived here, in the same ...'

'That's enough, inspector.' She stood up from the chair, and her air, and tone of voice, was of unqualified dismissal. 'I don't know who killed my sister. I'll be honest ... I don't much care. As a citizen—as a tax-payer and rate-payer—I'm prepared to give what information I might have ... and I've *given* it. My sister doted on men

... which, almost by definition, means she disliked women, and women disliked her. I certainly disliked her, and make no secret of the fact. We lived together for purely economic reasons ... nothing more. We shared no secrets ... nor ever wanted to. She tarted herself up. Tried to look ten years younger than her true age. She wore ridiculously modern clothes. She was a fool. A clown. Man-mad. As far as I know there was only one man she ever criticised ... and that, because she had no real option.'

'Who was that?' asked the D.I.

'Crickett, I think—no ... *Crispin*. And that was years ago. Years ago.'

Patience ... it catches more crooks than all the forensic parlour tricks ever invented; to forget the hours—to forget the calendar—and, with each small eternity, to ease a fraction of an inch nearer to the man you're after. To ask questions—sometimes progressively logical questions, sometimes apparently random questions—and, very often, to ask them without *seeming* to ask them; to hide them in small-talk, or conceal them in throw-away remarks. And to be able to recognise the answers, which aren't *real* answers, and tabulate them away, like the jumbled pieces of a jigsaw puzzle waiting for the key-piece to fall into position and, thereafter, all the other pieces to unscramble themselves and complete the picture.

And no copper who seeks and finds and, in finding, knows the pure gold of success, ever again grows weary. No matter how prolonged the enquiry—no matter how physically tired he becomes—the thought of calling it a day and granting the crook the accedance of victory never once enters his head. Because he knows, the next question might be *the* question ... the next answer might be *the* answer.

Which is one reason why Lennox and the W.P.S. seemed to be there for the night.

'Y'see, luv ...' Lennox sipped at his tea, swallowed, then said, 'Y'see, we think the same bloke who shot your hubby also shot this Miss Bentley, at Ashfield Comprehensive School.'

'I—er—I didn't know,' muttered Muriel White. 'I—I haven't looked at the newspapers. Or listened to the wireless. Or ...'

'No—of course—you wouldn't,' said Lennox, soothingly. 'Nobody's suggesting—y'know ... But this lady—this Miss Bentley—was shot, earlier today. Killed ... like your hubby, I'm afraid.'

'Oh, dear. The poor woman.'

'Aye.' Lennox nodded sympathetic agreement and his multiple chins wobbled solemnly. 'But—y'see, luv—we know it was the same gun. So we *think* it was the same man.'

'Well—yes—that's, y'know ... obvious. Isn't it?'

'We think so.'

'But—but *why*? Why should anybody want to kill White and this other lady?'

'Can *you* think of a reason?' asked Lennox, gently.

'Me?'

'Ashfield Comprehensive, for example. Was your hubby connected with it in any way?'

'No. No ... I'm sure not.'

'Didn't go there—wasn't a pupil ... before it went comprehensive, of course?'

'Oh, no. It was a little school, up in the dales. White hadn't much book-learning, sir. He was clever—I'm not saying he wasn't clever ... but it wasn't *book*-learning.'

'All right,' said Lennox patiently. 'Let's look at it from the other side. Ashfield Comprehensive—or even Ashfield Secondary, before it went comprehensive—any connection—any connection with High Dale Farm? However remote?'

'No ... none.'

'Rambles—y'know ... nature rambles? They go in for those things, these days?'
'No.' She shook her head. 'Not across *our* land.'
'Field Days? School sports? Y'know ... hare and hounds stuff? Paper-chases? That sort of thing?'
'No.' She continued to shake her head. 'White was always very down on trespassers.'
'All right ... trespassers? Anybody, recently? Anybody who might have been connected with Ashfield School? Some of the kids? Some of the teachers, even?'
'I—I don't think so. He never mentioned ... and I think he would.'
'The golf club ... that's virtually next door. Right?' She nodded.
'Any of them? Looking for lost balls? Straying beyond the course? That sort of thing?'
'No, sir.' Her voice was plaintive. Almost pleading. She said, 'Look, sir—if I could help you ... If I could, I *would*.'
'Yes.' He sighed, and his expression of sadness was genuine. 'I know you would, luv. And don't think I'm enjoying this ... but it has to be done. You're a brave lass, missus. It's appreciated. These things happen. Normally—death comes to all of us, I know ... but at least we're granted the privacy of sorrow. We can grieve, without making a public exhibition of ourself. Without having flatfooted coppers pestering us with questions we can't answer. That's the hard part, when death comes this way, luv. I know it. Every copper in his right mind knows it ... and hates it. And he's grateful when he has to deal with somebody like you. Anything we can do ... I don't have to tell you. Anything! I know there rarely is—but ... y'know.' He stood up from the chair and, despite his ludicrous suit of checked cloth, despite his bow tie, despite the obesity of his figure—despite all these things—

there was solemn dignity, and a touch of old world charm, in his half-bow of leave-taking.

It was another midnight talk-session. Gum-bashing by the can-carriers, and supervised by the can-carrier-in-chief himself. It would be wrong, and an overexaggeration, to describe the atmosphere—the tone of their conversation—as bordering upon panic. One of the main qualifications required for the size of rank held by Gilliant, Sullivan, Bear, Harris and Sugden was phlegmatic unflappability. They kept their 'cool' ... externally. And the other four—Rucker, Lennox, Blayde and Preston—kept what stomach-flutterings they may have had under strict control.

Nevertheless, there *was* an atmosphere.

It reminded Lennox of the war years; those few seconds of breath-held silence, between the cut of a doodlebug's engine and the blast of the explosion. The life-or-death question mark. Will it, or won't it? How far, how far? Is this the last, or just the beginning?

No panic ... but a great deal of apprehension.

Blayde's office seemed overcrowded, and the overcrowding was emphasised by the fact that Sullivan, Sugden and Preston had all refused chairs; they prowled the office, like a trio of caged and frustrated animals. Sullivan and Sugden drawing furiously on their pipes. Preston with his hands deep in the pockets of his trousers.

There was definitely an atmosphere.

Gilliant sat at Blayde's desk and he, too, smoked. Jerky inhalations of a cigarette then, when he'd half-smoked one cigarette, he chain-lit a new one and screwed the first cigarette into the desk ash-tray with slightly unnecessary violence.

'Three murders,' he said, with soft deliberation. 'The same murderer. Let's not waste time discussing "chain reaction". I want to hear no "carbon copy" rubbish. One killer—one man ... that's what we're after. He's killed three times, in less than forty-eight hours. There's a thread, somewhere ... however tenuous, there must be a thread.'

'Unless he's mad,' said Bear.

'In that case, it's a mad thread. An insane thread. But, before we can move, we have to find it ... sane, or insane. Three killings, gentlemen. Let's take them, one at a time. The murder of William White. Anybody prepared to stick his neck out, and volunteer an opinion?'

Blayde said, 'I've read all the statements taken, so far. I've read, and re-read, them. Shall I start the ball rolling?'

Gilliant nodded.

Blayde leaned forward in his chair a little. He spoke slowly and carefully—weighing each word and pausing between each sentence—summing up much of the data which had already been filed away in the Information Room.

He said, 'For the sake of our own peace of mind, we'd better start with an assumption. That these aren't haphazard killings. That we aren't dealing with "murder for kicks". That there's a reason—however obscure a reason —and that White was killed *for* that reason. From this, it follows that the murderer knew White. It's no big step from that to say that White knew the murderer. Maybe a friend. Maybe a mere acquaintance. But, for my money, White and the man who shot him weren't strangers.

'Now, White's owned High Dale Farm for the last seven-to-eight years. He, and his father, bought it, from Appleyard. But White's *worked* on that farm for nearer twenty years. He was Appleyard's stock-man. He lived in a tied cottage ... a cottage now occupied by one of White's own employees. Appleyard emigrated. White convinced the bank that the farm was a good investment, and secured an overdraft. What I'm getting at is this ... *twenty years.* When a man lives in one spot for that length of time, he gets to know a lot of people. Locals. Visitors. Chance acquaintances. Hundreds of people. And, no matter how good or how popular that man is, he can't like them all ... and they all can't like him. He *has* to make enemies.

'We're told White didn't bear grudges. That he wasn't that sort of a man. But that information comes from the widow ... and, although she may be telling the truth, she may also be biased. That has to be taken into consideration. She admits that White kept himself to himself ... which, in affect, means he was somewhat secretive. He certainly wasn't very demonstrative. Throughout her statement, Mrs White refers to her husband as "White". I've checked with the officer who took the statement. That's the expression she always used.'

'I can verify that,' rumbled Lennox.

'Not a sign of open endearment,' continued Blayde. 'Not even "Mr White". Not "Bill" ... not "William". Always "White". It's still done, in the country ... therefore it may not count for too much. But it's only done by country people who refuse to move with the times. A wife calls her husband by his surname. Rarely—very rarely—by his Christian name. It's old-fashioned. It's also a pointer to the status of the man, within his own household. The master. Strong-willed. Never to be disobeyed ... and a man with that sort of inbuilt personality has to cross swords with *somebody*, over a period of twenty years.'

'The personality of the victim,' said Gilliant. 'I'm inclined to agree ... with reservations. Beyond that, what? What facts?'

'Facts,' ruminated Blayde. 'It seems a fact that the murderer knew the route White was likely to take, across his land. That he knew *when*—within reason—White was likely to come through that gate. There's a tree—about sixty yards from the gate—and we've found marks from golf-shoe spikes near the trunk of the tree. A perfect hiding place. Behind the tree, waiting for White to reach the gate. A fact—at least calculated guesswork—that the murderer studied White's movements. Habits.'

'That the killer knew White,' said Gilliant. 'That White must have known his murderer.'

'Possible,' agreed Blayde. 'Even probable. Certainly a careful watching of White's movements. Over some period of time. This, to me, suggests that the murderer is local. If not local, that he's been living in this district for some time. Watching White ...'

'And Bentley? And West? He's been a very busy little man, chief superintendent.' The interruption, heavy with contempt, came from Rucker.

'For the moment, let's concentrate on the White killing,' said Gilliant, coldly. 'And—er—Mr Rucker without sarcastic asides, if you don't mind.'

'That's about all, sir.' Blayde continued his summary, as if the interruption hadn't happened. 'The shoes—the prints ... that ties the killer to the golf club, on the face of things. If so, he's pretty sure of himself. Most people know about footprint casts, these days. Unless, of course, he was surprisingly devious.'

'I'm sorry.' Bear frowned apologetic puzzlement. 'I'm not with you, chief superintendent. *How* "surprisingly devious"?'

Blayde said, 'Golfing shoes. Anybody can buy them. You don't *have* to be a member of a club ... or even play golf. It's possible he wore the shoes deliberately. Knowing they'd leave a good imprint. Knowing that the imprint would point us to the golf club.'

'But not being a member of the club?' murmured Bear.

'It's possible.'

'It's possible,' chipped in Sullivan, 'but I don't go along with it. It shows too much planning. Anybody being *that* cunning wouldn't have left an empty cartridge case at the scene. No ... I'll plump for the simpler explanation.

That the murder was committed about a mile—slightly less—across the fields from the fourteenth hole. And that, to get *to* the fourteenth hole, he had to make believe he was playing golf. Wear the gear ... all the rest of it. The shoes were part of the gear. He didn't forget them—forget he was wearing 'em ... he just forgot to remember.'

'That's as neat a piece of hair-splitting as I've heard for a long time, Mr Sullivan,' smiled Gilliant.

'Like cricket,' explained Sullivan. 'A batsman—a county player, say—gets so used to wearing batting pads, he doesn't even notice they're there. The same with the golf shoes. My bet says he's so used to wearing 'em, he isn't conscious that they're any different from normal shoes. He's no super-mind. Otherwise, he wouldn't have left the cartridge case ... otherwise, he wouldn't have shot a dead man through the forehead.'

'Okay, sir. He's no super-mind.' Sugden paused in his prowling. 'But—whatever else—he's a damn good shot. The White killing—even counting that as an easy target, which it wasn't—one shot. The Bentley killing ... one shot. The West killing—again, one shot ... and one hell of a shot! Whoever he is, he can handle a .22.'

'Telescopic sight,' said Sullivan.

'Still one hell of a shot,' insisted Sugden.

Sullivan grunted reluctant agreement.

'One thing for sure.' Harris added his contribution to the free-for-all discussion. 'When we nail him, we've *got* him. He hired that car the day before the Bentley murder ... presumably *for* the Bentley murder. In the early afternoon—*before* the White shooting—and that's premeditation, with knobs on.'

'Which,' sighed Gilliant, 'brings us full circle. Why White, *and* Bentley?'

'*And* West?' added Bear.

Sugden growled, 'The West killing ... it's hardly off the ground, yet. We may come up with a common denominator, when we've pushed that one a bit harder.'

Gilliant said, 'Right ... let's start with a basic proposition. That they're not random killings. The deliberate hiring of the car tends to rule that out. The hiring, and the time of the hiring. He intended shooting White. He intended shooting Bentley. He intended shooting West. Which means he *knew* them. He *chose* them. For whatever reason, he had a grudge against them.'

'Or *thinks* he had a grudge,' said Sullivan.

'All right,' agreed Gilliant, 'or thinks he had a grudge.'

'I only hope,' sighed Bear, 'that he doesn't "think" he has a grudge against many more people.'

'For Christ's sake, be cheerful,' grunted Sugden.

'It's a possibility,' said Harris sombrely.

'The grudge—the imagined grudge—whichever ... it's the link,' said Gilliant.

Blayde said, 'The Bentley woman ... there's an almighty contradiction as far as she's concerned.'

The others waited.

The Beechwood Brook chief superintendent continued, 'Statements, and the initial report of the D.I. who interviewed her sister. The people she worked with swore by her. A wonderful worker. Efficient. Popular. Well-loved. You name it ... if it's complimentary, that's what she was. She lived with her sister—Violet Bentley—and, according to the report from the D.I., she was anything *but*. A tease. Everything short of the complete whore. The two things don't tally. There's maybe a midway mark ... if so, it has to be pinpointed. The pupils of Ashfield Comprehensive have yet to be interviewed. With luck, we'll get nearer the truth with some of the older pupils.'

'The "mystery woman",' murmured Rucker. 'That's all we're short of.'

Bear said, 'Sisters ... they either love, or hate. They often keep their hatred under wraps. But it's either one or the other. Every time.'

'I take it,' said Gilliant, 'that nobody's suggesting the *sister* killed the Bentley woman?'

'No, sir,' said Bear. 'A general observation ... that's all.'

Blayde said, 'There's no obvious link between the Bentley woman and the golf club ... at least, not yet.'

'Bentley and White?' asked Sullivan.

'Again, no obvious link ... not yet.'

'We'd better *find* that link,' said Gilliant, softly. 'It's there—it has to be there ... the killer hired the car for the Bentley killing, before he shot White. There *is* a link, gentlemen. When we find it, we're a long way towards solving the puzzle.'

So easy ... so obvious ... frustrated, treadmill talk, parcelled up in cigarette and tobacco smoke and, always, the talk went full circle and ended with the link. The connection. The thread.

Three murders. One murderer. Three victims ... therefore, on the face of it, one motive.

The session broke up, after almost two hours of fruitless conversation. Two hours of non-productive chat, by the big-wigs of a new Metropolitan Police District.

The whodunit ... but, this time, for real.

And the only thing they were sure about was that, *this* time, it wasn't 'the butler' ... and that, only because there *wasn't* a blasted butler!

After the session, all eight of the aforementioned big-wigs drove home, in the hope of catching a few hours sleep, before the manhunt was notched one gear higher.

Three of them were unlucky.

'Queen Selene of the Don,' said Mrs Lennox, firmly.

'Not *again*!' groaned Lennox.

'She has beautiful babies. They're always ...'

'She's a bloody sex maniac.'
'She has her quota of kittens. No more. And they're all ...'
'I'm shagged,' said Lennox ... and sounded it. 'I've had a long day. I need bed. The last thing I need is ...'
'Selene requires our help,' insisted Mrs Lennox.
Lennox grunted, 'Look—why the hell not just *leave* her? As far as she's concerned, it's as easy as podding peas. They just pop out ... and that's it.'
'Potential prize-winners,' said his wife, coldly, 'do not just "pop out". The mother needs somebody with her. To give her confidence.'
'We count 'em,' argued Lennox irritably. 'That's all. Every bloody time. And always at some unearthly hour ... *always*. I've never known a more inconsiderate cat. Last time, it was four o'clock in the morning. Why the hell she can't ...'
'This time, too, by my calculations,' murmured Mrs Lennox.
'Oh, my Christ!'
'And she needs us there.'
'Not me. I can't see what the hell *I'm* ...'
'Her mummy and daddy.'
'Speak for yourself,' grumbled Lennox. 'I'm not the "daddy" to a damn moggie.'
'A *what*?'
'All right! All right!' The butterball detective held out pudgy hands, as if to ward off an expected attack. 'Not exactly a "moggie". A prize-winning Russian Blue ...'
'Who, in her own way, contributes almost as much to the communal purse of this household as you do.'
'... but, for all that, only a bloody cat.'
'*Only?*'
'And I don't have fur and whiskers.'
'ONLY?' repeated Lennox's wife, in a more powerful —more penetrating—voice.

'Only a cat,' insisted Lennox doggedly. 'She fornicates. She enjoys herself ... at least, I reckon she does. And, for doing what she enjoys doing, she gets better treatment in this place than I do.'

'She mates easily,' said Mrs Lennox, coldly. 'Which is why she's a priceless queen. Surely, even *you* can see that?'

'Y'mean,' growled Lennox, 'she's a bit of a feline slag.'

'What on earth I ever saw in a coarse-minded oaf, like you, I'll never know. Why I ever married ...'

'Because,' said Lennox, nastily, 'you ain't Queen Selene of the bloody Don ... and never were. It wasn't my money. Sure as hell, it wasn't my looks. Unlike the blasted cat, you couldn't just lie back, enjoy it and watch the banknotes roll in. So-o ... there's only one reason left. A meal-ticket.'

'I'll ignore that outburst,' snapped Mrs Lennox. 'I'll excuse it, because you're tired. But—be warned—don't go any farther. And you'll be on hand, when the kittens arrive ... whatever time it is.'

'Like hell I will,' rumbled Lennox.

But he *was*.

Yes ... and even deputy chief constables are subjected to the rough edge of their wives' tongues. Even super-duper deputy chief constables, like Sullivan.

As he walked into the massive living kitchen of the miniature mansion which a grateful (albeit misguided) Police Authority had allocated to him as rent-free living quarters, for himself and his family, upon his previous promotion to A.C.C. (Crime) of the old Lessford City force, Mary Sullivan greeted him with angry eyes and a waspish outburst.

'You and your infernal ceiling,' she snapped.

'Eh?' Sullivan stared.

'Of course, you *had* to do your own decorating.'

'For God's sake, what's ...'
'And you *had* to be smart and sarcastic to Steve.'
'Look—what the hell ...'
'And now, he's in hospital—in pain ... thanks to *you*.'
'He's in ...' Concern filled Sullivan's eyes, hoarsened his voice and cloaked his expression. He said, 'Mary—for Christ's sake—what's happened?'
'Those steps. They weren't safe.'
'I know, but ...'
'You *knew* they weren't safe.'
'Yes—all right—I knew they weren't safe ... but what's happened?'
'And telling him he wasn't helping with the new house.'
'I didn't. When did I ...'
'And now this.'
'What's *happened*?' pleaded Sullivan, desperately.
'He—he wanted to finish the ceiling for you.'
'Oh!'
'And he fell off the steps.'
'Oh!'
'And—and broke his leg.'
'The clumsy young bugger.'
'Well! Of all the ...'
'Well ... isn't he?' Sullivan's concern for his son rebounded, did a back-flip and transformed itself into snarling disgust. 'I've been up and down those bloody steps a couple of hundred times. They sway a bit ... that's all. All *he* has to do is go up 'em once, and he's a hospital case.'
'Of all the callous, self-centred ...'
'Don't talk like a hysterical schoolkid.'
'Richard Sullivan, you disgust me. D'you know that? You absolutely disgust ...'
'Holy cow,' bawled Sullivan, 'you're a copper's wife. Remember?'
'I'm also a mother. But have you ...'

'A copper's wife ... and you behave as if a broken leg's a blasted terminal disease. He's bust his leg. So what? Which leg?'

'The right leg, if you're so interested. But, as far as I can see ...'

'All right. He's bust his right leg. It'll hurt a bit. But it'll teach him a lesson ... not to monkey around with things beyond his limited capabilities. Christ, if he can't even paint a bloody ceiling, without breaking his stupid neck ...'

'His leg. That's all, thank heavens.'

'... he isn't fit to be allowed on the street, without a nursemaid. Some bloody architect! What happens, if he has to climb up onto a roof?'

'And that's all, is it?' gasped Mary Sullivan.

'Eh?'

'That's the sum total of your concern, when your own son suffers a serious injury while trying to ...'

'I'll be back.' Sullivan turned to leave the kitchen.

'Where are you going?'

'To the hospital. Where else? To see how the young fool's getting on.'

'Oh, don't bother. He's only your son. Don't inconvenience yourself on *his* ...'

Sullivan glared, and said, 'I think as much about him as you do. He's a nut case—that's all ... but that doesn't mean I think any the less about him.'

Mary Sullivan took a deep breath, closed her eyes, momentarily, at the unfathomable intricacies of the male mind, then said, 'At this time? They won't let you in. You won't be able to see him.'

'This fancy rank of mine carries *some* privileges,' growled Sullivan. 'This is one of 'em. They'll let me in— they'll let me see him ... that, or I'll have somebody's tripes, with onions.'

'I'm coming with you,' declared Mary.

'There's no need. I just want to ...'

'Don't you *dare* go, without me.'

'All right,' sighed Sullivan. 'But—as a personal favour —don't give him the impression he's at death's door. And don't treat him like a bloody hero. He's a ham-footed clown. Must be. Don't leave him in any doubt ... else, next time it might *be* his neck.'

Preston sat on the cane chair, in the bedroom, and fumbled with the laces of his shoes. He hadn't switched on the light; there was sufficient glow from a nearby street lamp with which to undress, don his pyjamas and climb into the comfort of his twin bed.

The truth was, he didn't wish to awaken his wife.

This, for a number of reasons. If she was asleep, she was asleep, and there was no reason to disturb her slumber, merely because he'd had a particularly late session. And, if she awakened, she'd talk—and talk—and talk ... and the talk would be the same old roundelay. The same old gripe. The same old bitterness. The same old disappointment ... as if he *hadn't* been disappointed.

Preston was kidding himself.

From the gloom of the farther bed, his wife's voice mumbled, 'Is that you?'

'Uhuh.' Preston jerked at an awkward knot in the lace of the left shoe.

'What time is it?'

'Two o'clock. Just after.'

'Oh, my God.'

'Sorry. It was a late session.' He gave up the struggle with the knot, and eased his heel clear of the shoe, without untying the lace.

'Was *he* there?' It was an overloaded question ... the start-gun for the marathon he'd been fearing.

'Uhuh.'

'Having a lot to say for himself, as usual?'

'Not much.' Preston unknotted his tie and folded it carefully, before placing it on the bedside table.

'Crawling, I suppose?'

'He's no crawler ... whatever else he is, he's not that.'

'In that case, how the dickens did he ...'

'Drop it,' said Preston, wearily. He stood up from the chair and began to unbutton his shirt.

'He got your job,' she said, bitterly.

'*You* think so.'

'Don't you?'

'Maybe.' He slipped the shirt from his arms and draped it over the seat of the chair. 'Who the hell knows?'

'*I* know.'

'Who the hell *ever* knows?' He unbuckled his belt, lowered the zip and stepped out of his trousers. As he folded the trousers, he murmured, 'This job ... who the hell ever knows? You gut yourself. Work yourself to a standstill. Then they hopscotch somebody over your head, and you're taking orders, when you should have been giving 'em.'

'Crawlers,' she insisted, with quiet fury.

'Not this time.' He placed the folded trousers on top of the shirt. 'Anything else. But not a crawler.'

'What else, then?'

'I dunno.'

'You're weak,' she sneered. 'You let them wipe their feet all over you.'

'No.' He sat on the empty bed and began to peel off his socks. 'Nobody reaches detective superintendent by being a doormat. That's one comfort.'

'Men!' she said, scornfully. 'They forgive so easily. All pals together. Somebody pinches your job, and ...'

'That's not true.' He stood up and padded, bare-footed, into the bathroom. 'You take the rough with the smooth —that's all ... now, drop it.'

When he returned from the bathroom, she said, 'What did *you* say?'

'Eh?'

'This discussion thing. What did *you* say?'

'Not a lot.' He slipped out of his underpants, reached his pyjama trousers from the bottom of the bed and threaded his feet through the legs. He added, 'There wasn't a hell of a lot *to* say.'

'You just sat there, like a good little boy,' she said, contemptuously.

'Drop it, pet ... eh?' he pleaded, wearily.

'I bet *Rucker* found enough to say for himself.'

'Not too much.'

'*I'll* bet!'

Preston jerked the string vest clear of his body, tousled his hair and punched his fists through the sleeves of his pyjama jacket. He grabbed at his rising anger, and held it in check ... but only just.

She was a fool; she hadn't the sense to realise that she'd pushed him to the limit, and that one more scathing comment would be one too many.

She sneered, 'Big man. Detective Superintendent Preston ... but not big enough to stop a smooth-talking hound like Rucker from ...'

She ended the outburst with a quick yelp of terror as he vaulted the empty bed, grabbed her nightdress by the neck and hauled her into a sitting position.

His voice was choked with anger as he poured his frustrated fury out at her frightened face, from a distance of less than six inches.

He rasped, 'Listen, cow. This was something I was keeping under wraps. Forgetting—y'know ... ignoring. Kidding myself it was a flash in the pan. Not too much to worry about. Something that would burn itself out ... that you'd come back to normal, and be a moderately decent wife. But—okay—you want it ... you've asked for it. So, here it comes.

'Kitley—you and that bloody dentist, Harold Kitley ... I know about it. I know *all* about it. Don't bother about *how* I know. I *do* know—I'm a detective superintendent, remember? ... it's my job to know things. All sorts of things. Like, when I'm on a late session—like tonight—and the Kitley bastard comes calling, with his cock hanging out. He's been here, earlier ... a thousand pounds to a bag of peanuts. Like the time you went to Southport for a break. Four days, last May—with your sister ... but your sister only stayed *two* days. The second two days belonged to Kitley. I'm getting through to you, I hope. You're getting the picture. That you're a whore ... and that I *know* you're a whore. And that I'm so pig-sick of it all—of *you*—that I don't give a damn. Didn't. But—okay—you want to play silly buggers. You want to twist my tail, because Rucker dropped for the job I should be holding. You can't leave the subject alone. Okay. *Okay!* So, you won't mind too much if I take a turn with the thumbscrew ... right? You enjoy making me sweat. Great—two can play at that game ... so, now, I make *you* sweat. And Kitley sweat. I may not be Head of C.I.D., but I'm still a detective superintendent. And Kitley's one of the local jet-set tooth-pullers. The yellow rags'll have a flag day. All the mucky details ... I'll make damn sure they get *them*. And pictures. The copper's wife who can't keep her legs crossed. The "with-it" dentist who goes through life with a permanent hard on. My oath ... I'll make you two weep blood.

'And why? Not because you've been whoring around. Not that. But because I gut myself, trying to do a good job—trying to do what I'm paid to do—and, when I come home, dead beat, I can't even find peace of mind. You can't shut up. You can't resist the blasted needle. You can't *leave* it.

'Well—that's it, sweetheart ... getting married was a mistake. But you won't live quietly with the mistake. You have to pick the scab off the sore, at every opportunity. And that's it. That's *why*. And, when your boy friend asks, tell him ... it was fine by me, if you'd kept your bloody trap shut about other things.'

He flung her back onto the pillow, turned his back on her, and climbed into the other twin bed.

Two more people—one more copper and his wife—who didn't sleep that night.

And, at 4.am that same morning, a cow had some slight difficulty in bringing a calf into the world. A farmer heard the mournful bellowing, dressed and trudged into the stackyard, on his way to the cowshed. He saw a man, asleep between bales of hay.

The farmer did what he could for the cow, while his wife telephoned for the police.

And, at 4.23.am, precisely, Crispin was nicked, bundled into a squad car and driven towards the nearest police cell.

Nor was Queen Selene of the Don any more considerate in her timing than was the cow.

'There must be a better way to *do* these things,' wailed Lennox.

Mrs Lennox watched her beloved cat, and murmured, 'Nature takes its own course. Its own time.'

'When you mate the bloody thing ...'

'She is not a "thing".'

'... surely to Christ it's possible to time things better. You're the expert. It takes so long to—to—to ...'

'The gestation period.'

'Aye—the gestation period—surely to Christ it's possible to *time* the thing better.'

'To the hour?' said his wife, scornfully.

'I'm damned if I see why not.'
'You're an idiot.'
'I *must* be. Fannying around, at this hour, watching a cat have kittens.'
'Helping her,' corrected his wife.
'Helping? You won't let me within three yards of the damn thing.'
'Your presence helps. That we're both here ... that helps.'
'I'm buggered if I see how. She hasn't even looked at us, for the last half hour.'
'She's watching her babies. She's amazed. Can't you see it in her eyes ... she's *amazed*.'
'In God's name, why should she be amazed?' demanded Lennox. 'This is her tenth litter ...'
'Eleventh. As you'd know, if you were even half-interested.'
Lennox said, 'That's what I mean. Eleven bloody litters. Why should she be "amazed"? As far as she's concerned, it's as natural as you, or I, brushing our teeth. What the devil has *she* to be amazed at?'
'Careful.'
'Eh?'
Mrs Lennox leaned closer to the cat, and said, 'There's another coming. Any minute ... another little darling's going to see the world for the first time.'
'Twenty quid coming up,' murmured Lennox, irreverently.
'Reach me the brandy.'
'The what?'
'The brandy.'
'Why the deuce do *you* need brandy. It's the cat who's ...'
'It's *for* the cat.' Mrs Lennox held out an impatient hand. 'She's been working very hard. She needs a spoonful of brandy in her milk.'

'Where is it?' asked Lennox.

'What?'

'The brandy. The brandy bottle. Where is it?'

'I—I ... Oh, you pot-bellied fool. I told you to bring it along.'

'Oh, no,' protested Lennox.

'I *told* you. I remember, quite distinctly ... I told you to bring the brandy.'

'I must have forgot,' sighed Lennox.

'You forget very easily,' she snapped. 'I sometimes think you forget on purpose ... just to make things more difficult.'

'All right. I'll fetch the brandy. You keep a weather eye on the mother of—what is it?—quads ... so far.'

Sullivan loathed hospitals. Especially in the small hours. He'd spent too much of his life sitting by beds, waiting for some would-be suicide to regain consciousness, and thereafter stumblingly try to explain to a happy man what depths of misery can prod a person to the brink of self-destruction ... and, always, Sullivan had listened with sympathy, but had never fully understood. He'd sat at other bedsides, too. He'd witnessed the silent agony of men whose bodies had been mangled in gangland feuds. He'd watched the fear in the eyes of victims of criminal assault. He'd seen the end-product of back-street abortion. Crimes against the person—the official jargon used to describe varying forms of pain—and the end of the line some hospital ... with some copper sitting at the bedside. And Sullivan had been one such copper far too many times.

He loathed hospitals.

Sullivan and his wife followed the night porter along the dimly lit corridors, to what was obviously a ward sister's office. The porter switched on the light, waved a hand towards the chairs at, and around, the small desk and, with a worried expression, muttered, 'He'll grumble. He'll gripe like the very devil.'

'Will he?' said Sullivan, in a non-committal tone.

'He don't like bein' disturbed.'

'Really?'

Mary Sullivan looked embarrassed, made as if to say something, then decided to remain silent.

'He might not even come,' said the porter.

Sullivan growled, 'He'll come ... pronto. Tell him that, if he seems to have any doubts. That he'll come, *now*. Or I'll make it my personal business to see he has more trouble that he ever knew existed.'

'He won't like ...'

'I don't give a damn what he likes. Get him!'

The porter moved his shoulders, resignedly, and left.

Mary said, 'You shouldn't talk like that, Dick. These people work long hours. They're ...'

'They're not alone. They like to think they are. But he's in bed—remember? ... and, so far, I haven't even *seen* bed.'

Mary Sullivan knew her man. When he had the bit between his teeth, he couldn't be argued with ... and God help any young doctor who even tried.

Fifteen minutes later, the young staff medic exploded into the office. He was a coloured man—a Pakistani—and, like a certain type of self-opinionated young man (regardless of skin pigmentation) he had the arrogance which only experience, and enough wrong decisions, can destroy. His hair was unkempt. His angry eyes were slightly blurred from interrupted sleep. He pronounced Sullivan's name 'Salluvin' ... which, in turn, did nothing to cool down the exchange.

'Are you Sullivan?' he snapped, irritably.

Sullivan stood up from his chair.

'I'm asking you a question,' rapped the medic. 'Are you Sullivan? Are you the foolish man who's ...'

'Aye,' growled Sullivan. 'I'm "Sullivan". And there's a "Mr" in front of it. And don't call me a fool a second time ... otherwise you'll know what the expression "doctor cure thyself" really means.'

'Are you daring to threaten me? Here? In my own hospital?'

'*Your* hospital?'

'I'm the doctor in charge here, at this moment. You would do well to remember that fact. And I don't take kindly to being awakened by panic-ridden parents, when there's no cause ...'

'How the hell do you know there's no cause?'

'I won't argue with a man like you. I have better things to do with my time.'

The medic turned for the door, but Sullivan beat him to it. Sullivan slammed the door closed and leaned with his back against it.

'Let me out of this office. Immediately.'

'Sonny.' Sullivan's voice was low, and dangerous. 'I don't often pull rank ... but this time looks like being the exception. Aye—my name's Sullivan ... Deputy Chief Constable Sullivan. Which means that, in this town—and that includes this hospital—I carry enough weight to screw you into the dirt. And *will* ... if your manners don't improve. You've just been pulled out of bed. Congratulations. I've been on duty as long as you ... and I haven't yet *been* to bed. My son—Steve Sullivan—he was admitted, earlier today ... a broken leg. I want to know how bad.'

'You can't possibly see him, at this time in the ...'

'I want to know how bad,' repeated Sullivan. 'Then *I'll* tell *you* whether, or not, I'm going to see him.'

'You can't possibly see him at ...'

'*How bad!*' exploded Sullivan.

The medic backed off a pace, and some of the fight—and a percentage of the arrogance—was missing

when he said, 'A broken tibia. That's the shin ...'
'I know what the tibia is.'
'Nothing serious. Nothing at all serious.'
'Especially,' snarled Sullivan, 'when it's not your bloody tibia.'
'It happens all the time. We have them every day.'
'Other people. Not *you*. Grab that, sonny ... and you may end up a fair-to-moderate doctor. At the moment, we're not discussing "other people". We're discussing my son. How is he?'
'He's as well as can be ...'
'"Expected"?' Sullivan's lips curled. 'Don't give me the usual text-book pap. I want to know how he is. His condition. Whether he's comfortable ... whether he's asleep. And whether there are likely to be complications ... and, if so, what those complications are likely to be.'
'How do I know?'
'You should know. You've just claimed to be in charge of this damn hospital ... so you *should* know. If you don't know, find out. Fast! Otherwise, I'm on a phone and I'll have *your* gaffer out of his bed and down here ... and you'll tell *him* what the tax-payers are paying you for.'

The medic moistened his lips, breathed deeply, then said, 'If you'll let me out of this office, please.'

Sullivan stood away from the door.

As the medic left, Sullivan warned, 'And don't get any stroppy ideas, sonny. Ten minutes. And, if you aren't back here, with all the answers, I start using a telephone.'

When the medic was out of earshot, Mary said, 'Dick ... that was uncalled for.'

'No. It was necessary,' contradicted Sullivan, grimly. 'They're public servants. Like me. Like every other copper. Like every other man, or woman, who earns public money. They forget that, too easily. They need

reminding, periodically ... otherwise, these places turn into assembly-line shops.'
'They're—they're overworked.'
'Aye ... aren't we all.'
'No, I mean ...'
'I know what you mean, pet.' Sullivan smiled his understanding at his wife. 'But—look—I wouldn't have talked to a crook the way he was going to talk to us ... and I'm damned if he's going to talk to *me* that way. It's a "calling". So they tell me. Fine ... but part of that "calling" includes sympathy and understanding. Y'never know. Maybe he's learned something tonight. If he has the gumption, it might make him a better doctor.'

Three coppers, then, had one more sleepless night. Three coppers, and their respective wives. One officiated at the birth of Russian Blue kittens. One worried himself out of a night's sleep, because his son had broken a bone in his leg. One tried to sleep, but couldn't because he was haunted by the nagging hurt of his wife's infidelity, plus the injury to his self-esteem at the thought of Rucker occupying an office which (had there been any justice in the world) would have been his.

The man-and-wife talk bounced around, between this trio of mixed couples.

And, without realising it, mention was made of what was, perhaps, the biggest clue in the triple killing of White, Bentley and West.

Deputy Chief Constable Bear slept well, therefore Deputy Chief Constable Bear was first of the brass hats to enter the Information Room ... and, thus, was first to see the latest reports from the Forensic Science Laboratory.

He studied those reports and when (half an hour later) Blayde joined him in the Information Room, Bear had already decided upon a plan of action.

He handed the reports to Blayde, who dutifully scanned the somewhat unworldly gobbledegook used by scientists the world over, before returning the reports to Bear.

'The foot pedals and the carpet of the Capri,' murmured Bear.

'I noticed,' said Blayde.

'Grass cuttings. Soil. Sand. Bracken.'

'Golf links.' Blayde obligingly provided the common denominator. 'There's a good percentage of bracken in the rough.'

'The boffins can pull one out of the bag, occasionally,' grinned Bear.

'Occasionally,' agreed Blayde.

'So-o ... we concentrate on Beechwood Golf Club. Everything.'

'A mere five hundred suspects.'

'Better than the whole world,' said Bear, optimistically.

Blayde said, 'Rucker was handling the golf club side of things.'

'I know.'

'And Rucker,' said Blayde coldly, 'is a great tearer up of trees.'

'Shall we forget you said that?' suggested Bear, quietly.

'Why? I said it. I mean it ... and he'd be the first to agree.'

'The tone, chief superintendent.' Bear looked directly into Blayde's eyes as he delivered the mild reprimand. 'Personal likes and dislikes don't come into a murder enquiry. Shouldn't. We're a team ... that, or nothing.'

Blayde's smile was grim, and without humour.

'We *are* a team,' insisted Bear.

'Yes, sir.' Blayde became very formal. 'If you say we're a team, that's it. We're a team.'

'Without children.'

'Sir, that's a ...'

'Or grown men, who *behave* like children.'

It could have gone one way, or the other; Blayde's neck was stiff enough to have forced a minor showdown ... but his gumption, and his respect for this new Deputy Chief Constable, who commanded respect without throwing rank into the kitty, won the day.

He took a deep breath, his lips twisted, ruefully, and he said, 'Point taken ... I deserved that rocket.'

'Not a rocket, Mr Blayde,' said Bear, mildly. 'Just a reminder ... we all tend to forget basics, sometimes.'

Blayde walked to one of the table-desks which had been moved into the Recreation Hall. Bear followed.

Blayde touched a six-inch-high pile of typewritten sheets, on the surface of the desk, and said, 'Statements. Reports. From members and staff. Rucker knows how to make men work.' He hurriedly added, 'I mean that. He may not be popular—he doesn't try to be ... but, by hell, he can make men sweat blood, if necessary.'

Bear riffled the sheets of paper, thoughtfully.

'It could be in here,' he mused.

'What we're looking for?'

'The pointer. The hint.'

'Possible,' agreed Blayde.

Bear said, 'You and Preston. A thorough check. Every statement. Every report. Every word ... every innuendo. Boring. But necessary, I think.'

'Very necessary, in view of the lab report,' agreed Blayde.

'I'll leave it to you,' said Bear. 'Tell Preston, when he arrives. I think a master report ... one from each of you. Don't share the work. Duplicate it. What one might miss, the other might spot.'

Blayde nodded his agreement.

'Meanwhile ...' Bear chuckled, softly. 'A lot of people are going to be shouting "Fore" on the golf links, today.'

Men had spent all night searching the roofs and upper

rooms; possible firing points, from where it might have been possible to enjoy an uninterrupted aiming view of the stage door. They'd scrambled around the roofs, searching with high-powered torches. The Fire Service had helped, by providing ladders.

Dawn had come, and torches were no longer necessary, before they turned their attention to the multi-storied car park.

And, within five minutes, they found it.

There it was, behind the lift-head ... the spent cartridge.

Preston's wife heard her husband leave the house. She heard him open the garage door, start the car and drive away.

She pushed the sheets clear of her legs, swung her feet from the bed and reached for the telephone.

Her call was agitated—almost panic-ridden—and the man answering her call (the man called Kitley) did little to sooth her agitation. He was brusque. Almost sharp-tongued.

He ended the exchange with, 'For God's sake, you knew what you were doing. You're no starry-eyed virgin. So, stop worrying. There's a way out ... there's a way out of everything.'

Then, he hung up on her.

Meanwhile Sugden (as Assistant Chief Constable (Crime) in the Lessford Region of the newly formed M.P.D.) handled the West shooting. Having organised a token door-to-door-enquiry detail, he collected a detective sergeant and paid his respects upon the young man with whom West had been living.

Sugden (had you had the gall to ask him) would have insisted that he was a broad-minded man. A serious man —that, by all means ... but only because his profession was a serious profession. And yet, within the broad limits of that profession, an understanding man. A man not given to pre-judging other human beings. Indeed, a man who readily excused many things other policemen could never excuse.

Had you asked him, Sugden would have described himself thus ... and Sugden would have been kidding himself.

His very appearance was a contradiction of his own self-assessment. His iron-grey hair was worn short—almost crew-cut style—and, out of doors, always hidden under a conservative-coloured felt hat which gave the impression of having been positioned on his head with the aid of a spirit level. He wore dark, serge suits, complete with waistcoat, and black shoes whose toes were always polished to a patent-leather sheen. He walked 'like a man' (to use his own expression) ... which meant ramrod-backed and with long, determined strides.

He was a high-ranking copper ... and the impression was that he'd been *born* a high-ranking copper; that he had been lifted from a standard mould, and would die without once letting his hair down or relaxing his own, self-imposed discipline.

Given the oratory, Sugden would have made a first-rate hellfire-and-damnation parson. He had the build. He had the personality. But, above all else, he had the mile-wide streak of puritanism necessary for such a quasi-theatrical calling.

But he hadn't the oratory ... therefore he was a copper.

And now he had set himself the job of questioning a twenty-year-old 'with-it' young man who had been living, on homosexual terms, with the latest victim of the killer every man in the M.P.D. sought.

Sugden started the interview on what was (to him) rock-safe ground.

'Ten-forty-three ... exactly,' he said. 'This time we know when. Almost to the second.'

The interviewee's name was Dene—Chris Dene—of the shoulder-length hair, the psychedelic shirt, the skin-tight jeans, the sandals and the worry-beads. Chris Dene who, had hippies still been in fashion, would have been a hippy. Chris Dene ... of the tear-reddened eyes and the pallid complexion with the hint of unshaven bristle around the jowls and chin.

His fingers fumbled the worry-beads, and he muttered, 'Big deal, man. Eh? We know when, to the second. Big deal ... now, everything's okay.'

'When we find who killed him. *Then*, it'll be okay,' said Sugden.

'Yeah? That brings him back, does it? That makes the full resurrection job?'

The detective sergeant murmured, 'Easy, son. You've had a shock. We're not ...'

'Don't greaseball *me*, pig.' The heartbreak exploded into unbridled fury. Dene spun to face the detective sergeant, and snarled, 'You wanna do something to help, pig? That right? You wanna do something to help? Okay ... find the nearest corner, curl up and shit yourself. That might make me happy. Y'know ... that *just* might make me happy.'

Sugden compressed his lips, and said, 'That's enough of that talk, Dene.'

'You think so, man? You ...'

'I'm *telling* you.'

'You wanna ...'

'I want some questions answering.'

'Yeah? Well, lemme tell you, big man. You can go ...'

'Don't say it, lad.'

'Uh?'

'The tough talk. The dirty talk. Don't say it ... not to me.' Sugden's tone and eyes were hard and uncompromising, as he added, 'You're not big enough. You're not old enough. You're not important enough. We'll make allowances. Your friend's dead—so, we'll make allowances ... but don't run wild.'

The fingers fluttered wildly from bead to bead. He dropped his head forward, and the shoulder-length hair swung and almost covered his face. Then, he leaned back, with the nape of his neck resting against the top of the armchair's back and stared at the ceiling. The beads hung, between the thighs of the skintight jeans, and his fingers counted them—caressed them ... with the expertise of long practice and the restlessness of near-insane grief.

He whispered, 'Okay, man. Ask the questions. It ain't gonna help. But go ahead ... ask the questions.'

Sugden said, 'Where were you, when he was shot?'

'You think I killed him?' The counter-question was toneless, and without interest.

'I didn't say that,' said Sugden.

'Ten-forty-three? I was here ... where else? In the kitchen, making pizza.'

'For West? When he arrived home?'

'I make a good pizza,' droned Dene, tonelessly.

'For supper, when West arrived home?' insisted Sugden.

'Give him his right name, man.'

'West. Arthur West ... that's his name.'

'Arnold Westerfield.'

'His stage name ... surely?'

'He didn't go for the "West" name.'

'Nevertheless...'

'A guy can pick his own name, man. We got that much freedom left ... ain't we?'

'I—er—I suppose so. Just as long as it doesn't involve fraud.'

'You people stink ... y'know that?'

'It's an opinion,' said Sugden, flatly.

'He ain't here to defend himself. He ain't ever gonna

defend himself again. So, go ahead, call him bent ... he ain't gonna sue you.'

'I didn't say he was bent,' sighed Sugden.

'"Fraud." "Bent." Play around with words, copper. That's your bag.'

'All right.' Sugden shrugged. 'If it'll please you. "Arnold Westerfield." We'll call him *that*, for the moment.'

'Don't do me favours, copper.'

Sugden said, 'At the time he was shot, you were here? In the kitchen? Making supper?'

'Yeah.'

'He wasn't married?'

Dene hesitated. The worry-beads clicked busily as his fingers flickered across them, then he said, 'You're playing around with words again, man.'

'*Was* he married?' Sugden re-phrased the question.

'Yeah,' whispered Dene. 'We were married ... I guess.'

'"We"?'

'Yeah. To each other. We were lovers, man ... we were *lovers*.'

'Oh!'

'That ain't what you meant, though ... eh?'

'Not quite,' agreed Sugden.

'What the hell do you know about these things?' breathed Dene.

'Not a lot.'

'You shove your cock up some disease-rotten dame, and you think ...'

'That'll do!' snapped the detective sergeant.

Dene moved his head. Without taking the nape of his neck from the back of the armchair, he nodded, gently, at the ceiling.

Sugden allowed a few moments of silence to smooth balm upon Dene's outburst, then said, 'I'm talking about the more—er—*conventional* form of marriage. Was West —sorry, Westerfield—married?'

'No.'
'Was he *ever* married?'
'Yeah.'
'And?'
'She died,' said Dene, softly. 'She took dope ... she died.'
'Dope?' Sugden tried to hide the interest in his question.
'Too many bullets.'
'Bullets?'
'Caps.'
'You mean capsules?'
'Yeah?'
'What sort? D'you know?'
'Yeah. Red Candies.'
'Seconal?'
Dene nodded at the ceiling.
'Accidentally?' asked Sugden.
'What's your guess, man?'
Sugden said, 'Seconal. It's standard treatment for chronic insomnia.'
'Yeah.'
'She couldn't sleep?'
Dene muttered, 'The stupid bitch figured she wanted to sleep forever.'
'Suicide?' asked Sugden, quietly.
'Fifty.' Dene's mouth twitched, sardonically. 'Hell, you don't need *fifty*. Six—and a bottle of scotch ... and chances are you're way gone.'
Sugden said, 'Why suicide?'
Dene didn't answer the question.
'West?—Westerfield?' asked Sugden. 'Was he responsible?'
'Arnie,' mused Dene softly, as if to himself. 'Man, don't you knock my Arnie ... not now, not ever.'
'Was he responsible for his wife's suicide?' insisted Sugden.

'She made her own exit. She had a choice.'

'Answer the question, Dene.'

'Yeah.' Once more, Dene nodded at the ceiling. 'I guess. People like you might say that. It happens, man. Nobody *makes* it happen ... it just happens.'

'He drove his wife to suicide?'

'Who drives anybody?' countered Dene, sadly. 'We're all going. Some people choose their own time ... that's all.'

'And she chose then?'

'Yeah.'

'When?'

'Oh—y'know ... seven, eight years ago, maybe. Who knows? Who keeps diaries, these days?'

'Why?'

'We met ... that's all.'

'You and West?' Sugden was flicking the questions at the younger man with a staccato insistence they'd lacked before.

'I dunno any guy called "West", man.'

'Westerfield,' snapped Sugden.

The detective sergeant warned, 'Don't play silly buggers, Dene. You got the question ... just answer it.'

'Yeah ... me and Arnie,' said Dene, heavily. 'We met ... that's all.'

'Love at first sight, was it?' sneered the D.S.

Dene moved his head a little and looked at Sugden. He said, 'Hey, man. Do I have to take crap like that from this pig?'

'Not if you answer the questions,' said Sugden.

Dene returned his gaze to the ceiling, continued to finger the worry-beads, and said, 'Yeah. You ain't gonna believe it. 'Cos you ain't gonna *understand*. Ever! But—sure— you wanna put it like roses round some door, that's how it was. Arnie wasn't meant for no stinking woman. He didn't know that. We-ell—yeah, he knew it ... deep down, inside, he knew it. Like we *all* know it. But, he was living like he wasn't. Get me? Like he wasn't one of us. Like he *wasn't* gay.'

Dene stared at the ceiling and, slowly, his eyes brimmed with tears.

'And?' encouraged Sugden, flatly.

'We loved each other, man,' choked Dene. 'Dammit, you get me? ... We *loved* each other.'

At Beechwood Golf Course, the questions were still being asked. The statements were still being taken. Bear had been as good as his word. He'd more than doubled the men, and the handful of women, detailed to winkle answers from every club member, and the place swarmed with coppers.

In the locker-room ...

'Mr Conran?' said the detective constable. 'Mr Edward Conran?'

'That's me.' The man unlocked the steel door of his locker and pulled out an old jersey and shirt.

'It's about the White killing, Mr Conran. The day before yesterday.'

'Uhuh. I read about it. I can't see what ...'

'Where were you, at the time, please? Between four and four-fifteen?'

'*Me?*'

'Between four and four-fifteen?'

'Why? Why on earth question *me*?'

'Every club member, sir.' The D.C. smiled, reassuringly. 'Not just you—every member of the club, I'm afraid ... standard elimination procedure. That's all, sir.'

'We-ell, now.' Conran rubbed his chin, thoughtfully. 'I wasn't here ... that's a fact. This is my first visit this week.'

* * *

In the bar ...

A uniformed sergeant, working in plain clothes, was meeting difficulties.

'Excuse me. D'you mind telling me who you are?'

'Me?'

'Aye. Your name and address ... if you don't mind.'

'I *do* mind. Let me ask the same question. Who the devil are *you*?'

'Police. We're here on enquiries about the White-Bentley-West murders.'

'Indeed?'

'So—if you don't mind ... can I have your name and address, please?'

'I don't see the point.'

'*If* you don't mind.'

'I'm a solicitor ... does that put your mind at rest?'

'No. I'm afraid not.'

'Surely you haven't the impudence to ...'

'I'm here to ask questions. I want to know who's answering 'em. It's as simple as that. Now ... can I have some basic co-operation, please.'

'Officer—who the devil you are—for your information, I don't trust policemen over-much.'

'I'm sorry to hear that.'

'I've met too many.'

'If you're a solicitor, I don't have to tell you your rights.'

'Indeed you don't.'

'*Or* your duties. As a citizen, *and* as an officer of the court.'

'I've already told you. I don't trust policemen. They twist words. They indulge in—what's the official jargon? —"verbals".'

'That remark was a little uncalled for.'

'Think so? You should read up on the figures, officer.

The number of policemen who've been convicted for cooking the evidence.'
'Funny you should say that, sir.'
'Eh?'
'The other day. I was looking at some other figures. The number of solicitors, inside—doing time—for malpractice ... including Obstructing the Police. They outnumber the coppers, two-to-one.'
'Oh!'
'Now—d'you mind?—your name, your address and exactly where you were, between four and four-fifteen, the day before yesterday?'

On the practice putting green ...
'What a shot!'
'Yes, sir. Very good.'
'Tony Jacklin couldn't have done better.'
'I'm sure he couldn't. Now ... the day before yesterday. Between four and four-fifteen.'
'Lemme see, now. I was ... No—no, I wasn't.'
'Take your time, sir.'
'Quite. Ah, yes. The—er—the massage parlour.'
'The massage parlour?'
'Ye-es ... the one off Queen's Street. Up by the ...'
'I know it, sir.'
'I was there. There're a few very charming masseuses employed.'
'I—er—wouldn't know.'
'Take my word for it, officer. There's one called Paulette.'
'Yes, sir.'
'That's who I was with. From—let me see—about half-three until half-four.'
'With this "Paulette" lady.'
'Quite.'
'She'll verify that, of course?'

'If necessary. Er—*is* it necessary?'

' 'Fraid so, sir.'

'Ah, well. You're a man of the world, I hope.'

'Yes. You can be assured of that, sir.'

'What I mean is ... Y'know—my darling wife ... she tends to be a little stuffy about these things.'

'We're interested in murder, sir. That's all.'

'I'm obliged, officer.'

'And if you'll—er—have a word with this "Paulette" lady ... just to let her know we're not interested in *her*.'

'Eh? Oh—er—quite. It'll set her mind at rest, won't it? You young chaps are very considerate, y'know. Very considerate.'

Preston started his working day in a foul mood. This was understandable. He walked into the Information Room, scowled at the build-up of chaotic activity and muttered, 'Bloody hell! We *create* work. We're God's gift to paper manufacturers.'

The remark was triggered off by bad temper but (on the face of it) was not without some cause. Papers, reports, statement forms, flimsies, pads of foolscap ... the impression was that the converted Recreation Hall of Beechwood Brook D.H.Q. was knee-deep in them. And each minute brought its own increase as more statements, more reports and more flimsies upon which were scribbled telephone messages added themselves to the growing mass.

More than a dozen men and women—uniformed and C.I.D.—strove to keep the paper-mountain under some sort of control. Sorting, filing, cataloguing ... and always (or so it seemed) having to work harder and harder to keep pace.

In one corner of the room Detective Sergeant Tallboy had the sole service of a middle-aged, and very efficient, constable clerk ... and needed him. Each murder had its own Murder Log, and three Murder Logs—each itemising, to the minute (almost to the second) the enquiries and progress of its own individual manhunt—took some handling ... and, at the end of the day when, and if, the enquiries reached successful conclusions, those Murder Logs would be used as evidence upon which to base both congratulations and condemnations. They were an internal check upon the efficiency, and non-efficiency, of every man working on the cases.

Preston sighed his disgust and shook his head, wonderingly. He wouldn't have had Tallboy's job, for a mint of money.

'Ah, superintendent.' Blayde appeared at Preston's elbow. 'We've a job to do ... you and I. A careful check of all the reports and statements from the golf club.'

'I've already ...' began Preston.

'Personal instructions, from Deputy Chief Constable Bear, I'm afraid.'

'Why the hell concentrate on the White killing?' grumbled Preston.

'Same killer.'

'We *think*.'

'With some justification,' said Blayde. 'Same gun ... that much, we can prove. And there's a connection with the golf club.'

'On the face of it,' agreed Preston, reluctantly.

'So, that's our job. Fine-tooth-combing what we already know.' Blayde stepped to a desk and collected the bundle of statements and reports ... already an inch, or so, fatter than it had been earlier, when Bear had issued his instructions. He said, 'Not here, I think. We'll use my office. It'll be quieter.'

Preston grunted ill-tempered surrender and followed the Beechwood Brook Divisional Officer from the hurly-burly of the Information Room.

* * *

This (as the killer knew) was going to be his most difficult shot of all. His most difficult, and his most dangerous.

The long-empty, semi-derelict office block was the best he could do. From the first floor window, it was a fairly long shot ... especially as he must (for safety's sake) take aim from the shadows, and back from the open window. There was (agreed) an uninterrupted view of the hairdressing salon, but it was a busy salon and, when she arrived, she wouldn't (like West) pause long enough for a final second or two of accurate aiming. She'd turn into the shop, push open the door and be beyond his view. Beyond effective reach of the bullet ... just like that. It had to be a snap-shot. In the cross-wires ... and bang!

He could shoot—he had medals for shooting—but, because he could shoot, he recognised a particularly difficult shot for what it was. He wasn't fooled by the T.V. and cinema rubbish; where utterly impossible shots were triggered off with an almost nonchalant off-handedness ... and *always* hit the target. Two strides—three, at the most —and hurried strides, at that ... and she'd be moving away from him, at an angle.

It was going to be one hell of a shot!

She'd come. He had no doubts upon that score. She'd arrive ... punctually. Every fortnight. The same o'clock. A standing appointment. And, except when she was away on holiday, she always kept the appointment. She always parked her car on the British Legion car park. Always walked the two hundred yards, or so. Always turned into the salon with the springy step of a woman who knows she's about to be made to look a little more attractive.

Always!

One shot ... no more.

Then, down the stairs, into the toilets at the rear of the empty building, through the window and into the debris-cluttered yard, over the wall and into the ready-parked Mini.

Then, away...

Unless he tripped and fell, on the rubbish-strewn stairs ... he'd have to watch his step; take his time; not to make a hash of things, because of over-anxiety.

Unless he fumbled, when it came to climbing out, through the window ... for God's sake, that wasn't likely; he'd wedged the window open, with a batten of broken wood; he was a fit enough man; climbing through a blasted window wasn't likely to present any real problem.

Unless he ricked an ankle on the broken bricks and general muck, in the yard at the rear ... goddamit, he wasn't a two-left-legged fool; as an obstacle course the yard was a nothing—a *nothing*; a Boy Scouts' troop could nip across it, without even sweating.

Unless...

For Christ's sake!

He checked that the round was in the breech of the Husqvarna. Checked that the safety catch was 'Off'. Checked that the telescopic sight was at the correct focus.

Then he breathed. Deep, lung-stretching inhalations of air, which fed oxygen into his blood-stream and, gradually, fought the 'stage fright' and edged himself from the precipice of panic.

It worked, as he knew it would work. As he knew it would steady his nerves ... as he knew, from experience, that it *always* steadied his nerves.

He checked his watch, then waited ... knowing that he hadn't long to wait.

At 9.48 am—*exactly*—the police received their first real break ... exactly, because the information was important enough to make the detective constable who received it check, most carefully, with the wall-clock in the entrance hall of the old Lessford City Police Headquarters.

9.48 am ...

The man stood at the public counter, and stammered out his news.

He wore a stained, open-necked shirt, with the rolled sleeves showing muscular and tattooed arms. His trousers were uncreased and stained; the trousers worn by a man whose 'working tools' were his own strong arms and legs. Whatever else, he was no crank. He was as solid—as naturally honest—as an oak ... and what he had to say was worth listening to.

He said, 'I've—er—y'know ... just slipped out from work. From the fruit market. The boss knows. I told him ... and he said I should come down and mention it, see? About last night's shooting. The actor bloke ...'

'West?' said the D.C.

'I—er—I thought it was Westerfield. They said ...'

'That's his stage name. West ... that's his real name.'

'Oh! Well—y'see ... I reckon we must have seen him. See?'

'Sit down, Mr—er ...' The detective suddenly felt a little breathless, as he waved the welcome visitor towards a chair, on the public side of the counter.

'Walker,' supplied the man. 'Jim—James Walker.'

'Sit down, Mr Walker ... please.'

Walker sat down.

The D.C. scurried away into the innards of the building and, two minutes later, returned, accompanied by a large, prematurely bald man, who introduced himself as Detective Inspector Bruce.

Bruce nodded, treated Walker to a quick, tight smile, then said, 'One of the interview rooms, I think, Mr Walker. We won't be interrupted there.'

'I told the boss I wouldn't be ...' began Walker.

'*If* you don't mind,' insisted D.I. Bruce.

An interview room it was.

The slightly dazed—slightly apprehensive—Walker was settled into a chair, at a Formica-topped table. He was given a cigarette and provided with a cheap, tin ash-tray. Had he won the Treble Chance, he wouldn't have been subjected to more fuss and consideration.

Detective Inspector Bruce said, 'Now, Mr Walker ... in your own words.'

'The—er—the radio. This morning,' said Walker. 'I heard it ... see? About finding the bullet, on the roof park ...'

'Cartridge,' corrected Bruce.

'Eh?'

'It was the *cartridge* we found. The empty cartridge.'

'Ah—well ... *that*. And last night, we was up there.'

'Up where?'

'On the roof park. We was up there. We go there, sometimes. Fairly regular. It's—y'know ... private.'

'We?'

'Me and my young lady. We're gonna get married ... one day. And—y'know how it is—a kiss and a cuddle ... a bit of snogging. Well, that's where we was. Up on the roof park. In the back of the van—y'know ... stretched out, in the back of the van.'

'Go on,' encouraged Bruce.

'Well—that's it ... see? We—er—we heard this car drive up. A Mini, it was. And—y'know—you get some right berks up there, sometimes. Peeping into cars, and such. Seeing what they can see. Real dirty-minded sods, I reckon. I dunno what they get out of it, but they snoop around sometimes, and ...'

'We come across 'em, sometimes,' interrupted Bruce. 'You were saying ... about this Mini.'

'Well—y'know—we peeped out of the back window of the van ... see? Just to make sure. And this bloke parked the Mini, then lugged a cricket bag out, and ...'

'A *cricket bag*?'

'That's what it looked like. And he went behind that concrete thing. The top of the lift-shaft. He went behind there. I know Liz—that's my young lady—she said, "What's he gone there, for?" And I said I reckoned he wanted a pee. See? That seemed the only reason. But—y'know—we watched ... we even heard the bang. I reckon that was when he shot Westerfield.'

'You heard the shot? You actually *heard* it?'

'Yer.' Walker nodded. 'We didn't *know* it was a shot. How could we? It sounded—y'know—just a bang ... like a backfire. Then this bloke went back to his Mini ...'

'Still carrying the cricket bag?'

'Yer ... he still had the cricket bag. Walking fast—y'know ... not running, but walking fast. Then he put the bag back into the Mini, and pushed off.'

'Drove away?'

'Yer.'

'What sort of a Mini was it?'

'Red.'

'Did you get the number?'

'No.' Walker looked sad. Almost guilty. 'No—it didn't seem important ... not then. We wasn't interested in the car ... see? Just the bloke. In case he ...'

'What sort of a man was he?'

'It—er—it wasn't all that light, y'know. Not up there, on the roof park.'

'A general description,' insisted Bruce.

'We-ell—he was just a bloke ... y'know. Ordinary. Bit on the big side, maybe. Maybe not, though ... it was dark, and I wasn't taking too much notice. Just that he wasn't snooping around, looking into cars, and such. That's all. I wasn't—y'know ... really *looking*.'

'Where do you work, Walker?' asked Bruce.

'Down at the fruit market. I've already said ...'

'Which firm?'

'Southern's Fruit Stores. It's a ...'

'I know it.' The detective constable spoke for the first time.

'You'll need to tell your story to somebody higher than me,' explained Bruce. 'It may take time.'

'Look—I told the boss ...'

'I'll ring your boss,' said the D.C. 'I'll explain things to him.'

'He won't like it. He won't ...'

'I'll explain things. He'll understand. You're a material witness, Mr Walker,' said Bruce. 'So far, just about the *only* material witness. You're important.'

'Oh!'

'You, and your girl friend.'

'Oh, for God's sake, don't drag Liz into this.'

'Sorry.' Bruce smiled, apologetically. 'We've no option. She might have seen things you missed.'

'She didn't. I mean ... how *could* she?'

'She'll need to be seen. Where does she work?'

'Woolworth's. But they won't let her ...'

'Oh, yes they will.' Bruce turned to the D.C., and said, 'Get his boss on the blower. Explain things. That we're sorry, but he might be with us most of the day.'

'Yes, sir. Right away.'

'Then Woolworth's. Get the manager. On the Q.T. Put him in the picture ... as much as he needs to know, and tell him to keep his mouth shut. And that we need the girl. We'll collect her, on the way to Beechwood Brook.'

'Look,' protested Walker, 'I dunno much about these things, but I reckon you've no right to ...'

'Mr Walker,' said Bruce, gently, 'we have no option. It's inconvenient. But this is triple-murder ... and you, and your young lady, have actually *seen* the murderer. We *have* what you call a "right". We have a duty. But we prefer to do these things in a friendly way. Your boss'll understand. So will the manager of Woolworth's. You're important people, Mr Walker—both of you—and I'm only a detective inspector. You'll need to be seen by bigger men than me.'

'But, look, I'm ...'

'I'm not even on the murder enquiry, old son.' Bruce smiled a vaguely disappointed smile. 'I'm only holding the fort here, see? The murder job's centred at Beechwood Brook ... that's where all the griff's being gathered. Here ...' He shrugged his shoulders in a quasi-comical resignation to life's peculiar quirks. 'Stolen milk bottles. Broken-into gas meters. That sort of stuff. They still happen, y'know ... and that's what *I'm* expected to concentrate on.'

Walker sighed, and muttered, 'Y'know what? I almost wish I'd never bloody well come. And Liz ... she'll play hell.'

'Not a bit of it.' Bruce grinned, confidently. 'Rides in squad cars. All that red-carpet treatment. Real-life Z-cars ... she'll *love* it.'

'I wish,' grumbled Preston, 'that some of these so-called coppers would learn to take a decent statement. Just once in a while. Not the same old tired jargon. Who the hell "observes"? They *see* ... so why not say just that?'

'Any luck, so far?' asked Blayde.

'If I knew what the devil we were supposed to be looking for ...'

'Inconsistencies.'

'Is that all?' said Preston, sarcastically.

'Found some?'

'One lunatic says it was raining ... when we all know damn well it wasn't. One over-imaginative berk even claims to have heard the shot. He was in the bar, at the time—more than a mile from where it happened ... what the hell does he think was used? A howitzer?'

'You're liverish, this morning,' observed Blayde.

'You could be right, at that.'

'Why?'

Preston scowled, compressed his lips, then growled,

'Private reasons, Mr Blayde. Very *private* reasons.'

'Sorry.'

'But enough reasons. Believe me ... enough.'

'Leave 'em at home, superintendent,' said Blayde. 'We've a difficult enough job, as it is. There isn't room for private gripes.'

Preston breathed deeply, but didn't argue.

Why argue? What the hell was there to argue about ... supposing anybody wanted to know?

The killer held the rifle rock-steady. He squinted through the glass of the sight, and waited for the back of her skull to move within a fraction of an inch of the cross-wires.

He squeezed the trigger, and the Husqvarna gave its tiny jerk as it spoke its sharp, snap-like crack.

The woman was punched towards the glass of the salon door, before she folded forward in an untidy heap.

Then the killer ran. Down the stairs. Into the rear toilets. Through the window. Across the yard.

Then, he paused, muttered, 'Blast!' and jerked the bolt of the rifle, sending the spent cartridge into the debris which covered the flagstones.

He scrambled over the wall, sprinted to the parked Mini, threw the rifle on the floor, in front of the rear seat, and covered it with the blanket which was folded, and ready.

Then, away ... along the back streets—the little known, and little used by-ways—towards his neat 'estate semi', and the safety of his home.

'How far?' asked Gilliant.

Sullivan and Bear exchanged knowing glances. Gilliant's tone, as he asked the question, had that ragged edge which meant trouble. Gilliant was earning his salary ... which, at this particular moment, meant tail-twisting in the certain knowledge that lesser tails would, in turn, have sheepshanks tied into them, before the day was out.

'The golf club ...' began Bear.

'We were onto the golf club, at the White killing,' snapped Gilliant. 'Since then, he's shot Bentley and West. How many more corpses do we need, before we get within touching distance? Before we even have a *suspect*?'

Gilliant's king-size office was as luxurious as ever. Sullivan and Bear occupied comfortable armchairs. Gilliant was on his throne, behind the giant desk. On the face of things, everything looked cosy and very civilised ... but nobody was smoking, and nobody was drinking.

And nobody had doubts. This was a carpeting. A very high-class carpeting ... but, for all that, a very thorough carpeting.

'He's been lucky,' growled Sullivan.

'We *make* what you're pleased to call "luck", Mr Sullivan ... you've been a police officer long enough to know *that*.'

Bear tried.

He said, 'Sir—I don't have to tell you—there's virtually no real protection against a high-powered rifle, with telescopic sights. It's impossible to ...'

'A glorified pop-gun, Mr Bear,' snapped Gilliant. 'Please don't come to my office and talk about a two-two being a "high-powered rifle".'

Sullivan said, 'High-powered enough to kill. At least grant us that.'

'Only in the hands of an expert.'

Sullivan grunted, 'Aye. Even *we've* come to that conclusion.'

'Therefore, find the "expert" ... fast.'

'Judas Christ!' muttered Sullivan.

'I beg your pardon, Mr Sullivan?'

Sullivan ignored Bear's warning look, and plunged in. Sullivan had been up all night. He was worried about his son's broken leg. He'd crossed swords with a pompous, self-opinionated medic. He was in no mood to play the part of doormat ... not even to Gilliant.

He said, 'Three days—not yet *that* ... I know it feels like three years but, in fact, it isn't yet three days. That's how long we've been working on this case. You're asking for miracles ... and you won't get 'em.'

'You have a name,' said Gilliant, coldly.

'Aye. Richard Sullivan.'

'A reputation.'

'Reputations!' Sullivan's mouth curled in disgust.

'You're not proud of it?'

Sullivan snapped, 'I know its worth. I've been lucky ... and, Chief Constable, don't feed me all that guff about "making your own luck". I've been *lucky*. And luck comes, and goes, as *it* sees fit. And no man breathing can do a damn thing about it.'

'I don't agree.'

'No ... I didn't expect you to.'

Gilliant said, 'I've no doubt you're doing your best. Both of you.'

Bear and Sullivan spoke together.

Bear said, 'We're doing that, sir. I don't think you need our assurance.'

Sullivan growled, 'Well, thank *you*, sir.'

'But your best doesn't yet seem to be good enough.'

'Three days,' said Sullivan, stubbornly.

'Three *killings*,' said Gilliant. 'You count the days, Mr Sullivan. I'll count the killings. At the moment, we're neck-and-neck ... and that's not a situation I'm prepared to tolerate.'

'If you think we've missed anything,' murmured Bear.

'You must have missed *something*, Mr Bear.'

'What?' asked Sullivan.

Gilliant eyed his two immediate subordinates coldly, and said, 'That's a question I want an answer to, gentlemen. Find out *what's* been missed. *What's* been overlooked. *Where* this enquiry has become bogged down. Who's not ...'

'I'm not prepared to agree that it *is* bogged down,' cut in Sullivan.

'And I, Mr Sullivan, am not prepared to argue the point. I want action. And, unfair though it may seem to you two, I'm in a position to *demand* action ... or heads on chargers, if I don't get it!'

Ten minutes later two chastened deputy chief constables made their way along the corridors of forensic power, and towards their waiting cars.

'He can be hell on roller-skates, when he feels like it ... can't he?' observed Bear, ruefully.

'He's a raving lunatic,' growled Sullivan.

'It's what he's there for, Dick. It's ...'

'It's bloody ridiculous. You can't nail a murderer—not this type of murderer—in three days. We're within a golf-course length of feeling his collar. And *that's* bloody good going. Can't he see that? Can't he ...'

'I've known some very long golf courses,' observed Bear, drily.

'All right!' Sullivan's nostrils flared. 'He wants action. He wants fried balls, for breakfast ... he can have 'em. D'you want to share it with me, Winnie? Or would you prefer to stay popular?'

'Eh?'

'I,' said Sullivan, grimly, 'am going to go through this over-sized bloody police force, like a dose of salts. Everybody! Let me find one man—*one man!*—not gutting himself ... that's all. I'll drop the flaming town hall on the back of his neck.'

'And I,' promised Bear, solemnly, 'will follow it with the Municipal Art Gallery.'

Which (had he heard the remarks) would have delighted Chief Constable Gilliant.

The object of the high-level carpeting had been achieved.

Police Sergeant Poynings was shocked. Despite his profession—despite his rank—he was a kind-hearted man. Had the whole of his police service been taken up by escorting elderly ladies across busy roads, Poynings would have been a perfectly happy man. He'd often wondered why the hell they'd made him a sergeant. *Him* ... of all people. The seamy side of coppering saddened him; it sickened him to the stomach that men could be so deliberately wicked to their fellows.

And now this ... two shootings, in as many days.

Both women.

It was terrible. It was inhuman.

It was also grossly unfair ... because, on both occasions, he'd been Johnny-on-the-spot; responsible for deploying what few men he had at his disposal for those first few, vital minutes; easing the crowd back from the scene of the shooting; calming hysterical women, who'd been customers in the hairdressing salon; sending out the urgent call for an ambulance; notifying D.H.Q. of the latest abomination, and wondering where the hell the shot had come from *this* time.

Christ ... what a life!

Who'd be a copper, when they were crying out for deep-sea divers and steeplejacks?

The only silver lining was that (as with the Bentley killing) the first big-wig to arrive at the scene had been Lennox ... and Lennox, despite his music-hall appearance, was a very human, and a very understanding, man.

Poynings watched the ambulance drive away, and his face had an expression usually reserved for funerals.

'Bad,' muttered Lennox. 'Bloody awful, in fact.'

'Who's going to tell him, sir?' asked Poynings, miserably.

Lennox eyed the uniformed sergeant, contemplatively.
'Not me, sir.' Poynings shied away from the implied suggestion. 'I don't know him ... not that well. Don't ask *me* to do it.'
'Who does know him?' asked Lennox.
'He was county. Tallboy knows him. He was—still is—Tallboy's boss ... I think Tallboy's best.'
'County,' mused Lennox. 'Beechwood Brook?'
'Yes, sir. That was his division ... before the amalgamation.'
Lennox rubbed his bald pate and ruffled the whisps of hair around the tops of his ears.
He said, 'Tallboy? ... no-o. That's passing the buck, old son. Chief Superintendent Blayde, I think. And me ... I'd better be there, too.'
'Yes, sir,' agreed Poynings, almost eagerly. 'That's—that's the best solution, I'm sure.'
'Can you handle things here, till more weight arrives?'
'Yes, sir. I'll cope.'
'Good lad. Get on the blower. Use my name. Drum up as much help as you think you need ... and let the various specialist boys know they've more puzzles to play around with.'
'Yes, sir.'
'Oh—and, when you get the men—organise a search. Let's take it for granted it's the same lunatic. He shot West from above ... let's assume he did the same, here. Start by concentrating the search above ground level.'
'I'll do that, sir.'
'And good luck, Sergeant.'
'And—er—good luck to you, sir.'
'Thanks. I'll need it, son. Luck ... and the right words.'

The detective inspector was a man who chanced his arm a little. He was a 'loner', with a natural nose for scent the pack might miss. He worked to the rules, until the rules hindered progress ... at which point he ignored the rules. Two days before, he'd coaxed the name of Gascoinge from the landlord of *The Fighting Cocks*—then, he'd coaxed Gascoinge into parting with his ancient .22, for elimination purposes ... and now the D.I. was back in *The Fighting Cocks*, having another quiet, matey talk with the landlord.

It wasn't yet opening time, and the taproom was empty of customers. It smelled a little, of last night's beer and stale tobacco smoke—of washing-up liquid and aerosol wax polish—an odd, nose-tingling mixture of the old and the new ... but not unpleasant.

The two men stood, one at each side of the bar counter, smoked cigarettes and quaffed illegally-drawn bitter, as they talked.

'I have this nagging feeling,' said the D.I.

'What?' The landlord looked genuinely interested.

'That he comes here—that he's one of your customers ... the bloke we're after.'

'Not Harry Gascoinge, again,' protested the landlord.

'No.' The D.I. shook his head. 'Gascoinge's clear ... you've done him *that* favour.'

'Who, then?'

'Ah ... that's the big question.' The D.I. tasted his beer, then continued. 'Y'know ... something you said.'

'What?'

'This boozer. Not like a town boozer. Not really customers ... more like neighbours. Remember?'

The landlord nodded.

'I reckon,' said the D.I., slowly, 'this place gets more information—more parish-pump news—than the local rag.'

'Happen,' agreed the landlord, cautiously. 'But we don't spread it around. We don't tittle-tattle.'

'Uhuh. That's why you get to know things. Because you *don't* spread it around.'

'I reckon.'

'And the White killing. I dunno ... but there's loose ends.'

'Such as?'

'White—a countryman ... the other two, townies. The other two creatures of habit—predictable—certain places, at certain times ... White, a farmer who could be just about anywhere.'

'A man of habit,' corrected the landlord.

'Sure, but—y'know ... things happen on farms. Lambing. A tractor breaks down. Scores of things. It's *different*.'

'Aye ... I suppose.'

They drank in silence for a few moments, then the D.I. said, 'Tell you what ... why "Appleyard's" farm?'

'Appleyard used to farm it. Bill White was his man. Then...'

'Aye—I know that—but seven years. Christ, in seven years, it should have earned the right to be called "White's" farm ... surely?'

'Happen,' agreed the landlord.

'So, why not?'

'We-ell—y'know...' The landlord waved a vague hand.

'That I don't,' contradicted the D.I. 'And it interests me.'

'Don't rake over old muck,' murmured the landlord. 'It only disturbs the blow-flies.'

'Oh, no.' The D.I. shook his head. 'That won't do. I want to *know*.'

The landlord looked uncomfortable, then mumbled, 'There was this scandal ... that's all.'

'What scandal?'

'Appleyard's daughter ... that's why they sold the farm and emigrated.'

'What scandal?' repeated the D.I.

The landlord moistened his lips, and said, 'Her husband. He wasn't right ... y'know.'

'Mad, y'mean?'
'We-ell—not exactly mad ... although, I dunno.'
'Not certifiable ... is that what you mean?'
'No. Not "mad" that way.' The landlord looked acutely embarrassed, and said, 'Look—I don't want to talk about it. It's gone and forgotten. Let's leave it at that.'
'In a pig's eye.' The D.I. felt his nape hairs tingling. It was a sign—a sign which had never yet let him down—and if, as he thought, pay-dirt was on the way, the one thing he *wasn't* going to do was 'leave it at that'. He leaned fractionally farther over the counter, and said, 'Harry Gascoinge. Have you seen him, since?'
'Aye.' The landlord nodded.
'Did he say anything?'
'Aye.'
'What?'
'That—y'know—you're not like some coppers. You can be trusted.'
'Coming from Gascoinge, that means a lot, I'd say ... wouldn't you?'
'Aye. I'd say so,' agreed the landlord, miserably.
'Coming from a man like Harry Gascoinge,' insisted the D.I., softly. 'From a man who hates coppers. That's like a sworn statement on vellum ... right?'
The landlord sighed further agreement.
'Okay,' said the D.I. 'Go ahead, and trust me. Tell me.'
'It's old stuff.' The landlord put up a last, weak resistance. 'It's not gonna help you in this ...'
'I'll decide,' cut in the D.I. 'If you're right—if it doesn't help—I forget it ... it's never been said.'
'Madge Appleyard,' said the landlord heavily. 'She—er—did herself in.'
'Suicide?'
The landlord nodded.

'Why?'
'Her husband.'
'A wrong 'un?'
'A bad bugger,' said the landlord. 'Twisted. Y'know ... not natural.'
The D.I. frowned non-understanding.
'He was one o' *them*,' expanded the landlord, awkwardly. 'Y'know ... a queer sod.'
'You mean a queen? A joey?'
'I dunno what you call 'em. All I know is they're not *men*.'
'A homosexual?'
'Aye ... one o' *them*.'
'Y'mean on his wife?' asked the D.I.
'No! How the hell do *I* know?' The landlord looked confused. 'I reckon not. Knowing Madge ... I reckon not. She was normal.'
'All right.' The D.I. made a gentle beckoning motion with the closed fingers of his right hand. 'Give, friend. All the sordid details. I want the lot ... and don't worry about shocking me.'
The landlord capitulated. He swallowed a mouthful of beer, before he spoke.
He stammered, 'Seven years back—eight years ... maybe a bit more. Madge Appleyard. She was a married woman ... see? Everybody thought—y'know ... that it was *right*. Happily married. All the rest of it. We didn't know ... how the hell could *we* know? He was a townie. Some folks didn't like him for that, but—y'know ... townies. Get a few gates left open. Get a few hedges broken down. Get some damn fool block a ditch with rubbish. Y'know ... you get a bit biased.'
'And you?' asked the D.I.
'He was ... *different*.' The landlord moved his shoulders. 'He didn't come in, much. Couple of times a

year ... that's all. Into the village, while Madge visited her family.'
'Not him?'
'Eh?'
'He didn't go with her, when she visited her family? Is that what you mean?'
'No ... I reckon not.' The landlord scowled his misery at being forced to re-live ancient troubles. 'Appleyard wasn't all that keen ... see. Didn't approve. Didn't say much ... but we all knew. Madge's husband wasn't too welcome at the farm.'
'Go on,' encouraged the D.I.
'We-ell ... that's it.'
'No. I want to know what *you* thought about the husband. Before you learned he was a queer.'
'He was—y'know ... *different*. A townie. A bit overdressed ... by my standards, that is. Maybe all right, where *he* came from. But out here ... y'know. I know he once rolled up in a velvet jacket. Wine coloured. Bloody hell! We talked about it for days. And—y'know ... he used long words. Half the time, nobody could understand him. And he waved his arms about a bit, when he talked. Wore his hair a bit too long ... that sorta thing. I reckon we should have guessed.'
'That he was a queer?'
'Aye.'
'Then what happened?'
'He—er—he left Madge. Went to live with this other bloke ... a young chap. Little more than a kid. He left Madge, for him. And then—y'know ... she took the pills.'
'Sleeping pills?'
'Aye.'
'A deliberate overdose?'
'Aye.' The landlord nodded his head.
'A poor reason,' said the D.I. drily. 'A bloody poor reason for committing suicide.'

'D'you think so, mister?' The question was hard and challenging.

'Don't you?'

The landlord's tone was soft, but harsh—hard-packed with conviction—when he said, 'Mister detective, in these parts we're normal. A couple get wed. They go to bed together ... see? The man takes from the woman what he wants ... what nature *made* him want to take. And the woman gives it to him. Like nature *expects* her to give it to him. She makes him happy. She satisfies him ... and, if she doesn't she's a bad wife. If she can't—if she doesn't know her job—she's ashamed ... she doesn't blame her man, she blames herself. She tries harder ... and, if she tries hard enough, she wins him back. If she doesn't, she's a failure.'

'As a woman?'

'As a woman, and as a wife.'

'Jesus!' The D.I. stared near-disbelief. 'Talk about the Dark Ages. What about divorce, for God's sake?'

'That's not for us. Those vows mean summat. "Till death do us part" ... it *means* summat.'

The D.I. blew out his cheeks.

The landlord continued, 'And—y'know—when a husband prefers another *man* to his wife. That's an insult. A *real* insult. When he prefers a man's arse to what his wife's offering him ...'

'She commits suicide,' said the D.I. in disgust.

'She might as well. She's weighed down with enough shame.'

'Oh, my God!'

'Shame on herself. Shame on her family. Madge Appleyard knew that. She was a good lass. She did what she had to do.'

'She was a bloody fool,' exploded the D.I. 'You people ... you make me want to vomit. What the hell sort of moral code do you live your lives under? What sort of twisted mentality makes you ...'

'Mister detective,' interposed the landlord, coldly, 'I think you're treading ground you don't understand. You asked enough questions, and maybe I've given too many answers. Madge Appleyard tried to save her family from disgrace. She tried ... but she couldn't, so they moved out and left the country.'

'More fool they.'

'Oh, no. They'd never have lived it down. Even today —even now they aren't here—it's still "Appleyard's Farm" ... because of what happened. We have long memories, in these parts.'

'Poor old Madge Appleyard,' sighed the D.I.

'Aye ... you could say that. To be charitable, you could say that.'

'You wouldn't know how to spell the bloody word,' said the D.I., in disgust.

'What word?'

'"Charity". Your so-called "charity" can't swallow the simple fact that some women make mistakes. They marry homosexuals ... but don't know it, until it's too late. Even their husbands don't know it—won't admit it ... because, to bigots like you, it's unclean.'

'It's not natural ... if that's what you mean.'

'I'll not argue. It's wasted breath.' The D.I. turned to go, then stopped, and said, 'Madge Appleyard?'

'Aye?'

'You keep calling her that.'

'That was her name ... Madge, Appleyard's daughter.'

'Not her *married* name, for God's sake.'

'No.'

'Okay—what was her married name?'

The landlord hesitated, then said, 'West. But we don't...'

'*West?*'

'Aye—but we don't ...'

'You blithering idiot. You purblind, parboiled lunatic. West ... the name of the third person to be shot. And you've...'

'Westerfield,' frowned the landlord. 'That was his name. The papers all gave his name—Arnold Westerfield ... some sort of an actor. They all said ...'

'His stage name,' interrupted the D.I. 'His *real* name ... Arthur West. And—off the record—we already know his wife committed suicide, seven or eight years ago ... she swallowed fifty Seconal capsules.'

'Oh, my God!' whispered the landlord.

'*And* he was a bum-duster,' continued the D.I., mercilessly. '*And* he went to live with his boy-friend—little more than a schoolkid ... and that *that* drove his wife to suicide.'

The landlord's face was without colour. Eyes staring and mouth hanging slack.

'The code of the countryside,' rasped the D.I., sarcastically. 'It drives one woman to take her own life ... and it gets another man shot. So, where does White fit into the picture?'

'I—I dunno.'

'Where does Bentley fit into the picture?'

'I—I ... honest, I dunno.'

'You know so little,' sneered the D.I., angrily. 'What you *really* mean is you'll *tell* so little. But, be warned, friend. You are going to tell the lot. Everything! I'll be back—so do some heavy remembering.'

The D.I. turned and strode from the taproom.

Blayde dropped the quarto sheet he'd been studying, and reached for the desk telephone as its ring broke the silence of the Beechwood Brook chief superintendent's office.

He said, 'Blayde ... Yes, sir. He's ... Now? ... Right away, sir.'

Blayde stood up from the desk, and said, 'Lennox. There's something cropped up. He wants to see me. I'll be back, as soon as possible.'

Preston grunted, but without raising his eyes from the statement he was reading.

It was all happening at Beechwood Brook D.H.Q. that morning.

Sugden was telling the white-maned Harris about his interview with Dene.

'How long did he say he'd been living with West?'

'Seven years. Eight years. Thereabouts.'

'And he's twenty?—twenty-one? ... summat like that?'

'I know.' Sugden made no attempt to hide his disgust.

'He was a kid when it started,' growled Harris. 'Judas Christ! Twelve. Thirteen. He can't have been much more.'

Sugden said, 'Tell me *that* isn't a motive for murder. Moral corruption, if ever there was any.'

'Some relative of Dene's?'

'It's another alley that needs searching.'

'Except...'

'Except what? If some queer grabbed my son. My nephew.'

'If so, he's waited a hell of a long time.'

'There could be a reason.'

'And where does White and the Bentley woman come into it?'

'It's a motive,' insisted Sugden. 'The first fair-to-moderate motive we've come up with.'

Harris pursed his lips, and said, 'I'm not arguing ... I'm just saying, every alley could be a blind alley. Who the hell knows, at this stage?'

Rucker was making James Walker, and his girl friend, Liz, jump through the inquisitorial hoop ... to the disgust and embarrassment of Detective Inspector Bruce.

'You were both in the van?'
'Yes, sir.'
'Watching this character?'
'Well—yes—I suppose ...'
'Using your eyes?'
'Keeping an eye on him. Y'know ... keeping an eye on...'
'So, let's have a description.'
'I dunno. I keep telling you ...'
'The "invisible man"?' sneered Rucker.
'No. 'Course not. Just that ...'
'False whiskers? A putty nose?'
'Look—don't be ...'
'On stilts, was he?'
'How d'you mean?'
'With a sack over his head?'
The lady called Liz snapped, 'Do you *have* to be so nasty?'
'Naturally ... when I'm conversing with fools.'
'Don't call Jim a fool. Not while I'm ...'
'You're *both* fools. You're both as blind as bats. You see a man—a murderer—you actually *watch* him ... but you don't *notice* anything.'
'We didn't know he was a murderer. Not then,' protested Walker.
'How many legs had he?' asked Rucker, contemptuously.
'Eh?'
'How many arms? How many heads? Or didn't you even notice *that*?'
Walker took a deep breath, stuck out his chin, and said, 'Mister—we *saw* him ... that's more than you clever dicks have. He was ordinary. Like you ... very ordinary. It coulda *been* you, for all we know.'
'Careful, little man. Careful with the veiled suggestions.'
'All right ... just don't start pushing *us* around.'

'I'm warning you ...'

'Get stuffed!'

Liz said, 'Easy, Jim. Maybe he can't help being rude.'

'He'd better bloody-well make the effort.'

'Or?' purred Rucker.

'There's bigger men than you, I reckon. And if I'm pushed hard enough, I know how to complain.'

'Brave man,' murmured Rucker, contemptuously.

Detective Inspector Bruce put his career on the line, by saying, 'Not brave, sir. Justified. And, if he needs a witness, he can call me.'

In one corner of the Information Room, Lennox was holding a low-voiced conversation with Blayde.

Lennox said, 'You know him.'

Blayde nodded solemn agreement.

'Better than I do ... he's ex-county.'

There was another nod of frowning agreement.

'I'll be with you, of course.'

'Thanks,' said Blayde.

'But—either way—it's a hell of a job.'

'Therefore, the sooner we get it over, the better.'

'The sooner, the better,' agreed Lennox.

The Detective Inspector who'd just driven from *The Fighting Cocks* burst into the Information Room. He almost collided with Lennox and Blayde.

He said, 'Sorry, sir ... I'm looking for Superintendent Preston.'

'Not now, old son,' said Lennox.

'It's important, sir. There's a lead ... a real lead. I think...'

'Later.'

'Sir, it's red hot. It's about West, and ...'

Blayde waved a hand towards one of the few empty chairs, and said, 'Sit down, inspector. It'll wait.'

'No, sir. It ...'
'It'll *have* to wait.'
'Oh!'
Lennox said, 'I'll be back in a few minutes ... eh? Then you can tell *me*. Superintendent Preston's enough on his plate, at the moment.'
'Er—if you say so, sir.'
'Good lad.' Lennox smiled. It was a smile touched with sadness. He said, 'Keep it under wraps ... you'll know why, soon enough.'
The slightly bewildered D.I. nodded and made his way towards the empty chair.

In Blayde's office, Preston dropped the statement onto the pile of forms on his right, and picked up the report quarto from the pile on his left.
He began reading the report and, before he'd ended the second typewritten line, a scowl like thunder clouded his face.
'That sod!' he rasped, softly. '*That* bastard ... and he has the bloody impudence to be uppish with the copper who interviewed him. We-ell—we'll see just how stroppy he gets when *I* ...'
The door opened and Lennox and Blayde entered the office.
Blayde closed the door softly, but firmly.
Preston looked up from the report, and said, 'This hound Kitley—he's a club member—I'd like to ...'
He closed his mouth, before ending the sentence.
Lennox and Blayde looked worried. Awkward. Uncomfortable. There was something wrong—something *very* wrong—and Preston sensed that something terrible was on the way.
Blayde cleared his throat, then said, 'There's—er—been a fourth shooting, superintendent.'
'Oh?' Preston waited.

Blayde's voice was emotionless, as he said, 'There's no easy way of breaking this sort of news, Mr Preston. You'll appreciate that.' Blayde paused, took a deep breath, then ended, 'This time he shot at your wife.'

'My-my ...' Preston's eyes widened. His throat dried and the words wouldn't come.

'As she was going into the hairdressers,' amplified Blayde.

'Oh, my God!'

'Easy, old lad.' Lennox placed a thick arm gently across Preston's bowed shoulders. 'It's not quite as bad as it sounds. This time, he was a bit off target.'

'Y'mean he—he ...'

Blayde said, 'He hit her. But he didn't kill her.'

'Where?' breathed Preston.

'The face.' Lennox tightened his grip across his colleague's shoulder, slightly. 'She's ...' He swallowed, then continued, 'I'll not kid you, son. She's in a mess. She'll live—the hospital boys gave me that promise, before we came in here to tell you ... but it's still serious.'

'How serious?' croaked Preston.

'One eye's gone,' said Blayde, gently. 'The chances of saving the other eye are ... remote.'

Preston clenched his fists on the surface of the table. He dropped his head until it rested upon the pile of statement and report forms.

His shoulders remained steady. There was misery, but no weeping.

Lennox and Blayde gave him time to absorb the shock.

Then, Lennox said, 'That's it then, son. That's you finished until you've got yourself reorganised. Leave it—whatever it is you're doing—your wife needs you around, when she comes out of the operating theatre.'

Without looking up, Preston shook his head, slowly.

Blayde frowned, and said, 'Your wife needs you, Mr

Preston. This is just a job—just another job ... your wife comes first.'

Preston continued to shake his head.

'Hey, lad.' Lennox's voice held new concern. 'Don't be barmy. Don't make it worse all round. Well get the bastard—whoever he is, we'll get him ... and he'll pay.'

'He'll pay,' breathed Preston. He raised his head, and his eyes were wild, with a touch of madness, in his chalk-white face, as he looked first at Lennox, then at Blayde, and groaned, 'He'll pay. 'Cos now I know who the bastard is ... and he'll bloody well *pay*!'

Then, with all the unexpectedness of a hand-grenade, Preston exploded.

Preston was a big man. His stripped-to-the-skin weight topped the twelve stone mark, by a few pounds; it was magnificently distributed, and none of it was fat. In height, he touched the six foot point and he was superbly fit. He was younger than either Lennox, or Blayde ... and his sudden upsurge of madness more than doubled the strength of his not inconsiderable muscles.

Blayde made a grab, but missed. Lennox tightened his arm around Preston's shoulders, but was flung aside to land unceremoniously on his fat backside ... then Preston was beyond the door and racing along the corridors.

'Get him stopped,' gasped Lennox. 'He's round the twist ... for his own sake, get him stopped.'

Blayde halted his pursuit, before he even reached the still quivering door and, instead, scooped up the desk telephone.

Lennox hauled his bulk from the carpet and watched the Beechwood Brook chief superintendent as orders were barked into the mouthpiece.

As Lennox lowered himself into a chair, Blayde snarled, 'Damn and blast it! He's clear of the building ... his Vauxhall's just taken off from the car park.'

Lennox struggled to control his breathing, and croaked,

'An all cars call. Get it out ... no messing. Where the hell he's going I dunno. But, where the hell it is, he'd better not get there. Ram his blasted car, if necessary. But *stop* him. D'you see him? D'you see his face? Murder—we haven't enough of 'em ... it must be bloody contagious.'

Thus, one of the more dramatic moments of the enquiry.

But (as always) much of it was boring. 'Routine enquiries' ... that was the official jargon used to describe this great façade of busy non-activity. It had clipboards and shoe leather attached. It entailed the asking of thousands of questions ... or, to be precise, the same dreary set of questions, thousands of times.

Do you know White/Bentley/West (also known as Westerfield)/Preston?

Where were you at certain times during the last few days?

Are you a member of Beechwood Golf Club?

Have you any connection with Ashfield Comprehensive School?

Can you name any person who, in your opinion, might have a grudge against White/Bentley/West (also known as Westerfield)/Preston?

Such were the questions; permutated, re-phrased, vamped around a little, amplified occasionally and, sometimes, with an added question or two attached.

But, basically, the same old 'Do you?', 'Were you?', 'Are you?', 'Have you?', 'Can you?' chat on a thousand and one doorsteps.

As if His Nibs (assuming he answered the ring on his doorbell) was likely to trot out self-condemnatory answers ... as if *that* was even remotely likely.

Believe that, and fairies are a pushover!

But the rate-payers, and the tax-payers—the decent folk and the plain and fancy gawpers—the glorified sluts in their roller-curlers and aprons—the retired majors, hiding their stiff upper lips behind well-trimmed moustaches —the snotty-nosed kids, sucking their iced lollies—the white collar workers, with their fountain pens peeping from their breast pockets—the great unwashed masses ... the 'general public'.

They watched, and they were very satisfied.

Our policemen are wonderful ... the best in the world.

Look at 'em. Working their nuts off. Trying to trace some gun-happy lunatic who, apparently, wants to counter the population explosion.

Good luck to 'em ... they're a fine, hard-working body of men and women.

Sure they are ... but (although they don't show it) they're bored to tears.

Mind you ...

Some of the answers from the pupils of Ashfield Comprehensive raised a few eyebrows.

The questionees being young and innocent and, therefore, by all the laws of natural logic, more likely to be upset by the sight of size-twelve flatfeet playing havoc with the pile of the sitting room carpet, this was one aspect of the enquiry tackled (in the main) by policewomen.

A 'lady policeman' isn't *really* a copper—or, so goes the subconscious argument within the minds of those who don't know too much about these things ... she's only like 'our mam' dressed up in fancy clothes.

So-o...

'Come on, Lucy. Don't be shy. Tell the police lady all you know. You're father and I are here ... nothing's going to happen to you.'

'We-ell ... she was sweet on Mr Holt.'

'Lucy! That's not what ...'

'How do you mean, "sweet on Mr Holt"?'

'Look, if my mother's gonna ...'

'Your mother wants you to tell the truth. That's all.

She won't interrupt again. Now—come on—tell me.'
'She was sweet on Mr Holt ... that's all.'
'Mr Holt?'
'He's Boys P.T. A real drip, if you ask me.'
'And Mr Holt and Miss Bentley were friends?'
'More like lovers, if you ask me. Y'know—secret lovers ... I reckon they used to stay on, at school, when we'd all left, and ...'
'Lucy!'
'Aw, mam.'
'You'll—er—you'll have seen something? Something between them, which made you form this opinion?'
' 'Course. They couldn't keep their eyes off each other. And when Mr Holt had the boys out on the playing field —y'know ... doing P.T. Him with his big chest, and skin-tight shorts. I mean ... she couldn't keep *away*.'
'Look, miss, I don't think you'd better ...'
'I'm sorry, sir. But we have to ask these questions.'
'I know—I appreciate that—but our Lucy ... she's a very impressionable child. A very impressionable age.'
'I realise that, too, sir.'
'And I'm not gonna sit here and listen to you ask her dirty questions, either.'
'I'm sorry, ma'am ... but I don't think I have asked her a dirty question. Have I?'
'Aw mam—dad ... grow up. They fancied each other. That's all. If y'ask me, they were having it off, on the quiet.'
'For God's sake! What sorta school have you sent the child to?'
'*Me*? You had a say in the ...'
'You'd the final choice. I remember telling you ...'
'*You* said Ashfield was the best in the district. You said she'd be better off ...'
'Madam. Sir. It's better this way. Much better ...

believe me. Thirteen-year-olds use this sort of language in normal conversation, these days.'

'She didn't learn it from this house. That I promise you.'

'No ... from her friends at school.'

'Fine friends, I must say.'

'They talk that way, these days, ma'am. Now—if you don't mind—I'd like to ask her a few more questions.'

'Answer the lady, luv.'
'Thank you, Mrs Hartley.'
'Tell the truth, luv. Don't be frightened.'
'Now, Shirley, what I'd like to ask you is ...'
'Tell the truth, luv. Nobody's gonna be cross with you.'
'It's about ...'
'Your mummy's with you, luv. Nobody's gonna hurt you.'
'When Miss Bentley was shot. Were you ...'
'Just tell the truth, luv. That's all the lady wants you to do.'
'Just a few questions, Shirley. They'll not ...'
'So just tell the truth. Eh? There's a luv. Don't say owt you don't know—the lady doesn't want to hear what you don't know ... just the truth. That's all.'
'Mam.'
'Yes, luv?'
'I—I can't.'
' 'Course you can. What d'you mean, you *can't*?'
'I—I wasn't there.'
'C'mon, luv. Don't talk daft. Of course you were there.'
'No. I—I played truant.'
'You what?'
'I'm sorry ... but I played truant yesterday.'
'Well! Of all the two-faced little bitches. Of all the underhand little madams. By God, I'll skelp you're back-

side for you ... *and* your dad will. When he comes home, and hears about this, he'll ...'

'I—er—I think I'd better go, Mrs Hartley. Obviously Shirley can't help in this enquiry. If she wasn't at school. So ... if you don't mind.'

'She's a lying little trollop, anyway. You wouldn't believe. The dirty, underhand tricks we've found her out in. She isn't to be trusted. Not an inch. Not a bloody inch.'

Boredom. Umpteen man-hours of sheer, unadulterated boredom. Learning a little about life, perhaps ... learning a damn sight more about life than any psychiatrist can ever learn from a whole library of textbooks.

Routine enquiries—door-to-door enquiries ... the fancy names used to describe one prolonged yawn.

And yet...

Suffer it long enough—tap on a few thousand doors—and, gradually, you get to know people. You get to know what makes them tick; what goes on behind those lying eyes.

You get to *know* people ... not just names.

And, the better he 'knows people' the better the copper.

Therefore, boredom ... but the only infallible way of gaining police experience.

'What the hell sort of a cock-up is *this*?' snarled Sullivan.

Blayde composed his features, until they were as expressionless as a block of concrete, and said, 'Detective Superintendent Preston, sir. He's ...'

'Where the thundering hell's he hared off to?'

'That I don't know, sir. He said something about ...'

'You *should* know, Chief Superintendent. You're in charge of this place.'

'He just ran out. When we told him about his wife.'

'What about his wife?'

'She's the latest victim. We told him ...'
'Good God!'
'... and he went a little mad.'
Sullivan helped himself to a few lungfuls of air. He felt something of a twit. More than that, he knew he'd *sounded* something of a twit. The knowledge wasn't easy to stomach.
In a gruff voice, he said, 'Is she—er ...'
'She's not dead, sir.'
'Thank God for that.'
'Merely blind ... if that's a consolation.'
Sullivan looked at Blayde, and growled, 'All right, mate. Don't rub it in. Protocol demands I shouldn't apologise ... but we've just had an official roasting from the chief.'
'And you're here to disperse the heat.'
'Summat like that.'
'And somebody—presumably—has roasted him.'
'I shouldn't be surprised.'
'Some idiot who isn't a policeman ... if you'll forgive me for calling an idiot an idiot.' Blayde's mouth moved into a sardonic smile, as he added, 'Would it be satisfactory, if I accept what you've just said as a reprimand?'
'I'd take it as a personal favour ... and no hard feelings.'
Blayde nodded, and relaxed his expression.
Sullivan said, 'We'd better get to the hospital. Preston'll need what moral support ...'
'He's not *at* the hospital.'
'Oh?'
'He—er—he thinks he knows who's responsible. Who the murderer is. I have the unhappy feeling he's out, seeking personal vengeance.'
'The hell he is!'
'There's an all-cars call out, to bring him in ... before he wrecks his career.'
'Here?'

Blayde nodded.

'Keep your fingers crossed,' said Sullivan, heavily. 'He could be just daft enough to blow the whole thing to smithereens.'

'*And* his career.'

'Aye ... that, too.'

Sullivan chewed his lip, then said, 'Your office, I think.'

'It's quieter.'

'D'you mind if we sit in?'

'I was about to make the same suggestion.'

'Mr Bear and myself.'

'And Lennox ... if you don't mind.'

Sullivan said, 'Leave word. We'll meet 'em in your office.'

Bear had been a little less explosive than Sullivan when making his entrance into the Information Room. Bear, it must be remembered, ranked Sullivan, neck-and-neck—they were both deputy chief constables—but, whereas Sullivan's gingering-things-up tactics could be likened to The Charge of The Heavy Brigade, Bear's manner was slightly more subtle. He was very much the new boy in this three-in-one fusion of police forces. He was (to use the idiom of the district) a 'comer-in', and was aware of that fact. It wasn't that he was interested in the 'Most-Popular-Copper-Of-The-Year' stakes—he could sizzle whiskers with the best of 'em ... but, because of his nature (plus circumstances already mentioned) he liked to check the combustibility of the chosen whiskers, before he put a match to the blow-torch.

Hence his choice of target. Lennox ... who, at that moment, was having a particularly interesting tête-à-tête with a certain detective inspector who had recently been downing ale in *The Fighting Cocks*.

It was a lead. More than that, it was a *promising* lead ... it gave the West killing some sort of motive.

'Although, mind you,' grunted Lennox, 'I can't see old White being a poofty ... can you?'
'You never know,' observed Bear.
'Anything at all,' sighed Lennox. 'In this boss-eyed world—*anything* ... even bloody cats.'
'Cats?' The D.I. blinked.
'They keep you up all night, son,' explained Lennox. 'Kitling. Then the wife gripes her guts out because you're a lousy obstetrician.'
'Oh!'
Bear grinned ... the fat, pantomime-like detective chief superintendent was a living-walking-talking joke. Who the hell could pass rockets down the line, via *this* character?'
He said, 'Tell you what, Lenny ... have a trip to the golf club and check whether West—Westerfield, what the blazes he cared to call himself—was a member. Or, if not, whether he's been a guest.'
'Sure.' Lennox turned to the D.I. and added, 'You, too, son. You've pulled this particular lever ... any jackpot takings are yours.'
The D.I. smiled his satisfaction.
A uniformed P.C. approached, and spoke to Bear.
He said, 'Excuse me, sir. Mr Sullivan wants to know if you, and Mr Lennox, will join him in Chief Superintendent Blayde's office, as soon as possible.'
'Thanks.' Bear glanced at Lennox, and said, 'Why not now? Unless you've something more urgent you'd ...'
A second interruption came from a detective constable who'd just hurried into the Information Room. He held a .22 cartridge on the open palm of his hand.
He said, 'This, sir. They thought you'd better see it.'
'They?' Bear frowned.
'Dr Carr and his men.'
'Where's it from?' asked Lennox.
'A yard, at the back of some empty offices ... opposite

the hairdressers. We-ell, not quite *opposite*. But—obviously—where he was when he ...'

'Hold your hosses, son.' Lennox held up a fat-fingered hand. 'You said the yard?'

'Yes, sir ... behind the offices.'

'You can't actually *see* the hairdressing place, from where this was found?'

'Good Lord, no sir. You've to climb through a window, and up some steps before ...'

'That thing been dusted for prints?' Lennox nodded at the cartridge case.

'Yes, sir. Nothing.'

'Thanks.' Lennox lifted the cartridge case from the detective constable's palm.

The D.C. hurried away, about his business.

'Preston's wife?' murmured Bear, solemnly.

Lennox nodded.

'Terrible thing,' said Bear gently.

Lennox twiddled the cartridge between his fingers, and mused, 'He's screwy.'

'Obviously. Any man who ...'

'No—I don't mean *that* "screwy" ... I mean he's round the twist. Else he's trying to lead us up the garden path.'

The D.I. watched, and listened to high-level bobby-talk.

Bear said, 'You're a few lengths ahead of me, Lenny.'

Lennox tossed the cartridge slowly and, in a soft growled voice, which was not at all funny, said, 'Y'know what, Winnie? This thing's getting a bit too bloody personal. Shooting coppers' wives. Making the whole force look like so many broken-stringed yo-yoes. In the vernacular ... I think it's time we stopped arsing around, and slung this clever bastard on the wrong side of a cell door.'

* * *

The office had the feel of a condemned cell, and Preston had the look of the man about to be hanged. It wasn't deliberate. Sullivan, Bear, Lennox and Blayde were serious ... but compassionate. Nobody said 'sorry'—because it was too damn late to be sorry ... for anything. Coppers aren't supposed to crack, and Preston *had*. He'd committed the unforgivable police sin. He'd shown human weakness.

Sullivan was asking the questions.

He said, 'All right. Supposing you'd reached Kitley's surgery, before the squad car caught up with you. What then?'

'I—I dunno,' muttered Preston.

'You weren't going to *arrest* him, for Christ's sake ... were you?'

'I ... thought so. At the time.'

'For shooting your wife?'

Preston moved his head in a defeated nod.

'He was pulling teeth, at the time, for God's sake.'

'I realise that ... now.'

'Whoever was in the chair. His assistants. His receptionists. All there to prove he wasn't waving a gun around.'

'Yes, sir.'

'What the hell got into you?'

Preston raised his head and looked into the face of his deputy chief constable as he said, 'Sir—with respect—if somebody was shagging *your* wife, while you were out on duty working your guts to water ...'

He left the sentence unfinished.

'You knew about it,' said Sullivan, gruffly.

'Yes, sir.'

'All right ... take him round a corner and belt hell out of him. But in your own time. Don't drag the whole force into it. Don't jeopardise a murder enquiry.'

'My—my wife ...'

'I know about your wife. We're sorry about your wife —all of us ... but she's *your* wife, Preston.'
'Y-yes, sir.'
'We'll get whoever did it. And he'll pay.'
'Yes, sir.'
'You don't sound too damn sure.'
'I'm sorry, sir.'
'Do you have doubts on the subject?'
'N-no, sir.'
Lennox sniffed, loudly, and grumbled, 'You're a liar, old cock ... and I can't say I blame you.'
'What's that?' Sullivan swung his attention to the Head of C.I.D., Bordfield Region, and the tone of the question carried displeasure.
Lennox had a fat hide and a thick skin ... displeasure was a wasted emotion, as far as he was concerned.
He said, 'In old Preston's shoes, I'd be having a few doubts. I *had* a few doubts, until this little joker was found.' He tossed the cartridge case a couple of times, as he added, 'Plus certain info one of our brighter C.I.D. lads has sniffed out.' He turned to Preston, and said, 'D'you mind if I ask you a few questions, superintendent? A bit personal ... that's what they might seem to be. But necessary. I'm not being nosey. You have my word on that.'
'Ask your questions,' Preston said, heavily. 'What the hell have I to lose?'
Sullivan glared at Lennox, and growled, 'For Christ's sake, don't mind *me*.'
'Ta.' Lennox looked at Preston, and said, 'First thing. Your missus. Is she—er—*normal*?'
'Normal?' Preston looked puzzled.
'In bed.'
'What the hell has *that* to ...'
'I warned you they'd be personal.'
'If you mean, is she over- ...'

'Not "over"—not "under"... just *normal*. Heterosexual ... to use the technical lingo.'
'Ask Kitley,' muttered Preston, angrily.
'I'm asking you, old son. I'd like an answer.'
'She was normal,' said Preston, wearily. 'She wasn't a lesbian ... if that's what you're after. She knew which—which hole to use. She was *normal*.'
'*Is*,' said Bear, quietly.
'Eh?' Preston looked enquiringly at the deputy chief constable.
Bear said, 'You've slipped into the wrong tense, Preston. The hound we're after wasn't quite on target, this time. She's your wife ... and she needs you now, as never before. This isn't a marriage guidance pep talk, Preston. But—for the moment—concentrate on your wife ... forget your own self-pity.'
Preston took a deep, shuddering breath, then nodded.
Sullivan said, 'Lennox, I can't see what the devil these questions...'
'West was a queer,' said Lennox, bluntly.
'Oh!'
'It might have been the link. It's been known.'
'Oh!' repeated Sullivan.
'Not that.' For the first time Preston smiled. A twisted, non-humorous smile. 'If that's what you mean by "normal", she was—sorry, she is—*very* normal.'
'Thanks, old son,' said Lennox, solemnly. 'That question was just about as heavy to ask as it was to answer.'
'Any more?'
'Happily married?' asked Lennox.
'So-so.'
'What's that mean?'
'What yardstick do you use?' countered Preston. 'Who *is* happily married? Who just puts on a front?'
'But it wasn't a cat-and-dog life?'

'No ... not until recently.'
'Till Kitley moved in on the act?'
'Till then,' agreed Preston, flatly.
'Which means, for how long?'
'Six years ... nearly seven.'
'Good God, man,' growled Sullivan, 'you're still on your honeymoon.'

Preston rubbed the back of a hand across his mouth, then said, 'I wasn't going to get married ... y'know, being a copper. Ambitious. Wives hold you back. That was the argument. He travels fastest ... y'know the saying. I almost made it, too. I was well past the marrying age—a confirmed bachelor—that's what *I* thought ... then, I met Lorna.'

'Where?'

'The Assize Court—of all places ... before the Crown Courts came in.'

'Y'mean she was ...' began Sullivan.

'She'd been lumbered for jury service.'

'Jury service?' Lennox snapped out the question with the speed of a man swatting a fly.

'Lessford Assize Court.' Preston nodded. 'She was ...'

'*That's* the link!'

There was a silence, as every man watched the fat detective's face; watched the narrowed eyes and the slowly nodding head.

Then Sullivan said, 'All right. Is it a secret? Or, are we *all* allowed to know?'

Lennox muttered, 'White was on jury service. Lessford Assize ... his wife mentioned it. He was away from home, one day, and ...'

'The first day,' interrupted Preston. 'Crispin—murder, reduced manslaughter ... he earned himself twelve years.'

'Four years off, for good conduct,' mused Lennox. 'It fits.'

'Your case?' asked Bear.

'No.' Preston shook his head. 'I was county. I'd a housebreaking case ...'

'*Our* case,' interrupted Sullivan. 'I can remember Crispin. Hard as they come. A fight—a gang killing ... that's one reason why it was reduced to manslaughter.'

'It fits,' repeated Lennox.

Blayde spoke for the first time.

He said, 'It *might* fit. It *might* be the link.'

'The best, so far,' said Bear. 'The most promising.'

'Crispin should be out,' said Sullivan.

'And a member of Beechwood Golf Club?' asked Blayde, gently.

'Aah!'

'Quite.'

'All right,' agreed Sullivan, reluctantly, 'don't let's *make* it fit. But, at least, let's try it for size.'

'She was there.' Preston's eyes were slightly out of focus, and he seemed to be talking to himself. Reminding himself. 'Y'know how it is. Assize Courts. Crown Courts. The first day. Everybody milling around ... coppers, witnesses, jurors. A real shambles. And she was there ... with the jurors. Some of the other jurors. Lost ... asking what was happening. We—we got talking. We had lunch together ... down there, in the basement. The cafeteria thing they run, when the court's in session. Beans on toast. Jesus Christ! ... beans on toast. She was a widow ... 'bout two years since her first husband died. We—we got talking. I dunno ... these things happen. I was—y'know—settled ... a confirmed bachelor. And—and ...'

The tears spilled over. One from each eye. They rolled, unheeded, down his cheeks as his teeth clamped themselves onto his lower lip.

'Easy, son,' murmured Lennox.

Blayde touched Preston's elbow, and said, 'She'll need somebody around, when they tell her. You ... don't you think?'

Preston nodded, silently.

Sullivan said, 'Take a few days' compassionate leave. Till she's over the worst ... and keep us informed. We'd like to know.'

Once more Preston nodded, dumbly.

'C'mon.' Bear injected pseudo-business-like quality into his voice. 'I'll run you over to the hospital.'

Preston stood up and followed Bear from the office.

When the door was closed, Blayde raised his eyes to the ceiling, and said, 'Bloody women!'

'It can happen,' observed Sullivan.

Lennox gave a wry grin, and said, 'Not to me, it can't. I'm the safest bloke on God's earth. Supposing anybody was barmy enough to fancy *my* missus, he'd be wasting his time ... he'd have to fight his way through a wall of bloody cats.'

To use Sullivan's own expression, they 'tried it for size', and it fitted ... but, at the same time, it didn't *quite* fit.

A phone call to the Lessford Crown Court. A search through the records. And the jury which convicted Crispin had included White, Bentley, West and a Mrs Fairbanks ... who was later to become Mrs Preston.

A phone call to H.M. Prison Durham. Yes ... Crispin had served his time. He'd been out for more than a week ... ten days, in fact. Where was he? ... how the hell did *they* know? He'd done his stretch, he'd behaved himself ... why the hell should *they* worry?

Sullivan said, 'That's it, then. An all-forces alert. We want him picked up ... fast!'

That's how far it fitted.

It stopped fitting, within thirty minutes of the all-forces alert.

Wallace Crispin was in the jug. He'd been arrested in the

wee, small hours—at 4.23.am., to be exact—on the night of West's murder. He'd been arrested 'on sus' ... the old 'Ways and Means Act'. In a farm stackyard.

Unless he'd borrowed the Concorde, he couldn't possibly have clobbered West, and travelled *that* far after the shooting. And, as for Mrs Preston ... forget it, friend. He was being grilled at the time. A couple of detective sergeants were busy squeezing brother Crispin's balls, when Mrs Preston had had her face shot away.

'Blast!' muttered Sullivan. 'That explodes the best lead we've had, so far.'

'Partly,' agreed Bear.

'Look, Winnie, if Crispin was ...'

'They were all jurors—in the same jury box ... it has to mean *something*.'

Sullivan continued to look disgusted, but said, 'We'd better get the complete list. Shove a twenty-four-hour police guard on the rest of 'em ... and wait for His Nibs to take another pot shot.'

'Unless,' observed Bear, 'Lenny comes up with something.'

And, as for 'Lenny'.

Lennox was a very busy man. He used the D.I. as an unofficial chauffeur, while he slumped in the front seat of his ancient Alvis—one of the few automobiles capable of taking the strain of his own considerable tonnage, without noticing the undue weight—and, behind half-closed eyes, worked out permutations neither Littlewoods nor Vernons had ever heard of.

Lennox (as every copper who'd ever worked with him would have happily verified) was a one off job. Unique. The police forces of this world have very few niches into which the 'Lennox type' can fit, with any degree of comfort. He was the born man-hunter, encased in the body of an overgrown Billy Bunter; the complete ruthless bastard, imprisoned within the personality and external appearance of a stand-up comic.

Discipline—the caste system of the Police Service—proper procedure ... these, and similar things, were all so much useless crap as far as Lennox was concerned.

The bacon—and the delivery thereof—was the sole object of the exercise.

Nobody hated him. Who the hell can hate an animated bladder of lard, dressed up like a bookie's runner? But, at odd moments in his police career, people—people who had figured they could drive a double-decker bus through the laws of the land—had realised, with something of a shock, that they were terrified of him.

Behind that moon-round face—inside that balloon-shaped head—things happened. Thoughts—possibilities and probabilities—were filleted down to the bare bone. Inconsistencies were matched against inconsistencies. Inadvertent remarks were examined. Nuances were subjected to careful scrutiny. Tiny—almost invisible—straws were carefully gathered and, from these straws, bricks were built; and each brick was tied in with its neighbour, until...

Men serving time could have finished that sentence—and with a lop-sided grin ... because *nobody* hated Lennox.

First stop ... High Dale Farm.

First person to be questioned ... Muriel White.

Strictly speaking, it wasn't a 'questioning'; it was more of an informal conversation, between friends. As before, the conversation took place in the huge, stone-flagged kitchen of the farmhouse and, as before, Lennox's lap was claimed as a temporary resting place for one of the farm cats.

The D.I. watched, listened and learned.

'You'll have heard ... read about it,' said Lennox, sadly.

'All those other people?' Muriel White shook her head in bewilderment. 'Miss Bentley? Mr Westerfield? Who is it, sir? Why is he *doing* these wicked things?'

'Remember your hubby being on jury service?'

Muriel White nodded.

'So were the others. Same jury ... that's what they had in common.'

'Oh!'

'And a Mrs Preston ... wife of one of our colleagues. She was on the same jury.'

'Oh, dear. Has she been ...'

'Shot. Badly injured. But not killed.'

'Oh, I am glad. It seems so—so ...'

'Pointless?'

'Wicked ... *and* pointless,' she agreed.

'There's another link.' Lennox scratched the cat's ears. 'It's to do with the Appleyard family ... those who had the farm, before you. The daughter.'

'Madge West? Madge Appleyard-as-was?'

'Uhuh?'

'Oh, that was another terrible thing. Terrible!'

'Aye. We know. Your hubby ... he'd be working for Appleyard at the time?'

She nodded.

'Friends, were they?'

'Mr Appleyard and White?'

'Aye.'

'Great friends.' Her eyes stared into the past for a moment, then she added, 'White took it badly. When Madge did away with herself. He couldn't have been more upset, if it had been his own daughter.'

Lennox leaned forward, fractionally and the cat unsheathed its claws and clung to the cloth of his trousers.

He said, 'Take your time, old pet. But tell me everything. The marriage. The suicide. The funeral. Every little thing you can remember ... about everybody.'

Next stop ... Beechwood Golf Club.

Next person to be interviewed ... the club secretary.

Again (and to be precise) not exactly an 'interview'; more of a friendly chat, with Ingle fluctuating between half-hidden contempt for the obese and ludicrously dressed detective and an acknowledgement of the rank of chief superintendent of police.

'It's a favour, y'see,' explained Lennox, with a self-conscious grin. 'The use of the club house ... if you don't mind.'

'If it will help,' said Ingle doubtfully.

'Oh, I think it will. I think it will.' Lennox strolled around the airy office. Admired the view from the picture window. Ran his finger along the woodwork of one of the expensive desks. He said, 'D'you read detective stories?'

'Rarely,' replied Ingle. 'I find them rather contrived ... not my cup of tea. I prefer biographies ... and books on furniture restoration. That's my hobby. That, and golf.'

'This?' Lennox tapped the closed roll-top of one of the desks with the nail of his forefinger.

'Pure Victoriana.' Enthusiasm entered Ingle's voice. 'It was in a deplorable condition, when I found it ... at a jumble sale, of all places.'

'Good Lord!'

'Six months,' said Ingle, proudly. 'The work needed, to make it as good as new ... you wouldn't believe.'

'Nice,' observed Lennox.

Ingle said, 'It's not priceless. Victorian furniture never *is*. But, of its kind, it's as near perfect as you'll ever get.'

'That I believe,' murmured Lennox. He became more business-like, and added, 'About tonight. I'd like to ask a few—er—"guests" along ... if you don't mind. Not members of the club.'

'I see no reason why not.' Ingle moved his shoulders.

'And,' said Lennox, 'if you could pass the word to some of the members. There's a list here.' He fished a crumpled sheet of foolscap from his jacket pocket, smoothed it out, handed it to Ingle, and continued, 'Lemme see ... Procter —Harold Procter. The other Harold ... Harold Kitley. Oh, and the pro ... Grieve, isn't it?'

'Amos Grieve.'

'I'd like him there. And as many of the others as you can get word to. D'you mind?'

'No-o.' Ingle eyed the list. 'I'll telephone around ... but what shall I tell them?'

'Detective stories.' Lennox grinned, a little shamefacedly. 'Tell 'em it's the—er—"last chapter". Y'know ... "everything revealed". That sort of thing. They might be interested. Don't you think?'

'*Will* it be?' asked Ingle.

'We-ell ... y'never know,' hedged Lennox. 'Things go wrong. But he'll be there. Lay money on it. He'll be there.'

When they'd left the golf club, the D.I. couldn't resist the question.

'*Will* he?' he asked.

'What?'

'The murderer. Will he be at the golf club, tonight?'

'I reckon,' rumbled Lennox. 'By the time old Ingle's made all those phone calls—y'know ... His Nibs won't be able to stay away. He'll be too bloody curious. He'll *be* there. That ... or human nature's taken a turn in the wrong direction.'

Next stop ... Ashfield Comprehensive School.

'Nice place you've got here,' observed Lennox, chattily.

'Eh? Oh—er—yes ... very modern.'

The headmaster looked careworn and curiously bedraggled. Rather like a drenched bird.

Lennox said, 'We'd like you there. If you can make it.'

'Where?'

'The golf club. Beechwood Golf Club. The club house. At about nine o'clock ... if you can make it.'

'Why? What is there ...'

'What you might call a dénouement. With a bit o' luck.'

'A what?' Martin frowned.

'You read detective stories?' asked Lennox. 'Y'know ...'

'I've—er—read some,' admitted Martin.

'That's it, then.' Lennox beamed. 'The big trick. The rabbit out of the empty topper. That sort of thing.'

Martin stared, and said, 'You're serious?'

'You'd like to know who killed Miss Bentley, wouldn't you?'

'Er—yes ... Yes, of course. But ...'

'But what?'

'Well—real life ... you don't *do* it that way. Do you?'

'Why not?' Lennox raised the brows atop his bulbous eyes. 'Miss Christie did it, why can't we?'

'You *are* serious?' said Martin.

'Oh, I'm serious, all right,' Lennox assured him. 'It'll be quite a party ... if things go as I intend 'em to go. Quite a party. And—y'know—incomplete, without you.'

'Why, specifically, *me*?'

Lennox said, 'You'd like to know who killed Miss Bentley ... wouldn't you?'

'Well, yes. Of course.'

'That's a good enough reason, surely?'

'I—er—I suppose so,' sighed Martin.

'Good ... we'll expect you.'

* * *

Next interviewee ... Violet Bentley.

'I have far better things to do,' she snapped.

'Than shaking hands with your sister's murderer?' Lennox met kind with kind; shock-talk with shock-talk. It didn't work ... even when he added, 'To—er—*thank* him?'

'Don't be impudent.'

'From what I can gather,' grunted Lennox, 'you'd be *inclined* to thank him.'

'I've a good mind to report you to your superior officer.'

Lennox chuckled, and said, 'Go right ahead, missus ...'

'*Miss*—if you don't mind.'

'... It happens all the time. They're bored—they've damn-all to do—if a day passes without 'em having to compose some new apology for summat I've said.'

'You're an oaf, man.'

'Aye. Unfortunately, I've tried to live with it.'

'Are you trying to be funny?'

'Not deliberately.'

'Or is it natural bad manners?'

'Probably, missus ...'

'*Miss*.'

'... You should get together with my wife. Compare notes. That way, you'll reach some sorta conclusion.'

'Will you please leave this house,' she snapped.

'Don't you want to meet whoever killed your sister?'

'No.'

'You never know ... he might have a "thing" about the Bentleys.'

'What?'

'He might even have *you* in mind.'

'Look—if you're serious—if you've any reason to suspect...'

'Nine o'clock, at the club house. I think you should be there, missus.'

'*MISS!*'

Lennox paused at the door, tilted his head slightly and examined the face of Violet Bentley.

He murmured, 'Naturally ... *miss*.'

'D'you really think ...' began the D.I.

'I'm stirring it up, old son,' chuckled Lennox. 'That's all ... for the moment. The old wooden spoon technique. Get 'em on the hop. It does a power of good. It gets things moving.'

'No.' The D.I. hesitated, then said, 'What I mean is ... it doesn't *have* to be a man. Does it?'

'Some women can handle rifles,' agreed Lennox.

'So...'

'So, now,' interrupted Lennox, 'we're gonna chew the fat with your mate. The landlord of *The Fighting Cocks*. It's about time. I could just about do with a nice, cool pint.'

The landlord looked daggers at the D.I.

The D.I. quaffed ale, and pretended not to notice.

Lennox lowered his glass, and said, 'You keep a good cellar, cocky. That's as nice a drop as I've tasted for a long time.'

The landlord refused to be mollified.

He said, 'What was told to that officer was told in confidence.'

'Was it?' observed Lennox, without undue interest.

'He'd no right ...'

'He'd be up the creek if he *hadn't*.'

'If I'd known ...'

'And you'd be up the creek if *you* hadn't.'

'Oh!'

'So let's stop fannying around. There's a bloke I'd like you to meet.'

'Who?'

'He has a way with .22 rifles.'

'Y'mean...'

'Tonight at the club house. Nine o'clock. Beechwood Golf Club.'

'That's impossible. I have to be here.'

'What,' observed Lennox, with interest, 'would happen if he slapped a slug into *your* skull, before that time?'

The landlord blinked, went pale then gaped, open-mouthed.

'Is it—is it ...'

'You'd be a bit pushed to be here, if *that* happened,' observed Lennox.

'In—in—in that case ...'

'Aye.' Lennox nodded. 'Arrangements can be made. 'You don't *have* to be here. Pull your finger out, old lad. Make the necessary arrangements. And *be* there.'

'If—if you really think it's necessary.'

'Vital,' said Lennox, solemnly.

'Oh!'

'Be seeing you.'

Next stop ... a caravan.

And a different approach.

Lennox smoked one of his cheroots and, in a gentle voice, said, 'Look, old son, I know you reckon you represent an "oppressed minority"—and maybe you're right—but my mate, here, hasn't let you down. Nor will I.'

Gascoinge kept an expressionless face, and waited.

'People are getting killed,' said Lennox. 'Now, that ain't nice. It makes for panic. It makes for cockeyed accusations. And y'know what *that* means.'

Gascoinge moved his head in a nod.

'Stupidity,' said Lennox. 'It's even been known to lead to mob rule. Not this time—don't get me wrong, old son

—I'm not trying to scare you. But, I'd like you there. Personally. To scotch any behind-the-hand rumours. I reckon you owe it.'

'I owe you people nothing, sir.'

'Not *us*, Gascoinge old cock. Yourself. Your own people. I reckon the Romany people wouldn't mind. They might think it a good thing. To have a representative there ... see? To see the bastard nailed. To know—to be able to give evidence, if you like—that one "oppressed minority" isn't what it's cracked out to be.'

'They won't let me in, sir,' said Gascoinge.

'They'll let you in. As my guest.'

Gascoinge remained silent for a few moments.

Then, he said, 'How do I know this isn't a trick?'

'Would *I* be party to it?' countered the D.I.

Lennox blew foul-smelling smoke, and said, 'You *don't* know. You either take, for what it is ... a promise. Or, you call us liars. Both of us.'

'I don't think I should, sir.'

It wasn't an absolute refusal ... but the doubts remained.

Lennox pulled a wry face, and said, 'We-ell, we can't *make* you.'

'No ... you can't *make* me, sir.'

'If you make the wrong decision, you might regret it. You might wish you *had* come.'

'It's possible,' agreed Gascoinge.

'Whereas, if you *do* come—even if it's a waste of time ... no harm done. That's the way I see it, old son.'

Something not far from cynical laughter touched Gascoinge's eyes.

He said, 'You have the tongue, sir.'

'Is that a fact?' Lennox feigned surprise.

'You'd make a good trader.'

'We-ell—I dunno about that—but, if you say so.' Lennox grinned cheerful camaraderie.

Gascoinge hesitated, then said, 'I might be there, sir.'
'Good. I hope so.'
'As a favour to me,' added the D.I.
Gascoinge said, 'All right. I might be there.'

'Will he, d'you think?' answered the D.I.
'Oh, aye. Nothing surer.'
Lennox relaxed in the comfort of the Alvis's upholstery.
The D.I. said, 'You sound certain.'
'Curiosity, lad.' Lennox stomach wobbled in time with a silent chuckle. 'It does a damn sight more than kill cats. It's solved more crimes than Soft Mick. Just a bit o' luck ... it should solve this one.'
'Y'mean you think *Gascoinge*? You seriously think...'
'Last stop,' interrupted Lennox. 'That berk Freeman.'
'Patrick Freeman? The car hire proprietor?'
'As ever was. And,' continued Lennox, 'this time we don't use the soft soap. We *need* Freeman there ... otherwise, none of the others need bother showing up.'
'Y'mean *he's* ...'
'Patience, old son,' sighed Lennox. 'Periodically, I do things, and make a right old nadge-pie of an enquiry. But —y'know—if you're gonna be a twat, be a *big* twat ... that's my motto. Let everybody have a belly laugh. So-o, nine o'clock. Right? Then, if I'm up a rhubarb tree, you can laugh your socks off, with the rest of 'em.'

Last interviewee ... Patrick Freeman.
'That's impossible,' he began. 'I have an appointment...'
'At Beechwood Golf Club. At nine o'clock.' Lennox ended the sentence for him.
'Look. Don't be daft. I'm ...'
'You're living dangerously, old cock,' warned Lennox.
'Eh?'

196

'Calling a detective chief superintendent daft. That's *really* asking for grief.'

'No—I didn't mean ...'

'See that car?' Lennox jerked his pudding head towards a Ford Escort, parked in the huge garage.

'Sure.' Freeman looked perplexed. 'It's ...'

'Apart from the number plates—which, as we all know, can be changed as easily as a baby's nappy—that car answers the description of a nicked vehicle. Perfectly.'

'You *what?*'

'Perfectly,' echoed the D.I., from behind a stone-faced expression.

'You—you must be bloody barmy,' gasped Freeman.

'Daft. Now barmy. Y'know Freeman, old cock, I do believe you *want* trouble.'

'No! No!' Freeman backed off, in top gear. 'Not that. I don't mean that. Just that—y'know ... I have papers. Documents. I can *prove* it's my car. That's all.'

'Unless it *is* knock,' mused Lennox. 'And you knocked it. In which case, you'll have "papers". They all do ... forged to hell and back.'

'What the bloody hell ...'

'Knock,' murmured Lennox, drily. 'That car. I say it's knock.'

The D.I. contributed, 'Me, too. It answers the description down to a wheel at each corner.'

'You're—you're having me on,' breathed Freeman. 'You're—y'know—having me *on* ... aren't you?'

'No.' Lennox shook his head, slowly then, very distinctly, said, 'We're not having you on, lad. We're *fixing* you. You're gonna be at the golf club tonight. We're giving you a choice—that's all ... you're either going from here, or you're going from a police cell.'

'You can't ...'

'We can. We *have*.'

'Oh, my Christ!'

'So-o, get on that blower. Cancel that appointment you "couldn't" cancel. That, or get your coat and have your collar felt.'

'You are,' roared Sullivan, 'out of your tiny mind!'
'That could well be,' agreed Lennox.
'You're crackers.'
'Another possibility.'
'You're round the bloody twist.'
'I'm not arguing.'
Sullivan glared at the Bordfield Regional Head of C.I.D., sought words, gasped for breath then, eventually, said, 'For Christ's sake, sit down. Lenny—by all that's holy ... what the hell have you cooked up *this* time?'
'Ta.'
Lennox dragged a chair nearer to Sullivan's desk and lowered himself ponderously onto its leather-covered seat.

They were alone, in Sullivan's office; away from the 'officialdom' demanded by the outward appearance of every oversized police force. They were fellow-coppers—friends—and one of them knew he'd crawled out onto a limb, while the other concealed his concern behind an external display of blazing displeasure.

'Well?' demanded Sullivan.
'Off the record?' asked Lennox, quietly.
'Like hell.'
'So-o, I play it solo.' The obese detective chief superintendent sighed. 'It lengthens the odds. I'll not dispute that ... but it's still possible.'

He felt in his jacket pocket and produced a buff-coloured envelope. He dropped the envelope onto the surface of Sullivan's desk.

'What's that?' demanded Sullivan.
Lennox said, 'My resignation.'
'Why the hell should you ...'

'It's sealed. It carries today's date. I called at the typist's office, on the way up here. It lets you out—it lets *everybody* out—if things go skew-whiff.'

'They'll go skew-whiff,' said Sullivan, grimly. 'Nothing surer.'

'In that case.' Lennox nodded at the envelope. 'That puts everybody else in the clear.'

'Why?' asked Sullivan, heavily. 'In God's name *why*? We'll get him, in time. Whoever he is, we'll ...'

'I *know* who he is.'

'In that case ...'

'And this "time" you're on about. Time for what? To kill a couple more of that jury?'

'We've a police guard on 'em. They're safe.'

'Against a rifle bullet?' Lennox shook his head, sadly. 'You know better than that, Mr Sullivan. *Nobody's* safe against a rifle with telescopic sights ... not if the assassin bides his time, and takes enough care. And the hound we're after has waited eight years. He has patience, sir. More patience than we have. More patience than we can afford.'

'I notice,' observed Sullivan, 'that you've suddenly gone all coy and correct. "Mr Sullivan" and "sir". There's a reason ... presumably.'

'It's *on* the record.'

'That doesn't mean ...'

'It means it's my neck. Not yours. I'm not asking it to be yours, sir. I'm being strictly official ... then it *can't* be yours.'

Sullivan bought time for careful thought, by packing and lighting his pipe.

Then, he said, 'And, if it's *off* the record?'

'You're not far from retirement,' said Lennox. 'You're looking forward to it. Upper Drayson ... isn't it?'

'If it's *off* the record?' repeated Sullivan.

Lennox moved his fat-padded shoulders, and

murmured, 'I'm on thin ice. It might not hold two of us ... I'd be less than honest, if I said otherwise.'

'Meaning you've more guts than I have?'

'No, sir. Meaning my missus breeds cats. Russian Blues. They're pricey moggies ... and they bring in a fair lump of loot. At a pinch—if things go wrong—I can do without the pension.'

'Cut out the "sir", Lenny.' Sullivan grinned. 'It's off the record, as of now. So—come on ... open up a little.'

'I could use your rank,' admitted Lennox.

'Okay ... you've got it. Say what you want doing.'

'He's a crafty bugger, Dick,' warned Lennox. 'He'll *be* there ... as sure as hell, he'll *be* there. But I want a few things to hit him with. Talk ... okay, I'll provide the chat-show. But—over and above talk—I need a few surprises. Shocks. I'm out to trick a confession out of him ... in front of a roomful of witnesses.'

'It should be interesting. At *least* interesting.'

Lennox said, 'I'll hold the limelight, but I need some backstage jiggery-pokery ... see? Search warrants ... executed to the minute. Forensic science evidence ... ready for just the right moment. Like all conjurers, I need a damn good assistant. A whole army of assistants.'

'And?' asked Sullivan.

'We-ell ...' Lennox leaned forward, and the chair squeaked mild protest. 'What I have in mind is this ...'

Ingle took over the role of Master of Ceremonies. And, why not? This was the Concert Room, of Beechwood Golf Club, and the Concert Room had a small, but well-equipped, stage. The drum kit and the electric organ were, admittedly, covered by dust sheets, but the footlights and the centre-stage lighting had been switched on; the curtain had been raised and the microphone had been connected.

Ingle tapped, then blew at the microphone and, from

the strategically placed speakers, the required popping and hissing assured him that things were in working order.

He leaned towards the mike, and said, 'Ladies and gentlemen! Ladies and gentlemen ... your attention, please.'

At the tables around the room, soft-talking groups cut short their conversation. At the bar, which ran the length of the room, those who were drinking turned towards the stage, and the two bar-keeps paused in their gathering of orders.

Ingle waited for complete silence.

He smiled, then said, 'I—er—frankly, I hardly know how to word the introduction I am about to make. It concerns the killing—the shooting—of various fellow-citizens ... a matter of which you're all aware. A matter which has necessitated the questioning of members of this golf club by police officers. This has caused some inconvenience and—perhaps as a token gesture, and as a means of countering that inconvenience—the police have taken an unusual step. One might almost say a unique step. Certainly something *I've* never known before. The—er—the object of the exercise—as I understand it—is to name the culprit. Here. Publicly. Tonight. I—er—I'm almost tempted to add "before your very eyes".' He smiled at his audience, and his audience politely returned the smile. He concluded, 'That, then, is why we're here. And, to represent the police, might I present Detective Chief Superintendent Lennox.'

Ingle stepped away from the microphone and Lennox waddled onto the stage, from the wings.

In the audience somebody—one person—brought his hands together twice ... then stopped, as he suddenly realised that this *wasn't* a show, and that applause was very much out of place.

Ingle nodded at Lennox before descending the steps

leading from the side of the stage to the floor of the Concert Room.

Sullivan and Rucker sat at a table at the end of the Concert Room farthest from the stage.

Rucker's lip curled and he murmured, 'Wall-to-wall waistline. All he needs is a bowler hat, three sizes too small, and he's living proof that the burlesque show isn't dead. Those ridiculous clothes. That fatuous expression. And—God help us!—he represents law-enforcement. Will we *ever* live this pantomime down?'

Sullivan watched the murderer, without seeming to watch the murderer, and muttered, 'Cut it out, Rucker. Keep your eye on Freeman ... and be ready to jump, if he makes a wrong move.'

Lennox beamed at his waiting audience. He opened his mouth and spoke, but was far too near the microphone, and the speakers blared out an unintelligible blast of noise.

He stepped back a pace, grinned, and said, 'Sorry. These things are new to me. Now ... can everybody hear me?'

A murmur of assent rippled back from the audience.

'Good.' Lennox repeated the grin, and made a fresh start. He said, 'It's about these murders. White. Bentley. West ... most of you know him as Westerfield, the actor bloke. And a Mrs Preston ... wife of Detective Superintendent Preston. She's not dead, I'm glad to say. Chummy didn't do what he set out to do. Latest report from the hospital sounds more hopeful. One eye's gone ... but there's a good chance of saving the other. And cosmetic surgery can do things you wouldn't believe, these days.

'That's the background. That's why I'm here. That's why Major Ingle's been good enough to give me this platform. To explain things. Y'know ... to put you all in the picture. That's why we're *all* here. To see if we can stop chummy from making too much of a habit of this thing.'

He paused, then continued, 'It's fair to warn you. Parts of what I'm likely to say won't make nice listening. A bit bloodthirsty. And I see some ladies have come along for the show. It's *them* I'm talking to, now. I'm not saying don't stay. But I *am* saying be ready for some down-to-earth talk, if you *do* stay.'

Again, he paused, but nobody made as if to leave the Concert Room.

'Right.' He rubbed the back of his thick neck, and went on, 'Let's take 'em one at a time. White. Then Bentley. Then West. Then Preston.

'White was clobbered on his own land. On his own farm ... as he was opening a gate. He stopped two. The first one killed him. The second was for good measure ... straight through the forehead, at close range. The first came from behind a conveniently placed tree ... about sixty yards from the gate. That's a long shot, for a .22, without a telescopic sight ... so-o, we figured a telescopic sight. We were right, too. Even so, it's a damn good shot.

'You can kill with a .22, folks. That's been proved three times in the last few days. But it ain't easy. We're talking about a bullet with a smaller circumference than any of the cheaper cigarettes. A bullet that's usually used to kill rabbits—small game and vermin ... that sort of thing. Generally speaking, an assassin favours a bigger bullet ... a thirty-eight, a forty-five, a three-o-three. A .22 is a very hit-and-miss affair ... unless you're a *real* marksman. It has to hit certain vital spots. The pump. The brain—and right *into* the brain ... 'cos brain surgery can mend damage, these days, unless the victim's as dead as mutton.

'That was one hell of a shot that killed White, folks. He was dead, first go ... he didn't need the one through the forehead.

'It was an even *better* shot that killed Bentley. The distance was about the same. But from a car, and at a moving target. I'm not saying she was moving fast ... but she *was* moving. And the inside of a car restricts the aiming position ... see? So-o—all in all—that was a dinger of a shot. It *had* to be. 'Cos chummy had only the one go. He couldn't fire twice. He had to pull the trigger ... then, away. Real Bisley stuff ... and, if it wasn't for the fact that he was leaving corpses for us to collect, I'd be inclined to congratulate him.'

Blayde was in plain clothes. He shared a table with the headmaster, Martin, and Violet Bentley.

Martin was staring up at the stage, with a stunned expression on his face. Shocked, at the near-variety-turn with which Lennox was holding his audience; at the manner in which the fat detective chief superintendent was slipping colloquialisms, and personal asides, into the telling of the details of multiple murder.

'It's—it's disgusting,' he breathed. 'He's—he's talking about...'

'He's talking about an absolute cow, who deserved to die,' whispered Violet Bentley, furiously. 'Come out of that schoolroom atmosphere long enough to face the truth. She was a tart. She blinded you, with her fluttering eyelids and her simpering talk. She was ...'

'A little less,' muttered Blayde, warningly. 'We're here to listen, not talk. The man up there is doing all the talking necessary. He may *look* a fool ... but appearances can be very deceptive.'

The swing-doors of the Concert Room opened, then closed, silently as Sugden entered, holding Dene by the elbow.

The young homosexual seemed to be on the point of passing out, and Sugden guided him quietly, and unobserved, towards the wall facing the stage. Dene leaned his shoulder blades against the wall, dropped his head onto his chest and closed his eyes.

Lennox was saying, '... Which brings us to the third shooting. One more cracker of a shot. From darkness, into artificial light. And an angle-shot, at that. Chummy aimed from the top of a multiple-storied car park ... and at night. This time, his target was the brain of Arthur West ... better known as a local actor, working under the name of Arnold Westerfield. But—for this evening—we'll use his real name ... West. A long shot. An angled shot. A shot from darkness into light. Damn near trick shooting—the sort of stuff you see on the stage ... but chummy pulled it off. He drove up in his own car—a red Mini—parked it, carted his rifle to his chosen aiming point in a cricket bag ... then, after that one fantastic shot, went back to the Mini and drove home.

'Safe?

'We-ell, *he* thought so. But—y'see—he didn't have X-ray eyes. He couldn't see through the sides of a parked van. He couldn't see a young couple having a snogging session, in the back of that van. But they saw *him*. Both of 'em. They didn't see him pull the trigger. But they saw him leave the Mini, and they saw him come back to the Mini. They were—er—*interested* ... see? It's happened to all of us. A spot of slap-and-tickle and, at the back of your mind, the possibility that you're providing entertainment for some Peeping Tom. That's what *they* thought. They thought chummy was one more dirty old man ... so they watched him, through the back window of the van. They watched him ... but he didn't know he was *being* watched.'

Sullivan saw the tiny muscles tighten, around the jaw of the murderer. He saw the slight narrowing of the eyes ...

and, for the first time, Sullivan allowed himself the luxury of toying with the *possibility*.

Lenny just *might* pull it off.

Nobody else could ... but Lenny had the timing, and Lenny had the knack of telling the truth, but making the truth sound considerably *more* than the truth.

It was just possible ... and, with a following wind, Lenny *might*.

'Which ...' Lennox treated his audience to a quick, all-knowing grin. 'Which must be a bit off-putting for him. Eh? To know that he was actually *seen* at one of the killings. He's starting to sweat. Must be.' Lennox paused, looked around at the waiting, listening men and women—treated the murderer to what might, or might not, have been a split-second nod—then continued, 'A hell of a thing to have thrown in your teeth ... ain't it? I mean—just imagine—you're sitting there, all comfy and cosy. Feeling pretty pleased with yourself. Feeling pretty *sure* of yourself. Three quick, clean corpses ... and, suddenly, you're told you've been *seen*. You've been spotted. Just before, and just after, you splashed West's brains all over the landscape.'

'Shurrup!'

Every head turned at the screamed interruption.

Sugden tightened his grip on Dene's arm, and growled, 'Steady, lad.'

But Dene wouldn't be silenced.

He stared his half-crazed anguish across the Concert Room, and shouted, 'You there. Pig-man. You enjoying this? Arnie ain't around ... right? So you can throw shit over his name, like crazy. Who cares? *I* care, bastard. Y'know that, fatso? *I* care, when some crap-arsed fuzz-boy uses Arnie's name in some sorta kinky parlour game.'

The murderer said, 'I think that man should be

removed. We have ladies present. I don't see why they should be subjected to ...'

'No!' Lennox interrupted, and his voice had an edge it had previously lacked. He said, 'I gave a warning before I started. That it wasn't likely to be nice. That anybody who couldn't stomach the truth should leave. I want Dene here ... he's necessary.'

Ingle looked undecided for a moment, then nodded an acceptance.

He said, 'As you wish, chief superintendent. We can assume you know what you're doing.'

'I know what I'm doing,' growled Lennox.

'In that case, I rule that this Dene character be allowed to stay ... with the proviso that anybody who cares to leave, may do so.'

Kitley, the dentist, said, 'I disagree with that ruling. I think he should be thrown out ... now! In fact I think this whole charade is an insult to ...'

'This "charade" now moves onto the shooting of Mrs Preston.' The interruption was as sharp, and pointed, as had been the first. 'A subject which might interest you—personally—Mr Kitley. Or, conversely, a subject you might prefer to leave undiscussed.'

'You've had my ruling, Kitley,' snapped Ingle. 'Leave, if you wish. But Dene stays ... and the chief superintendent continues with his outline of the murders.'

Kitley compressed his lips, then rasped, 'I'll stay, I'll accept your ruling ... but, under protest.'

Ingle nodded at Lennox, and said, 'Carry on, please.'

'Neat,' murmured Sullivan, gently.

'Crafty,' agreed Rucker, reluctantly. 'Crafty ... or lucky.'

'A tacit acceptance of the inevitable. That's not luck, Rucker. That's knowing how to bluff the other man off the face of the earth.'

'But a long way from an admission of guilt.'

'But nearer,' said Sullivan, softly. 'Much nearer than we were when the show started.' He glanced around, and added, 'Let's have Freeman over here. I think the time's ripe for *his* little number.'

After Dene's outburst, and Kitley's explosion of anger, the audience was a little restive.

Lennox waved a podgy paw, and said, 'By the way ... don't let my jawing stop anybody from drinking. The bar's still open. The waiters are—er—"waiting" ... and, to be honest, I could do with a thirst-quencher myself.'

The waiters moved among the audience and took whispered orders, while Lennox continued his one-man performance.

And, having chopped Kitley down to size—having virtually *dared* him to object to a closely-examined exposure of the shooting of Preston's wife—Lennox merely mentioned it ... almost as an off-the-cuff remark.

He said, 'The fourth shooting. A slight dog's dinner, as far as chummy was concerned. He injured, but he didn't kill.'

Lennox rubbed his hands, grinned a little ruefully, and continued, 'Don't get me wrong, folks. Three, and a wounding, doesn't look nice on a crime sheet. It's three, and a wounding, too many. And—after the first two—we knew we were chasing one killer. One trigger-happy clown who had a grudge against more than one person. So-o ... we looked for the link. Two men, two women ... so sex discrimination went out of the window. Age didn't come into it. White was middle-aged to elderly. Bentley was no chicken ... but she wasn't yet a boiler. Even this place—this golf club—wasn't *the* common denominator ... although, at one time, we thought it might be.

'No—this golf club was important, because we were

pretty sure chummy was a member ... he'd left his hoof marks at the scene of the first shooting.

'But—y'know—he always left something else, too.

'One of these.' Lennox fished an empty cartridge case from his jacket pocket and twiddled it between his fingers. 'At White's shooting, he left one alongside the body. At Bentley's shooting, he left one in the car he used. At West's shooting, he left one on the roof car park. And, at Preston's shooting ... *there*, he left one away and gone to hell from where he was standing when he fired the shot.

'His trade mark. His—er—"visiting card". To link all the killings. To tell us. To make damn sure we knew ... that it was *one* man we were after. It also told us summat else. That he knew his onions about guns, because these ...' He held up the used cartridge case. 'They're like fingerprints. The breech of the weapon. The striking pin. The ejection mechanism. The same gun always leaves the same marks. Always! So-o ... even if the bullet was bashed around a bit, and couldn't tell us its tale, the ejected cartridge case could. Chummy ... every time. And he wanted us to *know*.'

Lennox beamed at his spellbound audience for a moment, then said, 'Easy ... ain't it? Except that it prompts a question. What the hell *did* chummy want us to know? Not his identity—that, for sure ... else, he could have sent us a postcard. Just that the same rifle fired all the shots. That White, Bentley, West and Preston were all victims of the same gun-happy lunatic. *That they had something in common.*

'That's all. He left an empty cartridge case, every time, just to make sure the dumb coppers latched onto the notion that they *weren't* chasing four killers. That they were after *one* man ... which, in turn, meant there was some connection between the victims.'

'Check,' murmured Sullivan.

Rucker nodded, rose from the table and, with a minimum of fuss, strolled to the door of the Concert Room.

He returned, re-seated himself, nodded, then said, 'They're ready.'

Sullivan beckoned the man Freeman, with his eyes.

Freeman came to the table, and Sullivan's voice was little more than a whisper, when he said, 'It's your turn Freeman. You know what to do—what to say ... go to it.'

The D.I. shared a table with Amos Grieve, the club professional, the landlord of *The Fighting Cocks* and Harry Gascoinge.

The D.I. was watching, and listening to, Lennox with something not far removed from hero-worship in his eyes.

Gascoinge rested his dark-skinned hands on the surface of the table, and remarked, 'He has the gift of tongue.'

'And how!' breathed the D.I.

'There's a natural concentration,' observed Grieve, softly. 'He knows *exactly* what he's going to do—going to say—next.'

'Every word.'

'Get rid of that gut, and he'd make a superb golfer. A real world-beater.'

The landlord grumbled, 'I still don't know why the hell *I'm* here.'

The D.I. took his eyes from the stage for a moment, stared at the landlord, and said, 'Sit tight, mate. Just hope *you* aren't the one he's going to name.'

The landlord paled, and breathed, 'Oh, my God!'

'... Which may sound clever. To *force* a bunch of thick-headed flatfeet along a certain line of thought.

'It took four cartridges to do it. To give us the connection, I mean. The connection between the four victims ... a connection, eight years old. They all sat in the same jury box. They all convicted a particular nasty piece of work to eight years behind bars. *That's* the link ... the connection. And that nasty piece of work is on the loose again. So-o, it could have been *him* we were after. It could have been *him* who's been evening up the score a little.

'Clever?

'What the detective story writers might call a "red herring".

'But, not so clever, folks. Not when you think about it. Not when you realise that this "red herring" needed four pieces of lousy luck. Four times, when he couldn't prove an alibi.

'Then, it ain't clever ... it's *dumb*. It's self-defeating. But—y'know—chummy *isn't* dumb. So, it leaves us with one more unanswered question. Why the hell play stupid? Why mess around, leaving false trails? Why not just clobber four—maybe more—victims, and leave it at that?'

The man wearing waiter's uniform touched the murderer on the shoulder, and said, 'Excuse me, sir.'

'What the devil ...' The murderer looked up, saw the man's face, closed his mouth and, at the same time, sighed in near-defeat.

The man said, 'Compliments of Deputy Chief Constable Bear, sir. And will you please join him, outside. By your car.'

The murderer nodded, rose from his seat and made his way quietly, and with as little fuss as possible, to the door of the Concert Room.

Sullivan watched the tiny enactment.

He muttered, 'Now, it's up to Lenny ... to mark time.'

'To *waste* time,' corrected Rucker.

'He can do it.'

'If this thing comes off,' said Rucker, with sour reluctance, 'I'm prepared to believe he can sprout wings and fly.'

'Dumbo could.'

'Maybe ... but this isn't Disneyland.' Rucker allowed himself a sardonic twist of the lips, and added, 'I dunno, though ...'

Lennox was saying, 'A thought's puzzled us all, since the beginning of this enquiry. The Appleyards. Why "Appleyards's Farm"? Why, after all these years, not "White's Farm"? There's a reason ... and I'll come to it, later. But, a secondary question tended to get between us, and a good night's sleep, too. Why *emigrate*? Lot's of folk sell their farms. Sell their businesses. But not too many leave the country. Especially the "Appleyard" type. They're country folk. They belong to the land. Lots of 'em feel uncomfortable, even when they take a holiday here, in England. They're busting a gut to get back ... to their own midden. So, when they move—when they have to move—they don't move far.

'The Appleyards left the country.

'Why?

'We-ell—as sure as hell—they didn't know what kind of country they were going to. And people like that aren't daft enough to believe all the garbage printed on brochures. Which means, they knew somebody—somebody they trusted—somebody who'd travelled around a bit, and seen these places ... somebody who could *tell* 'em. A close friend—a relative, maybe ... somebody they *believed*.'

Outside, it was dusk. Light spilled from the uncurtained windows of the Concert Room, and spread small illumination across the tarmac upon which was parked the cars.

Bear and Harris were waiting, alongside the murderer's Jag. Harris was holding a brief-case.

The murderer approached, and said, 'You—er ...'

'This is your car, sir?' Bear touched the roof of the Jag.

'Yes.' The murderer nodded.

'*And* this one?' Bear touched a red Mini which was drawn up alongside the Jag.

'Where ...' began the murderer.

'From your garage, at your home.' Harris didn't waste words. He answered the question before it was asked. He said, 'And don't get any wrong ideas. It was all done legally. Search warrants, and everything.'

'We found this in one of the bedrooms,' said Bear.

'This' was a Husqvarna M.1622, .22, 6-shot, clip-loading, bolt-action match grade rifle, with a Zeiss, Hensoldt Diatel D.6X telescopic sight attached. Bear balanced it, easily, in his right hand, and waited for the murderer's reaction.

'If I deny ownership?' said the murderer, carefully.

'That's your right.'

'For what it's worth,' added Harris, bluntly.

There was a few seconds of silence.

'Take your time,' said Bear, politely. 'Meanwhile, let's go back inside ... see how far Chief Superintendent Lennox has progressed.'

Sullivan saw the murderer return, and resume his seat at the table he'd vacated. He saw Bear join Sugden, alongside the youth, Dene, having first handed the rifle to Harris. He saw Harris stroll, unhurriedly—and without attracting attention—down the side of the Concert Room, and quietly place the rifle and the brief-case at one end of the stage.

Sullivan noted all these things and, at the same time, saw that Lennox, too, had noted them.

Lennox switched gear. The tone of his voice took on a subtle change. It became harsher, and less jovial. He was no longer a clown ... he was now an overweight, but utterly ruthless copper, moving in for the kill.

He said, 'Eight years ago. There was a jury ... but there was also something else. There was a suicide.

'Madge West—West's wife—killed herself.

'Madge West—Appleyard's daughter—hadn't the common guts to face up to reality. She took the easy way out, disgraced her family and forced 'em to emigrate.'

Lennox paused, then said, 'Lemme digress a little. Lemme talk about homosexuals. Nancy-boys. Queers. Brown-hatters. All the fancy names you care to dredge up. *Them!* They can't help it, y'know. To them, it's natural ... and they can no more control their feelings than they can change the colour of their eyes. Get that. To them, it's normal ... it's only *ab*normal because society says it's abnormal.'

Ingle spoke from the body of the hall.

He said, 'It's against nature, chief superintendent. More than that, to ordinary people, it's disgusting.'

'Maybe ... but, to them, what you call "natural" is equally disgusting. So who's right?'

'*We're* right.'

'You? Or have you elected yourself spokesman for all humanity?'

'You know what I mean,' snapped Ingle.

'Aye.' Lennox bobbed his head, solemnly but, at the same time, with mocking solemnity. 'I know *exactly* what you mean.'

'Softly does it, boy.' Sullivan mouthed the words, silently, as he willed success for the fat man who, by this time, had hypnotised every man and woman in the room into a state of nail-biting tension. 'Don't let chummy off the hook, by entering into some side-issue argument. Change the subject—get Ingle off your back ... *change the subject.*'

Lennox changed the subject.
 He said, 'Let's talk about parents ... and godparents. Specifically, about godfathers. I mean the real thing. Not the Mafia lunatics. I mean men who stand at a font, and accept a certain responsibility. Some of 'em go through the motions, but some of 'em *mean* it. To some of 'em it's as important—maybe even more important—than parenthood ... especially if they've no kids of their own.
 'Madge West had such a godfather. He was at the funeral ... Mrs White gave me that pearl of information, earlier today. He was at the funeral of his godchild, and —it doesn't take too vivid an imagination to reach the conclusion—he swore vengeance. However long it took. Whatever the price. The man responsible—the man *he* counted as responsible—was going to pay.
 'The godfather—chummy, in other words—advised the Appleyards about emigration ... but *he* didn't emigrate. He had work to do.
 'He planned. He waited. And he took a sheer coincidence of eight years back, and used it to his own ends.
 'Think about it. Think about it, as *he* thought about it. Twelve people—ten men, and two women—in a jury box ... and one of 'em was West. To hide a bean in a bag of beans. To hide a murder in a series of murders. To kill two perfectly innocent people—to attempt the killing of a third innocent person—just to get at the man he *really* wanted ... to lay a false trail. To send the wild geese flying. One bean, in a bag of beans. One murder, wrapped

up in a camouflage of identical murders. *That's* what we're dealing with.'

'Now!' Sullivan breathed the word as he clenched his fist and brought it down, a fraction of an inch, onto the top of the table. He watched the murderer, saw the crumbling façade, and whispered, 'You cunning old bastard ... *now!*'

'Or, never,' echoed Rucker, softly.

'We're also dealing with cowardice.' Lennox's voice had the lash of a steel-tipped whip. 'The cowardice of a man who can't face the truth. Of a man who cringes, and nurses his hatred, for eight long years until he can shove his guilt in another man's direction. The cowardice of a murderous hound who hasn't the plain guts to kill once, and have done with it ... who has to hide his killing in carnage. Who has to kill from a hiding place. Who has to kill innocent women. Who has to kill the friend of his own godchild, as a shield to his own rottenness.

'We're dealing with scum. Scum, to whom the words "courage" and "virtue" are mere entries in a dictionary. Without meaning. Without substance.'

The murderer pressed his left arm against his side and, against the upper arm, felt the reassuring hardness of what he knew must be his only remaining answer, if Lennox's tirade continued.

'... We're also dealing with the basic cowardliness of a woman. Madge West. A married woman who, because her husband found greater delight in the bed of a teenage youth than he found in his own, and with his own wife, tried to buy the pity of the world with sleeping pills. That she disgraced her family didn't matter a damn. She was happy to splash her inadequacy, as a wife, across the front page of the local scandal-rag ... just to get pity. Pity! If she'd had an ounce of self-respect—an ounce of honour —three murdered people would still be alive. A gutless hound wouldn't have had an empty excuse to go on a killing rampage. Had she possessed an ounce of common...'

'*THAT'S ENOUGH!*'

The murderer was on the stage, alongside Lennox. Spittle dribbled from one corner of his mouth and his eyes were wild with an uncontrollable madness. The Colt derringer had its hammer cocked, and its snub-nosed barrel was lined onto the fat detective's stomach.

Lennox ignored the derringer.

He nodded, solemnly, and said, 'Aye ... I think that's enough. Now, they all know what *she* was like. And what *you're* like.'

'It's a lie!' The murderer choked on the words, but every person in the room heard. 'Distortions. That's what you've been doing. Distorting the truth. She was a good woman. A fine woman. A beautiful woman. She didn't deserve the animal she married. He was unclean. He was foul. He was ...'

'And now, he's dead.'

'I should have killed him years ago. That much, I grant you. I allowed him to live too long.'

'And White? And Bentley?'

'We all have to die, eventually. What's death? What's a few years? *She* died young ... she had a whole life ahead of her.'

From the body of the hall Sullivan shouted, 'Don't be a bloody fool. Put that gun down.'

And every copper in the room was on his feet, and moving cautiously towards the tiny stage.

The murderer stepped away from Lennox, brought the derringer to his own temple, and whispered, 'I am *not* a coward. I *have* honour.'

The last thing he heard, before the single shot ripped his brain to shreds was Rucker's contemptuous, 'We will now have two short choruses of "Oh, Let Me Like A Soldier Fall".'

'I'm—I'm speechless,' snarled Gilliant. 'I honestly don't know what the hell to say.'

Which, in view of the fact that he'd been ranting for the best part of thirty minutes, was a bit of a daft utterance to make.

'Why?' he demanded. 'In God's name, why do it *that* way? You could have been wrong. You could have cocked the whole case to hell and back.'

'With *those* shots?' murmured Lennox. 'It had to be somebody who could handle a rifle. *Really* handle a rifle. We knew from the White killing—from the prints of the golfing shoes—that it was somebody from the club. Ingle ... who else? Trained to handle a .303 ... which carries a fair old kick. A .22? He could take the pips out of a raspberry with *that* calibre.'

'And that's all?' mocked Gilliant.

Sullivan said, 'No, sir. We still needed positive identification. Freeman ... the only man who could give us it. We dressed him up as a waiter. We *didn't* tell him to go to Ingle. I handled that side of things. His instructions were implicit. To look around the room, and *if* he recognised the man who'd hired the Capri, to go to that man and tell him Bear wanted to see him, outside. A little unusual, I'll grant you ... but one hell of an identification parade. He'd well over fifty people to chose from.'

Gilliant continued to breathe heavily.

Lennox said. 'We knew—correction, *I* knew—before I set up the pantomime. Freeman—remember?—he described the man's hands. Dirty. Oil and grease, worked into the skin—that's how he put it ... but qualified it with "washed", but still "discoloured". It's in the report.

And that office ... it stank of beeswax and linseed oil. Furniture restoration. It calls for beeswax. It calls for French polish ... which needs linseed oil. Use that stuff, day after day—week after week—and the hands become stained ... and you can't wash it off.'

Lennox took a cheroot from his pocket and began to strip the cellophane.

'Don't,' snapped Gilliant, 'smoke that foul-smelling thing in *my* office.'

'Sorry.' Lennox slipped the cheroot back into his pocket.

After a few moments of silence, Sullivan said, 'The rest you'll find in the report, sir.'

'Oh, I read the report,' said Gilliant, with heavy sarcasm. 'It tells me just about everything ... except *why?*' He waved a hand at the rifle, the derringer and the brief-case, placed in a neat line across the top of his desk. 'Why—for example—not go about things in a more normal way? The gun could be matched up with the bullets. With the cartridge cases. The scrapings—there, in envelopes in the case—they could be matched up with the pedals of the Mini. Everything! He was on toast ... so, why the hell do things *that* way?'

'Those were back-up troops,' rumbled Lennox. 'In case I couldn't break him ... summat else to throw in his teeth.'

Gilliant raised disgusted eyes at the ceiling, and said, 'That's what I'm getting at, chief superintendent. Why was it *necessary* to break him.'

Lennox rubbed his bald pate, and said, 'Y'want the truth?'

'I'd be obliged.'

'We-ell, discounting Freeman—who could make a positive identification ... and we all know what a good defence lawyer can do with an identification parade. But —discounting that—pretty well everything else could have been explained away, in court. Even the Mini ... it could have been claimed to have been pinched. Even the rifle ... coppers *have* been known to plant evidence. A damn good lawyer could have twisted every piece of evidence, and made it fit one, or more, of the other members of that club. It's always the same with a murder case. That so-called "element of doubt" ... God Almighty, the lawyers can make a hair-line might-have-been look like a yard-wide plank. You've seen it. I've seen it. Every senior copper, in every force, can name some bastard who's killed, and got away with it ... thanks to some dim-witted jury and some smart-talking lawyer. So-o—this is a new force, and it wouldn't have looked too smart if a three-time killer had got away with it ... which meant he had to be clobbered the fancy way.'

'And that's your excuse?'

'It worked ... *that's* my excuse,' grunted Lennox.

For a full minute, Gilliant gazed at the Head of Bordfield Region C.I.D. A series of qualities chased and displaced each other across Gilliant's expression. Outrage and admiration. Irritation and amusement. Even a touch of genuine anger.

Then, Gilliant sighed, and said, 'All right ... smoke the damn thing, if you must.'

'Ta.' Lennox grinned a fat-faced grin and slipped the partly-unwrapped cheroot from his pocket.

Gilliant spoke to Sullivan.

He said, 'You were in on this forensic parlour trick, of course?'

'Yes, sir.' Sullivan nodded.

'And Bear? And Sugden and Harris? And Rucker?'

'All of 'em,' agreed Sullivan.

'But not me ... so, why *not* me?'

'You might not have approved.'

'I wasn't given the chance.'

'And,' added Sullivan, wrily, 'somebody had to be

around, to boot us all out of the force, if things had gone wrong.'

'And don't think I wouldn't have,' said Gilliant, grimly.

'We all knew ... that's why we left you out.'

'There'll be a stink,' sighed Gilliant. 'The coroner will have some very pithy remarks to make.'

'They always do—they always have—they always will ... but who the hell takes 'em seriously?'

'There'll be a Home Office enquiry. Bound to be.'

'True. But look at the publicity. We'll be the best-known force in the country ... in no time at all.'

'Questions asked in Parliament.'

Sullivan said, 'Lenny's already put it in a nutshell, sir. It *worked*. That's our excuse. That's our answer ... to everything.'

'God save me from crazy policemen,' breathed Gilliant. He looked at each man in turn, then said, 'That's all, gentlemen. You may now leave me to sweep up the debris.'

Sullivan and Lennox turned and walked to the door of the office.

Just before they left, Gilliant said, 'Oh and—er—Lenny.'

'Sir?' Lennox turned to face his chief constable.

'No more ... please,' said Gilliant. 'It really isn't your forte.'

'If you say so, sir.'

'I *do* say so. Agatha Christie did it infinitely better than you'll *ever* do it.'

'Yes, sir,' grinned Lennox, as he closed the door.